D1413959

Dim Sum
Dead

Also by Jerrilyn Farmer
in Large Print:

Sympathy for the Devil

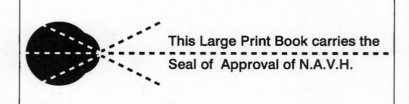

JERRILYN FARMER

DIM SUM DEAD

A MADELINE BEAN CULINARY MYSTERY

Thorndike Press • Waterville, Maine

This is a work of fiction. Names, characters, places, and incidents are products of the author's imagination or are used fictitiously and are not to be construed as real. Any resemblance to actual events, locales, organizations, or persons, living or dead, is entirely coincidental.

Published in 2003 by arrangement with Avon Books, an imprint of HarperCollins Publishers.

Thorndike Press® Large Print Mystery Series.

The tree indicium is a trademark of Thorndike Press.

The text of this Large Print edition is unabridged.
Other aspects of the book may vary from the original edition.

Set in 16 pt. Plantin by Liana M. Walker.

Printed in the United States on permanent paper.

Library of Congress Cataloging-in-Publication Data

Farmer, Jerrilyn.
    Dim sum dead: a Madeline Bean culinary mystery / Jerrilyn Farmer.
        p. cm.
    ISBN 0-7862-4754-1 (lg. print : hc : alk. paper)
    1. Bean, Madeline (Fictitious character) — Fiction.
2. Caterers and catering — Fiction. 3. Los Angeles (Calif.) — Fiction. 4. Chinese Americans — Fiction. 5. Women cooks — Fiction. 6. Cookery — Fiction. 7. Large type books.
I. Title.
PS3556.A719 D46 2003
    813'.6—dc21   2002073236

To Evelyn Kobritz and William Sarnoff,
my role models —
for Evelyn's beauty and strength
and Bill's jazzy spin on life

ACKNOWLEDGMENTS

There would be no Mad Bean books without my closest advisor, my wonderful husband, Chris. Through some insanely dizzy days, he encouraged me to do more than I have ever before attempted, and then tirelessly cleaned up the wreckage when, on occasion, I hit the wall. The result: cities were visited and signings were held; a successful mystery writing class was taught at UCLA Extension; another fabulous season of *Supermarket Sweep* was written; two healthy, happy boys excelled in grades 1 and 4; and the completion of this book you are now holding. My luckiest day was the day I met my husband. This book is for Chris, with my love and deepest thanks.

I am also happy to acknowledge the contributions of Chef Nick, who learned to read while this book was being written, and to Strategy Advisor Sam, whose deep philosophical conversations kept his mom's brain percolating. This book is also for Sam and Nick, with my love.

I have to thank all my cousins, but particularly Emily Silver and Miriam Becker, for showing me how strong and accomplished the women in our family can be. This book is for Emily and Minky and the Sarnoff/Sornoff cousins, with love.

As always, I must thank my editor, Lyssa Keusch, for her exceptional talent and a friendship I treasure. I must also thank my excellent literary agent, Evan Marshall, whose advice and jokes and gossip and brilliance I cannot do without.

Lastly, I would like to thank my brother, Richard Klein, for bringing home intriguing tales of China, and also the many friends I've made in the book and mystery communities, including Linda Urban, Dawn Weiss, Joan Wunsch, Audrey Moore, Linda Bivens, Terry Baker, MaryElizabeth Hart, Patsy Asher, Joanne Sinchuk, Diane Plumley, Diane Bouchard and the L.A. chapter of Sisters in Crime, Jan Burke and the SoCal chapter of MWA, Erica Bailey Rudnick, Al Howard and Elyssa Lenard and all my friends in the "Big Sweep," Linda Venis at the Writer's Program, dearest mollyemma, and, of course, the fabulous Julie Klein of The Julies.

And if that is surely not enough, I owe an enormous debt to the daily doses of friendship I receive from Margery Flax and my online buds who enjoy tea.

Chapter 1

"I hate surprises." I do. Hate 'em.

My best friend and partner, Wesley Westcott, had just arrived at the Santa Monica Farmer's Market to meet up and buy supplies. He pulled off his backpack and propped it up next to a dark forest of fresh romaine and a spiky rustle of gray-green endive.

"You always say that," Wes said, "but this one is different."

"I don't think so."

Our breath misted when we spoke. Southern California in January. Who said we don't have seasons? But, of course, the day would warm up. As soon as the sun burned through the fog, we'd make it up to seventy degrees, warmer inland.

I put a crisp Chinese cabbage back down upon a perfect pyramid display of similar heads. "Really, Wes. I hate surprises."

Wes began to unzip the black bag now resting on the outdoor vegetable cart. "Stop saying 'hate.'"

"Okay. I don't want to be negative. Negativity sucks. But . . ."

A small man, examining some chard, looked up. His dark eyes gave me a once-over before they returned to their careful examination of greens.

I lowered my voice. "I just want to point out that surprises are highly overrated. In my opinion."

"You just like to know everything ahead of time. That's the control freak in you." Wes pulled out a large package and began unwrapping it.

"Control freak? I am *not*." Really.

I picked up one perfect bunch of basil from the large selection of fresh herbs on display. This stand was but one of hundreds that made up the vast Farmer's Market held near Arizona and Second Street every Wednesday and Saturday morning. All around was a feast for the eyes. Ripe and juicy and picked at the peak of flavor only hours before up in central California's Conejo Valley, this produce rocked the senses. But then, you can probably tell I am wild for fresh ingredients.

Wait, now. There, on one inner basil leaf, was a teeny, tiny brown spot. I put the minutely damaged bunch of basil into a plastic bag anyway. Control freak? I think not.

The chard shopper shot another quick glance my way. I noticed the sun glint off his gold ring as he put down another tightly banded bunch of chard.

I shifted my shoulder bag. I looked at the plastic bag. Quickly, I untwisted the twist tie and removed the slightly imperfect bunch of basil.

Wes caught my eye. "You were saying . . ."

"I just have rather high standards for things, that's all."

"Right," Wes said, with his basketball-size surprise just about unwrapped. "Excuse me. Totally different thing."

Aha! My eyes were always darting around at the Farmer's Market. Who could tell where the next treasure was hiding? Now *here* was the perfect basil. The rich green, purple-veined leaves were large and moist, full and soft. I raised the thick bunch of basil to my nose. The heavenly aroma of the Mediterranean was intoxicating. I popped it into a fresh plastic bag, cheerfully twisting and tying.

I looked up.

Wesley stood there looking back at me, a breeze whipping his long brown hair back. Wesley Westcott is my best friend — my business partner, actually — and an excellent gourmet chef. Together, we have

11

started a catering and event-planning firm called Mad Bean Events, which Wesley insisted we name after me. I thought we should call it Madeline Bean Events, because, you know, it sounds more dignified. He didn't think dignity "sells" particularly well here in L.A. Perhaps he's right, because we are doing just fine as Mad Bean Events, catering Hollywood parties and planning a kicky range of ultra-high-end special events.

For Wesley and me, the Santa Monica Farmer's Market is one of our Wednesday morning rituals. It's something we've done since we moved down to L.A. from Berkeley nine years ago. We both love food and we both love to shop — so this was just about heaven for us, if you didn't mind thousands of other shoppers elbowing you aside to get the last ripe Haas avocado.

The early-morning bustle on Third Street, closed off to car traffic, was getting thicker by the minute. Tight throngs of well-dressed Westside gourmets scoured the finest and freshest fruits and vegetables of the season. One could people-watch for hours.

There were the young couples, holding hands, their heads close together as they whispered about dinners they would share.

There were men, serious home cooks, who shopped in silence. There were lots of attractive women — young moms pushing tots, and media career types, and others we like to call forty-and-holding — everyone carrying designer water bottles and dressed casually, perhaps on the way to workouts with their trainers. All over the Market, you'd see them, lifting a melon up for a quick sniff, squeezing a lemon lovingly, and tucking their dawn buys into the latest lavender Kate Spade totes.

Shopping along with the neighborhood regulars, of course, there were a goodly number of us professional chefs, and we all knew each other. The outdoor Market was a natural place to meet and gossip in the chilly, overcast mornings, and then to vie like schoolyard bullies for first pick and special buying privileges from our favored grower/vendors.

"Excuse me." A young mom stepped up to the stall and grabbed a bunch of basil, and resumed talking a kind of baby talk to the infant she had strapped to her chest in one of those contraptions. "La-la-la-la-la" this young woman burbled to the infant. I looked closely at the baby. He or she seemed like every other baby. Big round head, that sort of thing. I know the sight of

13

babies makes many women weak in the knees. But I guess my knees were built steadier. Like I tell people, I'm too young. I'm not ready.

Wesley looked down at me from his six-three height and just waited, bringing back to mind his threatened big "surprise."

"Maddie," he said, "I dragged this thing over here this morning just so I could show it to you."

"Okay." I was resigned but gracious. "Let's see."

He pulled off that last piece of newspaper wrapping and revealed a small wooden chest — quite an old-looking thing with a brass handle. "Is this not cool?"

At last, Wes had caught my attention. "Oh!"

But life at the Market goes on. At that moment, Maria, who works behind this particular produce counter, left her last customer and smiled up at me. My turn.

Wes continued his story as I took care of business.

"You'll never guess where we found this."

"Where?" I handed Maria a five and turned back to Wes.

"In the master bedroom. Raymond had just pulled back the wallboard — you know that awful stuff that covered the west wall?

14

And behind that old ratty board was a fireplace."

"You're kidding."

"We saw the double flue in the chimney, so it only made sense. There had to be another fireplace. And it's original. Can you believe anyone in his right mind would want to board it up and hide it? Poor house."

Wesley's latest passion was an amazing older home he was renovating in the Doheny Estates area near Beverly Hills. The house had been designed by Paul Williams, famous architect to the stars. Wesley often had a rehab project going on the side, but this house was the largest and most financially draining project to date.

Maria counted out my change and then I gave the beautiful discovery my full attention. I touched the smooth surface of the old rosewood case. "You actually found it hidden behind a false wall?"

Wes nodded.

I noticed it was covered with Chinese designs and lettering. "This," I said, studying it, "is very cool."

Wesley leaned the box on a corner of the vegetable stand. He fiddled with the brass lock for a second, then slowly raised the lid. I moved closer.

There, inside the dark case, were stacked

dozens of beautiful small white tiles, about three-quarter inch by one and a half inches. They looked like bone or ivory. Hand-etched and colored on the face of each tile was a Chinese character, or a number, or a lovely Asian picture.

"A mah-jongg set." I held out my hand and pulled the brass handle on one of three slender drawers. It slid easily to reveal more of the lovely tile pieces. "And it looks very old."

Wesley smiled.

This happened to be a sweet stroke of serendipity. For the past six months, Wes and I had been catering the very private Sweet and Sour Mah-Jongg Club up in the Hollywood Hills. You may remember mah-jongg if you have any old aunts of the Jewish or Chinese persuasion — in which case, you are now shaking your head. I know. But it turns out the kitsch old game of mah-jongg has become the new hipster obsession. Perhaps it's the hint of the Orient, or the intricate strategy, or the luck, or the gambling. Whatever. Our young clients were hooked.

They had organized a weekly MJ party, which they held at a large estate belonging to a hot young music video director, Buster Dubin, the leader of their pack. They played mah-jongg. Mad Bean Events provided the gourmet grub. It had become one of our smaller but steadier gigs.

I touched the mah-jongg case and picked out one of the tiles. It was exquisitely smooth and cool to the touch. Etched in red on one side was a Chinese pictogram of a sword.

"Wes, this is beautiful."

"The Red Dragon. Yes. I didn't have time to check out the entire set. We just found it an hour ago."

"You were doing demo all night?"

"We've got the plasterer coming in two days. Our schedule is tight. I'll crash on the weekend."

I played with a few more tiles. Beneath the top row, there was a second row of tiles. "Is this set complete?" I asked.

"I don't know anything about it. I was just shocked as hell when the crowbars came crashing down and there was this fully intact fireplace with a masonry surround waiting to be discovered. We were pretty stoked. And then I noticed it. Sitting there, right in the center of the fireplace, was this box, wrapped up in a blanket. You know, I think someone put it there to hide it. Although I can't imagine why."

As Wes talked, he pulled open the second drawer and picked out another mah-jongg tile. In the ancient game of mah-jongg, these small ivory tiles are used as game pieces. Like cards, the tiles are marked in suits. He showed me the Green Dragon tile, with its pictogram of an arrow about to leave the bow.

I pulled open the bottom drawer, getting into it now.

"This is odd," I said. "Doesn't it seem like this drawer is deeper?"

"Let me see." Wes pulled out a handful of tiles and put them in his jacket pocket, then he began emptying out the rest. But between my pulling out the drawer and Wes reaching in, the lovely old chest began to tip off its perch.

"Wes!"

He grabbed the box before it fell. Unfortunately, I grabbed for the box, too. The almost empty bottom drawer fell to the sidewalk.

"Oh, no." I knelt quickly, gathering up the fallen mah-jongg tiles and righting the overturned drawer. And then I saw that a tiny patch of wood had been dislodged. There was a false bottom to the drawer, and I pulled it out.

"Did it break?"

I stood up, bringing the drawer to show Wes.

"Wow," he said.

Inside, something other than a row of bone and bamboo tiles glinted in the morning light. It looked like a slim, silver box engraved with Chinese Dragons. Wesley lifted the silver box from the deep recess at the bottom of the drawer. It was about nine inches by five inches and only about an inch high. Beneath it, at the bottom of the drawer, was a small book, possibly of mah-jongg instructions, bound in red leather.

"What if it's a jewel box filled with diamonds?" I asked.

Wes tried to loosen the silver lid of the box, but couldn't. He shook it and we heard the muffled clank of metal on metal.

"Does it have a lock?" I asked. A few people in the crowd around us began to take an interest.

There was no lock that either of us could see. I told Wes to hold the small silver box steady, and I edged my thumbnail under the rim of its tightly stuck lid. As he braced the silver case, I pushed up on its lid as hard as I could.

With all that prying force, the lid swung back on its hinge and out flew the contents, landing at our feet. I looked down.

A drop of blood flecked the pavement. And then a few more.

"Maddie, you're hurt!"

"I am?"

I looked at my ankle and noticed the thin red gash, felt the throbbing pain, watched as the drops of blood splashed down on my Nikes. It was true. I had been cut.

A woman a few steps away gasped.

On the pavement lay the object that had fallen from the silver box. It looked very old. It had a long curved blade. It was an antique Chinese dagger with a handle carved in the shape of a dragon.

I hate surprises.

Chapter 2

The noisy crowd of shoppers seemed to back up and quiet down.

"Are you all right?" Wes went down on one knee and checked my ankle, and I sat down on the pavement beside him.

"A little blood. A cool scar someday. Nothing major."

Wes picked up the dagger lying there and quickly shut it away in the silver box. Then, he put the silver box and all the tiles he'd unloaded before back in the mah-jongg case drawers and hooked them all shut.

"I was just thinking —" I started.

"You want a doctor to take a look? St. John's is closest."

Wes was taking this way too seriously.

"No. It's okay, Wes. It barely scratched me. I was just thinking that the dagger could be worth something. Do you know anything about Chinese antiques?"

"So you're okay?" Wes asked. And we both stood up.

"Yes. Fine. Recent tetanus shot. Don't

worry so much," I said. The shoppers nearest to us had been openly eavesdropping, so I said it again, loudly and with perfect enunciation. "I'm fine."

They took the hint and went back to their own business.

"But maybe . . ." I took note of the splotch of red on the bottom of my jeans. "Maybe, I should be getting back to the house." Our business was located in the bottom floor of my house, and that was where I was headed anyway.

And then something magical happened. My focus abruptly shifted from my ankle to my left hand as something lovely and warm clamped onto me in a tight, hot grasp. I looked down. A perfectly beautiful, towheaded child of about three was hanging on to me for dear life. The child had simply grabbed on as he looked around the open-air market, his attention fastened to the large Gala apples on the stall beside us. I was astonished. Did children this little really have such strength? Such heat?

Just then, the boy looked up into my eyes. His were a clear and brilliant shade of soft denim blue. I looked down in surprise on his lovely face.

His expression froze. I was not his grown-up. His mother, paying for some purchases a few feet away, must have been the intended target of that tight little hand. He let go of me fast, and the electricity in our connection vanished. I watched him, blond and angelic, as he quickly found his mommy, and she soon felt the warmth of her baby's hand.

Wesley, missing that little scene, was staring at me. "You look weird, Mad. You sure you're okay?"

Was I? I was having a strange moment, that's for sure. But it had nothing to do with the nick to my ankle. So, is that what some women feel about babies? That fierce thrill? I had to wonder.

"Wesley?"

We both turned. The voice belonged to a friend of ours, Jody Silva, a grower with a stand a few steps away.

"You got a minute?" Jody asked. She had come out from behind the stall. She was a young woman who was built on a heavy frame, but a strong one. Her muscles had been developed not on a weight machine but by lifting crates at her family's farm and loading them into her truck. "We've got a lady customer. She bought a case of potatoes for this camp she runs for sick kids. We give her a real good price, but she needs to get the load over to her pickup."

"Would she like a hand?" Wesley asked, looking up and spotting the customer, standing by her crate of potatoes not far away.

"Could you do her this favor?" Jody asked.

"Of course." Then Wes turned back to me. "But you need to get home," he said.

"Why don't you meet me back at the house," I said, improvising. "I'll take care of this stuff." I waved at the mah-jongg case and the backpack.

"You'll be all right?" he asked. "With your ankle?"

"Yeah. Right. I'm hobbled." I smiled at him. "You moron. Go and do a good deed for sick children."

We gave a little hug, because I'm a hugger, and Wes, after nine years of me, has gotten used to being hugged in public.

I watched him walk off, noticing a few other pairs of eyes following his lean body in his perfectly hanging khaki cargo pants. Well, this is L.A. We watch. Wes picked up the crate with one strong move and then trudged off through the crowd as the thankful woman accompanied him off to some distant parking spot.

I was standing near the corner of Jody's very large stall, beside her bountiful displays of six types of onions and two types of leeks, in addition to carrots in several astonishing colors.

"Hi, Maddie!" Jody called out. She was now back behind her stall.

A dozen shoppers were looking over the rutabagas and radishes on Jody's stall. Jody's sister was down at the other end, weighing tomatoes. A tall man in a hooded sweatshirt stood waiting for Jody's attention. We both noticed him at the same time. I stepped back and looked down, ready to pick up my crocheted shopping bag, Wesley's backpack, and the rest of the stuff I'd left at my feet.

That's when it all started. The shoppers who were thronged three deep around Jody's booth all of a sudden began yelping, swearing. People were being shoved. I was just bending down to pick up the old mahjongg box when the sudden pushing in the crowd began.

"Hey!" I felt myself begin to trip. I reached out to catch myself. And then, just before I could grab hold of the side of the vegetable cart, a man's hand shoved me hard, right between the shoulders.

I tumbled down, crashing against the corner of the vegetable stand, throwing a hand up at the very last second to prevent the sharp wooden rim from poking out an eye. Under the sudden weight, the leg beneath the table buckled. I heard Jody's voice, now shrill. "Stop that! Get security! Stop him!"

I tried scrambling up to my feet, as the squash and cucumbers toppled down onto me. The sweatshirt man, standing close by, tried to help me up.

"*Maddie!* You okay?" Jody called, her voice full of tension.

Jody's sister started screaming from the other end of the booth. "I told you. It's not safe here. The homeless! They're everywhere in Santa Monica . . ." She continued rattling on more of the same, as her urban paranoia ratcheted up to a dangerous high.

I looked back to the ground to pick up my things.

Hell.

"Wesley's case! *Hey!*" I squinted after the form of a short man walking fast as he disappeared into the thick crowd down the lane. "That guy who was pushing — he took off with my stuff!"

"What?" Jody looked in the right direction but it was too late to see him by then. At the top of her lungs, Jody began yelling, *"THIEF! Thief!"*

People nearby stopped talking. Some

helpful souls had been righting the tipped produce stand, arranging to fix it to stand level again. Meanwhile, Jody began blowing a high-pitched whistle. "They'll stop him, Maddie," she said, and shrieked her whistle again.

I didn't stick around to find out if the law of the Santa Monica Farmer's Market would work its magic. I took off after the man, who by now had gotten lost in the crowd.

I picked up some speed, cutting to the center of the road, avoiding the stalls and the main clusters of shoppers. I couldn't see the thief, but there was no place for him to have turned off, yet.

I should have been more careful, more alert. I usually was. I was engulfed by the crowd, now, unable to see two feet in front of me. Damn!

If I hadn't been caught off-balance like that, I'd surely have been able to keep from falling. I was disgusted. Me, Madeline Bean. Urban warrior. I don't leave my things just lying around for someone to steal.

I cleared a large group of mommies pushing strollers, balancing large Starbucks cups. *There.* I thought I saw the guy, walking fast, up ahead about twenty yards. Then the crowd closed around him.

It was difficult to dart through the shoppers without accidentally stepping on someone. They were not on the lookout for young women dashing a little too fast for safety. I ran too close to an elderly man and almost smacked into him as he stepped off the curb right into my path.

"Whoa!" I said to the old guy, sweeping my eyes up ahead, near the last place I'd caught a glimpse of the mugger. There he was. And, just as I spotted him, the guy turned his head, checking back. It was the chard guy. Damn. He spotted me spotting him. At once, he took off again, running, turning left at the first street. For a moment, I could even see our damn mah-jongg case in his hand. Creep! And then he disappeared around the corner.

I followed, squeezing between several shoppers, dashing into a clearing, gaining a little. I was almost up to the corner, breathing heavily, running now. I was just picking up some speed, when a large man stepped out directly in front of me. I stopped just short of plowing into him and stepped to the side, but the man moved over and wouldn't let me pass.

"Excuse me," I shouted, adrenaline pumping, "I've got to —"

"Running isn't safe in the Market. Better walk."

I looked up, sputtering. Before me stood a large immovable object — a big guy I'd seen around here for years. I think his wife worked the family bakery stand, but I'd never seen this guy do much of anything.

"Did you see that man who just ran by here?" I shouted. "He stole my box. Let me go."

"Look," the fat man said, reaching a log of an arm out to hold my shoulder. "I'm just saying, someone could get hurt with you running . . ."

I pulled away from him. More time lost.

I backed up and spun around off the curb, but before I could take off down the road, I was intercepted again. This time, by another man. Only this man was sitting on a bicycle — a young, good-looking man wearing shorts, with the kind of thigh muscles that could make a heart flutter. Not that I notice these things. I was now looking at a sworn officer in the Santa Monica Police Department Third Street Bicycle Patrol. His badge read, "Stubb."

Officer Stubb pulled to a stop beside me. "Your name Maddie?"

"Madeline Bean, how . . . ?"

"They gave a description," Stubb explained.

"What?"

"Your long braid. Your gray jeans. Your great . . ." Stubb stopped the description at the point of embarrassing himself. "One of the vendors reported the theft. We've got our guys out on bikes, but there are a lot of people here at the Market today. We've got to take it slow."

"I just saw the jerk," I said, frustrated as hell. "He went there, off to the left. We've got to move fast."

"We're on it," Stubb said, resisting my command to move fast or even budge. "I've got two officers on that part of the Market. They'll get the guy. It's hard to run through a place like this without attracting attention."

"They've just got to find him," I said, more to myself, and took another quick glance at Stubb.

I knew about the Santa Monica cops on wheels. They were a PR guy's dream: seventeen hunky officers selected for their interpersonal skills and riding ability. They were highly visible — a comfort to any nervous sightseers about to leave their tourist dollars in the beach city that was also known for its homeless "element."

But I was freaking out, just standing around, doing nothing. I looked up and read concern in the nice brown eyes of young Officer Stubb.

"Sorry," I said. "I have got to get that box back to my partner. I'd better go out there and look for it."

"Miss Bean," Stubb explained calmly, "agility, maneuverability, and knowledge of the area permit our Bike Patrol to be more effective. All of us ride specially equipped police bicycles. Believe me, bikes rule."

"I'm sure they do." They must make the guys memorize this stuff. "But —"

"Our team's response is fast yet silent. If that guy is still in the area, we'll find him."

"Okay," I said, giving up. "Okay."

I'm not a big fan of cops, really. I don't like it when someone tells me to cool it. But then, Officer Stubb wanted to calm the nerves of a crime victim, as I'm sure he was instructed to in Bike Cop School. So, I had better show him that my nerves were freaking calm. Or he'd never leave.

"What did he take?" Stubb asked. "Your purse?"

"He stole my friend's mah-jongg set."

Stubb looked at me with concern. "March on? What is that?"

"Can't you call someone? Radio someone? Please. I can probably give you a better description of the guy. He was short, maybe five-five, and had black hair, dark eyes. He was wearing a tan jacket and gray

31

pants. He was shopping for Swiss chard."

The seconds were speeding away. I was going to scream.

Just then, Officer Stubb's radio sputtered. "Be right with you, there, Madeline," he said to me, and he picked up his radio from his belt.

I could hear the other officer informing Stubb that there was no sign of the assailant. No one matching the description of the suspect, as given by vendor, was on foot, running. They would continue their search.

Terrific. *Like maybe about five years ago* the suspect had been running on foot. By now, he had surely jumped into some waiting getaway Honda Civic or whatever. He was probably tooling his way up Wilshire by now, for all the effectiveness of the fast yet silent Bike Patrol.

Stubb said something and there was a bit of conversation I didn't follow as I felt my pulse slow down and my breathing get more regular. Ah, hell.

Officer Stubb looked back at me, and said, "Sorry about that. Why don't I just go down the street there" — he gestured to the left — "and maybe we'll get lucky."

"Sure."

"So, what is it I'm looking for? The stolen property?"

"Mah-jongg tiles. It's a game. They were in an antique Chinese chest about this big." I made a halfhearted gesture showing him about eighteen inches high and twelve inches around. "It's an old wooden box with brass hooks and latches. My friend left it with me for a minute, and then this bizarre little man shoved me down and grabbed it."

"Okay, then. I'll check it out."

Young, huge Officer Stubb had the decency to look rather pink about the face as he wheeled his bike around in the proper direction. He spoke into his radio once again. Perhaps he was finally calling in some megawheels backup, like a patrol car, to head the guy off. But I wasn't counting on it. After all, I'd only lost a "march on" set. This wasn't grand theft, auto.

But what was I going to tell Wesley?

I trotted down the street, passing vendors and shoppers, looking ahead for any sign of the missing thief, or Wesley's antique mah-jongg set, or Officer Stubb's police buddies. In about a block I reached a dead end and I could only turn left or right. In such cases, I make it a habit of always turning to the right. I jogged down the stalls on the one side, and wove my way through the stalls on the other. Nothing. *Nada.* Zilch.

I should have turned left. Figures. It was

just that kind of day. I doubled back and raced over to the next block, feeling the sense that too much time had slipped away and I'd never be able to make this one up to Wesley. I was just too lame. So of course, I kept running. I retraced my steps and did the entire circuit one more time, telling certain vendors I knew to keep a lookout for the box.

And when I found myself at the very end of the Third Street Promenade, all the way south, near the entrance to Santa Monica Place shopping mall, I stopped. I had been running around in circles for fifteen minutes, and running pretty hard.

I leaned over, hands on my knees, and gulped some air. My ankle hurt. In all my racing around, I hadn't seen Wesley, who I was sure must be halfway back to the house by then, unaware of this disaster. I was no longer chilled. My long hair was still pulled back in a braid, but now several stubborn wisps had pulled free and were curling up around my face.

"Madeline?"

Silently, Officer Stubb had glided to a stop beside me.

"Officer?"

I was waiting for my breath to slow down a bit and didn't look up directly.

34

"We've got everyone on it, but the fact is, we seem to have lost your man."

I nodded, head still bent over.

"We'll keep looking. I'll write up a report. You'll need it for insurance, that sort of thing."

When the nice cop starts giving you advice about insurance, you can pretty much kiss your stolen possessions good-bye.

"Okay. Thanks anyway." I stood up. "You want me to spell mah-jongg for your report?"

"That's a good idea. And I'm going to need a way to contact you."

"Right." In case they found my box? I wasn't holding my breath. I wrote down "mah-jongg" on one of my business cards and handed it to him. He thanked me again and pedaled away.

Well, that was that.

I had left my car parked in the oceanside parking structure, which I realized I could reach by cutting through the mall. I pulled open the glass entrance door and walked into Santa Monica Place.

The trilevel skylit galleria was designed by architect Frank Gehry. Like most of L.A.'s landmarks, Santa Monica Place looks familiar to out-of-towners. It was the mall in *Terminator II* and was often seen on *Beverly*

Hills 90210. Yes, I'm afraid even our shopping plazas have screen credits. I checked my watch — twenty past ten. The large shopping mall had just opened for business.

I stopped inside the entrance and flipped open my cell phone. I had to tell Wesley the bad news sometime.

"Wes here," he said. That's his phone schtick. I liked it, so businessman and cordial.

"Madeline here," I replied. "I'm still in Santa Monica."

"Whazzup?" He said it in that disgusting, guttural slangy way that had become popular in a series of beer commercials. We are annoying in this way. We pick up on every fad and buzzword and insist on torturing each other with them. Yes, we are cruel.

"Whazzup?" I said back, being as obnoxious as he was. "Wes, get ready for a big fat horrible story." I was standing near a large planter in the mall.

"What's up?" he asked, his voice instantly full of concern.

I told him the tale.

"So that's it?" Wes asked when I finished. "Your cute bike cop didn't come through?"

"I wish Stubb hadn't stopped me, Wes. I was this close to grabbing the guy." Okay, slight exaggeration. "And I recognized the son of a bitch."

"You did? What do you mean?"

"That guy fingering the chard — did you notice that guy? At Maria's stand. What was his problem?"

And as I was venting and generally acting cranky, standing just inside the mall entrance with shoppers flowing by in ones and twos, I looked up. And there he was. The son of a bitch. He was walking out of Robinsons-May, holding something bulky in a large navy blue Robinsons-May shopping bag.

"Wesley, Wesley, Wesley," I hissed rapidly into the phone, interrupting whatever he was saying. "It's him." He was only about a hundred feet away, walking deeper into the mall, away from where I stood.

"Call the cops." Wes had that stern sound I rarely hear.

"Call you back," I said, and clicked off.

I followed the chard guy, but it was easy this time. The mall was hardly busy this early in the morning. And, even better, the chard guy wasn't on alert. He hadn't seen me. He didn't think he was being followed. He was acting all normal, walking slowly, trying to fit in.

I tried to stay back, walk softly, and match his pace as he strode past the shops. I made sure I was never close enough for my reflection in the window to bounce back at him as we passed by Brookstone, Card Fever, and The Limited. I was careful not to tip him off. Soon, I had followed him all the way through the mall, and we were coming to the opposite entrance.

I crept a little closer. Not a great move.

My cell phone rang. *Wesley.*

Chard man stopped and began to turn.

I peeled off neatly into an open doorway. Lenscrafters. Swell. I punched the YES button, which answers my cell phone, and then immediately punched the NO button hard, holding it until the cell phone was shut down. I had no time to argue with Wes.

And when I'd managed to shut my phone up, I peeked out the door.

He was gone.

What can I say? I ran out after him, but he had vanished. And, believe me, I instantly began to doubt myself. Had I really seen him? Was I post-traumatic nuts? I stood at that mall entrance, looking up and down the walkway. Nothing.

And then something caught my eye. A school-age kid was standing by the parking structure not far away. He was pulling a bag out of the trash can by its cord handles. The top of a large Robinsons-May bag emerged.

"Alex!"

The boy's mom called his name sharply.

"Mom, I found something," he said, pulling the bag out.

I ran over to the boy, desperate to check that bag.

His mother yelled, "Put that back, Alex. Don't take things out of the trash."

"That's my bag." I heard my own voice ring shrill across the sidewalk as I rushed up to the trashcan.

"It's *mine*." Alex held on to it with both hands.

"No, kid, it's mine," I shouted, grabbing for the handles.

The mother hustled herself over in a few steps. "Look, lady," she said to me. "My son found —"

"That's . . . my . . . bag." I shouted, emphasizing each word. "It's mine. Look in the bag if you don't believe me."

The mother was in a difficult spot. On the one hand, she rightly bitched to her kid that he shouldn't be taking trash out of trash cans. On the other, she couldn't stand to have some stranger take something away from her boy. The life of a parent is terrible 'ard, I say.

But I was bigger than Alex, and I was

more determined. "Let *GO!*" I pulled at the bag with force.

"Hey, hey!" The mother was aghast at my rudeness. She suddenly realized I was going to escalate this fight over trash. "Let go of the bag, Alex," she instructed her kid more urgently. What a monster I was. I was willing to steal garbage from a baby. "Let go. This woman is crazy. Let her have all the trash she needs. Remember what I told you about Santa Monica?"

Oh, my word.

"Aw, Mom." But Alex obviously remembered how homeless people dig in the trash. He let go of his prize.

They both glared at me with Republican stares, but I didn't care. I turned my back on them and started to look inside the Robinsons-May bag.

It was there. My box. Wesley's box. The hidden-behind-a-wall box. The stolen box. I had it back at last.

Chapter 3

"Something was definitely wrong about that guy," I said as I moved around my kitchen looking for a big bowl.

Holly looked up. "Yeah, I'll say."

Holly Nichols, tall and fair-skinned and currently platinum blond, has been our full-time assistant almost from the beginning. Over the past seven years, she has received frequent promotions and various impressive job titles because she has proven to be indispensable. Holly is that perfect catering chameleon. No matter the party need, she ably tends bar or twists balloon animals or sallies forth to collect a delinquent bill with awe-inspiring enthusiasm.

Holly, wearing hot pink capri pants and a pair of stacked platform thong sandals, gave me a look. "Like, he stole your stuff."

"More than that," I said.

"Okay." Holly paused in front of the glass door to the large pantry. "Like he stole your stuff and then left it in the trash."

"Well, it's obvious. He saw the dagger and

the silver case. That's all he wanted. So he had to ditch the mah-jongg set. He just hid it in that department store bag until he could find an inconspicuous place to dump it." I looked over at Wes, who was brooding as he worked. "What do you think, Wes?"

"I think I was crazy to bring that stuff to the Farmer's Market in the first place. I was excited, and I wanted you to see it."

"Aw, Wesley . . ." I knew he was feeling bad.

"I didn't want to leave the case in my parked car," Wes continued. "I figured someone might see it and break into the station wagon. Great thinking."

"You can't blame yourself," I said. "We were out in public in daylight. No one can predict random crime."

"I hadn't expected we'd find a knife inside. So I didn't realize . . ."

Wes felt bad for getting me in trouble, and I felt bad for getting him in trouble.

"I'm sorry I lost your stuff, Wesley." Guilt is a really bad feeling.

"That stuff wasn't even mine, really," Wes said. "I was planning to give it back to the home's previous owner."

We'd been talking about this most of the day.

"Maybe we should put this aside for a

minute and get back to work," I suggested.

"Right. You're right."

Wes resumed measuring ingredients for the Chinese Turnip Cakes we were preparing. Tonight, being the first night of the Chinese New Year, seemed to demand we create something extra-special for the mahjongg club.

We were gathered, as we so often are, in the kitchen of my old Spanish house in Whitley Heights. I live in a historic area that straddles the Hollywood Freeway near the Cahuenga off-ramp. In the twenties and thirties, celebrities and film people built Mediterranean mansions and modest Craftsman-style bungalows side by side over the low brown-green foothills. These days, it's still a cool neighborhood, home to an eclectic mix of dog lovers and gay couples and studio folk, from art directors to musicians to that woman who does all the cartoon voice-over work.

Unfortunately, in the past fifty years, downtown Hollywood has taken a nosedive in class. The streets below Whitley Heights have become funky and colorful. Someone more sensitive to grime might even describe them as dirty and dangerous. But I like to think of the transitional nature of these streets as a blessing in disguise. To those of us who couldn't afford to buy a house in any other upscale section of the Hills, nearby Hollywood has kept home prices down. And here's the genius part. This area is poised to make a comeback soon. Really. I know I've been saying this for years but, believe me. And then who will have the prime real estate investment, eh?

My house is set up on its hillside perch amid old California live oaks. It has a lovely old red-tile roof and a rounded stucco wall and a dozen steps up to its arched front door. It was built years ago by Ben Turpin, the silent film comedian who was wildly popular for his "googly eyes." A few years ago, Wesley helped me remodel. After knocking out walls and running wild through a secondhand restaurant supplier, the meager-sized kitchen has been transformed. It is now one capable of producing professional quantities of our gourmet chow.

I looked over the kitchen, my spiritual center, really. The workspace was neatly fitted with brushed aluminum appliances, its walls a clean graph of white ceramic tiles, its counters made from yards of genuine butcherblock we'd recovered from an old bakery going out of business. And while I know it's not cool to become overly fond of

inanimate objects, I have a crush on my refrigerator. It's one of those Traulsen restaurant units — the kind you see in some delis.
The door is made of glass so you can see inside, and it's lighted. Wes tells me I like to
keep an eye on my produce lest it go limp on
me.

"So what about that chard guy?" Holly
asked.

"The cops never found him," I said, as
Wes pulled out his recipe book. He had less
curiosity than a mushroom.

"Well, it's not like it's a big mystery."
Holly had sifted a huge sack of flour out
onto her work surface and was now pushing
up the sleeves of her thin sweater. At close to
six feet tall, she was narrow as a breadstick.
She was letting her stick-straight whitish
blond hair grow out these days, and then
clipping it back in odd, off-balanced little
tufts, with several tiny barrettes in various
hues. "I mean, didn't you say the police took
that old antique case so they could fingerprint it?" she asked, making her point.
"They'll figure out who the chard guy is."

"Maybe." I looked up, struck again with
guilt. "But I doubt we'll ever see that old
Dragon dagger again. Or the silver case. I'm
so sorry, Wesley."

"Please, Mad. I told you. It was my fault."

Wes and I had spent most of the afternoon at the Santa Monica police station giving descriptions of what we could recollect. In the end, we were told to go home. They would keep the box, probably just overnight, and dust it for prints. They'd get in touch if they needed more information. One of the department's clerical people looked at my ankle. She had a first-aid box and gave me some disinfectant cream and a Band-Aid. And that was that.

As Wes and Holly kept reminding me over and over since we came home, muggings happen every day. I know that. It's just shocking, that's all. It's shocking when crime brushes against you, even petty crime. But we had a party to prepare for this evening. I had to readjust my focus. And so, we got back to work.

As befitted the Chinese New Year's holiday, our host requested a special feast. Buster Dubin asked us to prepare dinner for twenty. He expected to have four games of mah-jongg going at once, and was ready to set up a fifth if necessary.

"Holly, I think that's plenty of rice flour," I said.

She looked up from her work and said, "Cool." And then she sat down on a tall stool nearby. "So tell me all about this

Chinese New Year's thing."

I deferred to Wesley, a man with too many advanced degrees and the kind of memory for detail that can be infuriating when he's remembering *to the word* what you said to him nine years ago, but in all other regards is quite a lovely resource. While Wes explained Chinese New Year, I turned on the computer at my corner desk and found the website I was looking for.

"Chinese New Year is like a combination of Easter and Thanksgiving," Wes said.

"Except, without the turkey, Pilgrims, or cross," Holly guessed.

"True. But food has high significance. Everything that is eaten during this two-week Chinese holiday holds auspicious meaning. Imagine that everything you eat or drink in the next two weeks will influence your life for the next full year."

As I clicked a few links on my computer screen, I quietly set down my can of Diet Coke.

Holly stared at her half-bitten peanut butter cup. "Gosh."

Wesley laughed.

I found what I was looking for on the 'Net. It was a clever little site that allows you to send a virtual fortune cookie by e-mail in honor of the Chinese New Year. I typed in

47

my message and chuckled. This would be fun. The recipients will check their e-mail before the party. They'll see a picture of a little golden fortune cookie. They click on the cookie and the animated cookie cracks open and reveals the fortune.

I tried it first before I sent the e-cookies out. My evil little message: *Be willing to taste anything once.* Well, what would you expect from me?

"By the way," Wes said, walking over and noticing what I was up to, "there is nothing Chinese about the fortune cookie. The fortune cookie is an American invention."

"But it's a lot of fun," I said, turning my mind back to predictions of the future. "It will put all the players in a good mood. And I've got a more authentic Chinese fortune-teller coming to the party — Lee Chen."

Lee was an old friend of mine. I could hardly wait to see her. She and I met several years ago, and although I hadn't seen her lately, I always felt a special bond with Lee.

"So," Holly asked, looking up at Wesley, "we're making . . . New Year's Turnip Cake?"

She had the list of ingredients and was measuring and setting them up on the kitchen's center island. She read off the ingredients to make sure she had them all.

" 'Eight Chinese dried mushrooms,' check . . . 'one-half cup Chinese dried shrimp,' check . . . 'two teaspoons *Shao Hsing* rice cooking wine,' got it . . . 'one tea-spoon sugar and two cups rice flour,' got it."

"Good."

"Now, what all is *this?*" Holly squinted at the page with my slanty scribbling on it. " '6 ounces *lop yok,* store-bought or home-made . . .' " She looked up. "Do we have to make some *lop yok* now?"

"I stopped in Chinatown. Look in the fridge."

"For?" Holly asked.

"*Lop yok* is Chinese bacon."

"Excellent." She brought over the raw bacon, along with a large glass pie pan that we needed to steam it before slicing.

"And the main ingredient?" Wes asked.

Holly scooted over to the list and read: "A two-pound law book." She grinned at him.

"That's *law bok,*" Wesley corrected promptly. "Chinese turnip."

Sometimes, whilst cooking, I do believe Wesley may on occasion lose his sense of humor. Holly and I shouldn't tease him, but it's so damn tempting to get a rise out of the guy.

"Not a law book? You're sure?" Holly looked at him.

"Turnip cake," he continued, "is made with Chinese turnip which is called *law bok*. It's a type of *daikon* radish. There is also a *daikon* radish called Japanese *daikon* radish, which is similar to the Chinese turnip in appearance." Wes snickered to himself. "Actually, to make matters even more confusing . . ."

"Could they be?" Holly whispered to me.

". . . translated into English, *law bok* means turnip. Some produce vendors do not realize there is a distinction."

I could imagine the illuminating lectures to which Wesley Westcott must treat such poorly informed vendors and smiled.

"Is it this ugly thing?" Holly asked. She held up a mottled whitish root, about ten inches long and four inches around.

"Right, Holly. The Chinese turnip is more blemished-looking than the Japanese *daikon*."

Holly looked at the root, perhaps to memorize it.

I turned my attention back to the *lop yok,* quickly cutting the raw slab of bacon into thirds. Some people remove only the rind of the Chinese bacon, leaving all the fat. But I find this too rich. I discard the layer of fat under the rind as well. Steaming for about twenty minutes makes it soft enough to dice finely.

"So, Wesley," Holly said, "why do we serve *law bok* cakes on Chinese New Year?"

I loved to hear Wes talk food talk as we worked together in the kitchen.

"Eating cake is a ritual at Chinese New Year — very symbolic — but turnip cakes are a little more like fried polenta than your basic chocolate layer."

"That's the only trouble I have with Chinese food," Holly said, as she began to grate the fresh *law bok*. "Who can embrace a cuisine that doesn't glorify chocolate?"

"When our turnip cake is cooled," Wes continued, "we'll cut it up into bite-size pieces. Then we'll pan-fry it fresh when we get to Dubin's house, and serve it Dim Sum style, sizzling hot with oyster sauce."

"So what is the special meaning behind turnip cake?" Holly asked, putting a little more arm muscle into her grating.

"Ah, well. Rice flour symbolizes cohesiveness."

"Who couldn't use a little more cohesion," Holly commented. "That's nice."

"The round shape represents unity of family."

"Cute," Holly said.

"And the slight rising of the cakes indicates rising fortune," Wes finished.

"Wesley Westcott, you are freaky!" Holly said.

I nodded. Well, he is.

And I added, "That's what makes Chinese New Year's Turnip Cake the perfect dish to serve the mah-jongg group tonight. Gamers are so superstitious."

Carefully, I lowered the bacon on its glass plate into the boiling pot and replaced the lid. Meanwhile, Holly joined me at the stove. She placed all the grated Chinese turnip along with a quart of water in a heavy pot, and then set it on medium-high heat.

Wes was finishing up with the dried mushrooms and shrimp, placing each in a bowl of water for the thirty minutes it would take to rehydrate them.

I cleaned up a bit and worried a bit, too.

No matter how hard I tried to distract myself with work and cooking and friends, I couldn't shake the disturbing events of the morning. Surely, on the dawning of the Chinese New Year, this mugging must have some deeper meaning. And, as we finished preparing the Chinese Turnip Cakes, I hoped the signs for our own good fortune might be more auspicious.

"Did you ever get a call back from the police?" I asked Wesley.

He shook his head.

52

I thought it over one more time. The chard guy got rid of the mah-jongg game as soon as he could, but the dagger and the silver box were missing.

I felt really bad, and I couldn't tell what was making me feel worse — the idea that I had allowed myself to be ripped off in broad daylight at my favorite outdoor market, or the thought that another punk in this big, bad city had his hands on another weapon.

Chapter 4

Party planners are like vampires. We tend to be pale. We're willing to drink odd things. All right, I might be stretching it a bit. But we do stay up all night. We work late catering dinners, and wake up at strange times depending on if we want to catch the before-dawn arrival of fresh tulips at the flower mart or sleep in late after throwing an after-hours soiree. It is lucky that Wesley and I operate rather well on less sleep than most people do.

Our prep work for the upcoming Chinese New Year's party was completed by four and that left us a few hours before we had to set up the party at seven-thirty. Holly was going to run out and do some errands. It doesn't matter what time of the day or night she finds a few spare minutes. She knows exactly which hardware store, dry cleaners, and Bed, Bath, and Beyond are open twenty-four hours. Later, our bartender Ray would meet her back at the house to pack up for the party.

In the meantime, I had promised Wesley

I'd go over to the new place he was remodeling on Wetherbee. We took his station wagon — caterers tend to drive cars and vans that can schlep platters and coolers — and we drove west from my place.

As we cruised slowly in rush hour traffic, we watched the low-rent stretch of Sunset Boulevard metamorphose from grungy industrial to tacky motels. Here, naughty street corners had been known to lure idiot superstars to self-destruct. I might mention I almost never see hookers when I drive by, which I find vaguely disappointing from a purely sight-seeing perspective.

In only a couple of miles, however, the street turned trendy. There's a sudden pop-culture rush of giant billboards featuring three-story-high movie posters, or building-sized faces of rock stars. Wes calls this stretch of Sunset "bright lights/big egos." Only when you see a sixty-foot-high painting of Puff Daddy's nose on top of Tower Records do you really know Sunset has fully morphed into the Strip.

To the right of us as we drove slowly west, the Hollywood Hills rose in lumpy prominence. Their winding roads and exclusive neighborhoods were filled with celebrity neighbors. Having survived our bumper-to-bumper drive up Sunset, Wes turned his

Mercedes wagon up Doheny. We left the city below for a quick jaunt into the hills.

I looked out my window. Large homes were crammed right next to larger homes on either side of Doheny Drive. Many of the hillside communities placed a premium on land. In this neighborhood, you could buy a house that needed work for a million, and — if you fixed it up — sell it again for a million-three, or a million-five. Lots of upside potential here, the real estate brokers liked to say. I couldn't wait to see Wesley's fixer.

Wes turned onto Wetherbee, one of the narrow side streets that wound up to the right.

"It's a mess," he said. "We're doing everything — new electrical, new plumbing, new roof, new kitchen. We've been ripping the hell out of it. We just pulled out all the cabinets — these sad yellow plywood things put in in the fifties."

"Demolition is fun," I said.

Wesley loved houses. He hated to see a bizarre den addition or bathroom remodel from the dreaded sixties or seventies make a fool of a beautiful old home. It hurt him to discover some lovely early twentieth century architectural gem that had been anachronized over the years by owners who had "modernized."

Wes pulled his car into the driveway of a large Tudor-style house. Against the darkening sky, I could make out the metal Dumpster at the curb. After Wesley's busy week, I had no doubt with what the truck-size bin was filled: the debris of the home's remodeling errors-past and the detritus of several decades of out-of-date add-ons.

Wes turned with a smile. "We've got a lot of work ahead. I want your advice. And remember, Quita McBride is coming here at six."

Quita McBride. This was going to be tricky.

Quita happened to be one of the members of the Sweet and Sour Mah-Jongg Club, which is where Wes and I first met her.

"Did you tell her about the theft?" I asked.

"I thought it would be easier in person," Wes said.

"Oh."

Let me back up. The Sweet and Sour Club was a loosely organized group. It was mostly social. Its members included the usual Hollywood types, each with the proper fun-loving personality, the gambler's love of mah-jongg's intricacies, and an all-important adjacency to disposable cash.

Buster Dubin was the leader of the Sweet

and Sour Club, and Quita was his latest girl-friend. Buster tended to move through girl-friends rather quickly. He was that kind of guy. But in all fairness, it must be said that Quita had a pretty busy past herself.

Until recently, Quita had been living in this house on Wetherbee. She was the widow of the previous owner who had died only last year. Naturally, this was a whole story.

See, this new house of Wesley's was a "celebrity" home, which is really quite a real estate coup. A celebrity connection is just the sort of thing that gives homebuyers the tingles. It sells houses. In the case of this Wetherbee house, forties leading man Richard "Dickey" McBride was the famous previous homeowner. "Dickey McBride slept here" gave this address clout. The movie star's love life covered several live-in mistresses, five or six wives, and ended with Quita McBride.

Wes said, "Quita has never struck me as the brightest light on the dimmer board. But she's sweet."

Yes. Quita McBride had certainly been helpful. It was through her that Wesley first learned the Wetherbee house was coming on the market. But, in truth, we didn't know her well. We had never really wanted to.

"She's had a rough year," Wes said.

When Dickey McBride dropped dead from a heart attack last year, their old home had to be sold. Quita mentioned the news at one of the mah-jongg parties. That's how things get done here. Word of mouth. Naturally, Wesley became interested in the property as soon as she described what a wreck it was. And thanks to knowing Quita, he was able to make an offer on it well before it had a chance to make the *LA Times*' Hot Properties column.

"She's kind of a space cadet, isn't she?" I looked at Wes. He had gotten to know her better. They'd had a few conversations as the house moved through escrow.

"She seems spacey. I don't know if that's an act, though. She seems to take care of herself." Wes pulled out his key ring and opened the front door.

Inside, the house was gloomy and darkish. "Sorry. The lights don't work right now. We're in the middle of rewiring."

I walked through the empty entry hall and into the dusty living room. "Oh, Wesley! This place is wonderful."

"Do you like it?" Wes lit a candle and set it down on the mantel of a large fireplace in the living room. "It's got such good bones, don't you think? Look at the ceiling."

59

Large wooden beams crossed high above. "It must be two stories high."

"Sixteen feet. And we've been able to save the original finish on the beams."

"I love it." I gave my good friend a hug. "You have so much energy. You are amazing."

He folded his arms against the slight chill in the empty room and grinned.

Just then, there was a tap at the door. It had been so light I wasn't sure at first if I had heard anything at all.

"That's probably Quita." Wesley crossed to the entry hall and opened the front door.

In stepped a thin woman. She was "built," as they used to say. Her large chest was absolutely the first thing anyone noticed about Quita. She wore her thick blond hair longer and bigger than was fashionable at the moment. Her darkly tanned face looked like a kitten's with a pointy chin and a small mouth.

"Maddie," Wes said, playing the host, "of course you know Quita."

"Hi, Quita."

"Nice to see you."

Quita looked me over quickly and then followed Wes into the living room, which was now a huge hollow space, its dusty hardwood floors here and there covered in drop cloths, its walls in places open and exposed all the way to the studs.

Wes picked up a large piece of plastic sheeting. "Sorry about the mess."

"No, don't be," Quita said. Her voice was soft. She turned back to me. "You're Wesley's partner, the caterer."

"Yep." I'd only seen Quita every week for the past six months. But some in Hollywood don't notice the background people.

Quita looked around the empty space slowly. She wore a purply fuchsia-colored silk dress, which fit a little snugly in places over her ample curves.

"So," Wes said, "you got all of your furniture, right?"

"No."

"I beg your pardon?" Wesley looked concerned.

"No. I didn't. Actually." Quita turned her slightly unfocused gaze from the ripped-open walls of the entry and tried to settle them on Wesley. She just missed. "I think they took all of Dickey's and my things and put them in storage. Anyway, it doesn't matter. The lawyers are selling everything. Did you know that? They are. They'll have one of those fabulous celebrity auctions. And all the money will go to Dickey's estate, which comes to me. Only it

61

takes scads of time. It's ridiculous."

"Really." I couldn't help but be curious. So Quita, the last wife, was getting all of Richard McBride's money. According to the cover story in *People* the week he died, Dickey regretted never having children. With no other heirs, Quita was inheriting the lot. As she was forty-five years younger, it might even be argued that Quita was the "child" Dickey had dreamed of, but let's not go there.

"So your life is moving on," I said cleverly.

"Yes." Quita shifted her off-center gaze from somewhere in the vicinity of Wesley to make eye contact with me, almost. I noticed Quita had watery gray eyes. She was pretty, but something was slightly off, like her tiny kittenlike nose was just a smidge too tiny.

"I would have loved to have seen the house before everything was removed. Wes said it was filled with art."

"I have pictures. Somewhere. In one of my boxes. If you'd like to see them . . ."

"How cool."

I threw Wes a look. I really doubted I'd be spending much time with Quita McBride, going through old boxes and memories. But it was a magnificently odd thought. And Wesley and I love odd.

"I'd like to see any old pictures you have

of the place," Wes said. He was the consummate rehabber, always digging for historical references. He pulled out a business card for Mad Bean Events and handed it to Quita. "If you should find any pictures, please give us a call at the work number."

"Have you got anything at all to drink here?" Quita asked.

"Sorry," Wes said. "No. We don't have power right now. And the kitchen's been gutted."

"Oh, of course. That's right. Can I take a look?"

"At the kitchen? Sure. I was just going to give Madeline the tour." Wesley picked up a candle and handed it to Quita. "Just watch your step and follow . . ."

Wes was going to say, "Follow me."

I caught his eye. Damned awkward, if you ask me, leading a widow around her own house especially after one has just finished ripping the place up.

"This must be so horrible for you," I said to Quita, following her down the hallway. I noticed she was almost as tall as Holly is. Man, why is it that I am always surrounded by tall ones. I remembered something about her working as a model in the past. "It must be a shock coming back to your house and finding it under construction like this."

It is just my way. I don't like to dance around a dead buffalo, if one happens to be lying in the ballroom. I prefer to call everyone's attention to the dead buffalo and suggest it be removed.

Wesley, however, winced.

Some don't care for the direct approach. Some prefer to wait until the flies are so thick around the dead buffalo it can no longer be denied. Now, where's the sense in that approach?

"It is weird," Quita said. "I was just in here, getting a glass of juice for Dickey . . . was it really a year ago?" She stared at the gutted kitchen, without so much as a countertop or cabinet or appliance, its pipes exposed.

"Sorry," Wes said. "I thought it might not be such a good idea to meet at the house."

"No, no. I'm fine."

The three of us stood together in the middle of what had once been the kitchen, the candlelight flickering off our faces. Quita turned to me. "I did need to talk with Wesley about some of my property. But really, I wanted to see the house, too. I needed to see it. Dickey's gone. The house we shared is gone. I have to remember that it's all gone, now."

I don't know. There was something about

the pause that lingered an extra beat, her delicate chin in the air. I could have sworn she was ready for her close-up. But then, perhaps I was wrong. Perhaps this was what it took for her to come to terms with her new lot in life.

"It's all gone," she repeated, her eyes misting a bit.

Yes, but, what were we sniffling about here? The house Quita moved into with Buster Dubin was much nicer than this old house had been, even before construction started. And Quita hadn't wasted much time moving on to a new man with a new mansion. But don't mind me. I can be horribly judgmental at times.

We stood there in silence. Well, of course, the woman had been through an awful lot in the past twelve months.

"I'm sorry about your loss," I said to her. See. I could be nice. "Your husband died only a short time ago, I know."

"Eleven months ago." Quita looked at me and gave me a shy smile. "It was such a shock. So out of the blue. He was healthy. He was very healthy. And then, one night, he was . . . gone."

"So sad," I murmured. I had heard McBride had died in bed. With Quita. That had to be a shock. "How old was he?"

Quita glared at me, suddenly angry. "Yes. I know. He was seventy-five. Everyone talks about that."

Wesley gave me a look which I took to mean "shut up already," but I think people are too afraid of talking about feelings. Of course, Wes has on occasion suggested I am not afraid *enough* of these sorts of conversations, but so be it!

"I read about it in the papers. They said it was his heart."

"Yes, yes, his heart!" Quita tossed off the words. "And, yes, Dickey had a heart condition. I know. You are thinking that I don't want to face reality, and you know what? You are probably right."

I smiled at Wesley. Good therapy was going on here, in this darkened, demolished kitchen.

And then Quita burst out into loud sobs. She clutched at her leaking face with both overly tanned hands, but tears gushed out all the same.

"Oh dear."

I looked at Wesley, who really had the most smug, I-told-you-so sort of grimace on his normally handsome face. "Wes, don't you have any Kleenex?"

Okay, sometimes "good therapy" is wet.

Chapter 5

Quita was shaking with her sobs. I was struck with how rarely one hears a grown person crying hard. It's not a pleasant sound, with loud coughing, moaning outbursts, and harsh, rushing drags of air. In a few seconds, Wesley returned with a fresh roll of paper towels. I ripped off the cellophane, tore out a few sheets, and handed them to Quita.

Wes came close to me, and we both stood by as Quita eventually settled down.

"Don't worry, Quita. This is probably a very healthy thing. It's important to unload these feelings."

"Thanks." Quita tried to make eye contact, but failed miserably. "But I've been crying like this for the past . . ." She never finished the sentence, as new sobs welled up and drowned out her power to communicate further.

I stared at the bare walls and realized that I had developed, just in the past few minutes, an overwhelming desire to cook. This kitchen was weeks away from providing that kind of comfort. If only I could have baked something. Or put on a pot of tea, at least.

"It's not just the house that I miss," Quita said, picking up the story again. "And I know everyone is saying I wanted the money, but it's not the money."

Wesley looked mortified. All he could do was rip her off another paper towel.

"Look, none of this is your fault," Quita said, looking at Wes. "You bought Dickey's house, the house of the greatest star in Hollywood. Who could blame you for wanting it? Not me. And I guess you can do whatever you want with it. If ripping it up and redoing it is your thing, well go for it. You know? I just miss it. I miss my life. But that's the past. And now that I see it with my own eyes, I think I'm starting to believe it's really all gone. So, anyway . . ."

"Shall we leave the kitchen?" Wes asked.

He led the way back to the front of the house at a sprightly pace. That guy does not like a scene.

Quita's voice had settled down, and her tears had stopped pouring out. "I'll see you both at the party in a little while, right?" she asked us, remembering who we were and what she'd be doing later. "At Buster's house? Oh, I look disgusting. I've got to go change."

"There's time," I said. "Don't worry."

She turned to Wes. "But before I go. Where's my mah-jongg case?"

Uh-oh. We knew this was coming. See, Wes had found the antique MJ set upstairs in this house, in the wall of Quita and Dickey's old bedroom. This morning, just before he met me at the Farmer's Market, he had called Quita McBride to tell her the news of his astonishing find. Wes intended to give Quita the stuff he found. He didn't have to, legally. But of course he had wanted to. And now . . . Well . . .

"Quita, I wanted to tell you this in person."

"What?"

"It's about that old mah-jongg set."

"Yes. Dickey's old Chinese antique. I remember it. It was the one we played on when we were first dating." Quita sighed a pretty sigh. "Dickey taught me how to play MJ. I'm so, so grateful you found it for me. I'd been looking everywhere for it. Actually, it's been missing for years."

"Really?"

"That's why I was so annoyed at the Sotheby's people. They're doing the auction for us. The movers brought everything to Sotheby's, and I was sure Dickey's maj set would turn up in the mix. I specifically called and asked them if it was there. They haven't done a complete inventory, and they said I'd have to wait. But now, you found the old maj set! And hidden in the wall!" She shook her head. "My husband could be very secretive."

"Oh, I did find something else," Wes said, surely to postpone the inevitable. "In the garage we found a carton of paperbacks. Were those your husband's?"

"No. Probably mine. That's all I read," Quita said.

"Really?"

"They're great to take to the beach, you know? Dickey thought they were worthless, but I was always trying to find him a new property — something he could star in again. He preferred sci-fi. Did you know he was up for the part of Obi-Wan Kenobi in *Star Wars*? He turned it down. I think he regretted that."

No kidding.

"Remember *Kangaroo Planet*? That came out a little before. Dickey was magnificent in that one."

"Wow," Wes said. "Now that's a movie I haven't thought of in a long time."

Kangaroo Planet. What a hoot — an old-style goofy sci-fi flick. I remembered seeing it years ago. I must have been in second grade.

"That was when I first fell in love with Dickey, I think," Quita said. She seemed lost in her memories. "He was such a great actor. My sister and I were kids when our mom took us to see *Kangaroo Planet*. It was the first movie I remember seeing in a theater. What a trip, you know? I could never have guessed back then how I would move to California someday. Or that I'd meet — actually meet — the real, live Dickey McBride in person. Or that Dickey and I would someday . . . that we'd form such a close . . . bond."

"Who did he play, again?" I asked. It was on the tip of my tongue. "The big one with the floppy ear . . . Daddy Roo!"

"Yes! Wasn't he amazing?" Quita looked at me, happy to find a fellow fan of Dickey's with whom to share her memories.

"Of course," she continued, "I have the video. I make Buster watch it with me all the time."

That must be fun for him.

But really, I was being bombarded with bizarre. *Kangaroo Planet*. Big Daddy Roo. And then, that long-ago little girl Quita falling for an old guy who looked, in that film, more marsupial than man.

People are odd, I reminded myself for the trillionth time since I moved to L.A. But this

71

scene was taking odd to a totally new level. An all-time oddness high. I looked over at Wesley who must have been thinking the same thing.

Quita was hard to fathom. She currently had a cute new boyfriend — Buster Dubin, a guy we knew and liked. A young guy with plenty of money and talent. And yet, she still missed the old guy. Maybe love is blind. Or maybe there are some women for whom the best aphrodisiac is fame.

Dickey McBride. I suddenly recalled the bit in *Kangaroo Planet* where Dickey led them all in jet-powered hopping. Sometimes, practiced as I am in the art of restraint in the face of utter absurdity — after all, that is how I make my living — even I cannot keep a straight face. Wes, kindly, avoided making eye contact.

Quita looked out toward the purple and pink impatiens flower border that rimmed the sloped, grassy front lawn. She must have stood in this entry a thousand different times over the past decade, saying good-bye. Only on those other occasions, she hadn't been the one expected to leave.

"But now, about Dickey's MJ set," Quita said, bringing us to the unavoidable subject.

Neither Wes nor I said anything.

I took another tack. "I had no idea that

Richard McBride played mah-jongg. How amazing," I said.

"My husband had played mah-jongg for years and years. Literally, from before we were born. He played with some of his dear old friends. You know Catherine Hill?"

Everyone knew Catherine Hill. She was a child star at MGM along with Dickey when he was a young singing, dancing teen heart-throb. She played plucky orphans and poor cousins to Dickey's rich-boy parts in a long series of forties box office hits.

"Your husband played *mah-jongg* with Catherine Hill?" I was astonished.

"She was one of Dickey's regular mah-jongg buddies."

You never think of screen stars and what they do in their private lives, do you? Why shouldn't they shop at Ralph's or devour Sue Grafton novels or sit around passing the cashews while playing mah-jongg with the girls? They just want to have fun, like the rest of us. They have to do something. And an aging film star probably has more time on her hands than most, come to recon-sider.

"I was planning to bring the MJ set over to her house later. I'm sure that's what Dickey would have wanted me to do."

"You don't want to keep it?" I asked.

We were in luck. She was planning to give the old mah-jongg set away to Dickey's old mah-jongg buddy, Catherine *Freaking* Hill. So how bad could it be that we lost track of it for a little while this morning, eh? How hard would she take it that the set was currently being fingerprinted, but would be returned shortly? I started feeling a little better about our chances of avoiding an unpleasant scene. Wesley, the dog, looked equally relieved.

"So, really," I said, acting calm. "You plan to give the set away?"

"It was a nice set," Quita said, but her voice sounded as if it was not nice enough. "But then, the mah-jongg set Dickey bought for me was even nicer. Rarer. And I don't even think his old set was complete anymore. The value goes way down if you're missing pieces, you know?"

I didn't really. I did notice that some of the younger players like to own these wonderful vintage mah-jongg tiles and the prices had climbed in the past several years, they said. But just as likely the members of the Sweet and Sour Club would use new sets and have their names engraved on the White Dragons.

She shifted in the doorway. "You didn't happen to find my book, by any chance? I

74

know Dickey used to keep it locked away in that old case."

One of the drawers of the antique Chinese mah-jongg case had held a small book of game instructions or something. I tried to remember clearly. "I think there *was* a book."

Quita stared at me in surprise. "You don't mean to say that you found Dickey's lost novel! Covered in red leather?"

"I think it was a red book." I looked at Wes again.

"Dickey McBride wrote a novel?" Wes asked Quita. "I don't remember hearing about that."

"No, of course you wouldn't have. It was never published. That's the great tragedy. I urged him to write it. We talked about it, you see. Dickey McBride had many talents. He could have been a very great voice in literary fiction. I guess you might say I was his muse. Dickey and I worked on it together — well, I gave him a lot of encouragement. It was a love story. So it had certain meaning to me, you understand? But I never got to read the finished work."

"I see," Wesley said, looking suddenly glummer.

She took a deep breath and went on. "He worked on it for months, scribbling in longhand. He kept the project in a red leather-bound book I gave him as a gift that Christmas. When he finished, he didn't want me to look at it. I begged him to send it to his friend, Daniel Carter, who was the biggest literary agent in the country. It would have been enormous. Dickey McBride's first novel. But, unfortunately, Dickey had a true artist's temperament. Even though his prose was perfect, he himself wasn't pleased with it at all. Not the least little bit. He ended up telling me it was a big mistake. But I know that isn't true.

"He told me he was going to lock the book in his favorite old mah-jongg chest and put it away. I was terribly disappointed. But Dickey did what he wanted to do. I looked and looked for that old mah-jongg set and couldn't imagine where it had gotten to. Now, I realize my darling Dickey had it sealed up in the wall when we were remodeling. That was two years ago. And now, thank God, you have found it at last. May I have it?"

"Well, there is just one small problem."

"What problem?"

"We don't actually have the set Wes called you about. Not right here."

"What is this? Are you two shaking me down or something?" Quita's vague gray

76

eyes glistened with a certain sharpness.

"Of course not!" Wes was shocked.

"I don't understand," she said, her voice shrill. "You called me this morning, Wesley. You woke me up! You told me I could come pick my things up if I wanted to. Tonight!"

"Well, actually, I offered to bring the mah-jongg set to the Sweet and Sour club party tonight," Wes corrected. "You said you would rather pick it up early."

"Of course I did!" She was getting more upset. "Actually, I made a few phone calls about that old set. Now where the hell is it?"

"Look, Quita," I said, "someone attacked me this morning. I was supposed to be taking the mah-jongg set back to our office. It's a long story, but the book was in the mah-jongg case, and we were mugged."

"What are you talking about? What happened?" She looked frantic. "All this time you were just talking and talking and . . . Why didn't you tell me all of this before? When I first got here? What are you two doing to me?"

"I was going to tell you, but . . ." Wes said. It sounded lame.

"*Where?*" Quita screamed. Really, she should be mad. Sure. But this was getting strange now. "*Where was this?*"

"In Santa Monica," Wes answered.

"Madeline chased the guy but . . ."

"But *WHAT?*" Quita screamed at us again.

It hadn't been a random theft at all. It wasn't a street mugging. Quita was much too upset for that. Someone was after that case because they wanted that book. And it sure as hell wasn't a book of mah-jongg instructions, then, was it? And for that matter, I wouldn't bet the farm that it was any first novel, either.

Chapter 6

Quita stood outside her old mansion on Wetherbee and began breathing irregularly, hyperventilating.

"This man . . ." she said, between trying to slow down her breaths, ". . . who stole the case and the book . . . he . . ." She tried again. "Who was he?"

The chard guy. I knew there was a problem with the chard guy.

"That's the trouble," I said. "He ran off. The police have the mah-jongg case, now, and they're going to do a fingerprint test."

"Oh my God! Oh my God!" Quita had gone extremely white beneath her deep tan. "Tell me this isn't happening. What did he look like?"

"A smallish man, dark complexion. Late forties, early fifties maybe."

And then, right on the front step, Quita sat down hard, buckling into a heap, her purple dress hiking up, revealing long shapely legs.

"What's wrong? What's the matter?" I sat

down next to the woman, trying to see if this was one of those situations that required an ambulance.

"Please . . ." Quita gulped. "Please, help me . . ."

Wesley had run down the lawn to his car and fetched back a bottle of Deja Blue water. He untwisted the cap and held it out to the stricken woman seated on the pavement.

"Do you happen . . . to have . . . any Xanax?" She looked up at us, still hyperventilating.

"Sorry," I said.

Wesley and I were probably the only two people in the L.A. basin who didn't, but that's us.

"Valium?"

"Sorry, no."

"Zoloft? Wellbutrin?"

We looked apologetic.

She gasped for breath. "Maybe . . . a shot of Scotch?"

Wes gestured to the water bottle in her hand. "That's the strongest stuff I've got."

"Wes!" I felt a little stressed that we could do nothing to help. Now if I'd had a chance to bake, at least I could be offering her a cookie. But, no.

"I'm sorry," Wes said again. "Would you

like us to call you an ambulance?"

"No . . . no, thanks. I'm all right." Quita stood up, shakily, and steadied herself against the exterior wall to the right of the open entrance door.

"Quita," I said, "exactly what happened to us this morning?"

Wes and I stood there, waiting.

"Dickey's book. There's a fortune that could be made as soon as someone publishes Dickey's book," Quita whispered.

Uh-huh.

"Who knew he was writing a novel?" Wes asked. Good one.

"Well . . ." Quita was not the fastest thinker. "Maybe . . . Catherine Hill."

Catherine Hill? Did she expect us to believe that the legendary movie queen, Catherine Hill, sent some damn chard guy to attack me this morning, just to steal an unpublished novel?

"Okay. Don't believe me. Nobody ever does. Buster never listens to one word I say. But things are going wrong. Things are going to get worse. And I'm scared." Quita looked down at the bottle of water in her hand and took a tentative swig. "They're going to come after me," she mumbled.

"*Who* is?" I asked, stumped. "Catherine

Hill?" That legendary old queen bee was seventy at least.

Quita's unfocused gray eyes swept the street, as if there could be some long-retired leading lady out there gunning for her or something. She was sticking with this story. But it didn't make any sense.

"Hey, I'm in trouble here, okay? You don't realize what kind of trouble. I need help. Get that? Either Catherine Hill or one of the other crazy ladies that Dickey used to play mah-jongg with. They hate me. They'd like to see me dead. They think I purposely lured Dickey to have, you know, relations with me that night, even though I knew about his heart condition."

Ah. This was interesting.

"But it's all a load of crap. Look, I have to get away. I won't be safe at Buster's house now." She looked at Wes, her eyes pleading. "Hey, how about this? Let me stay right here at the house. Please. It's perfect. You aren't living here. Everyone knows the house was sold, and I moved out months ago. No one will think to look for me here." She sounded frantic.

I looked at her. Who exactly was Quita McBride really? I had not a clue. It's just a reminder that you never know. You never know who any casual acquaintance really is, do you? Those people who appear on the outskirts of your life, they're a mystery. They seem like anyone else — like your basic regular human. Well, in Quita's case, like your basic regular bored Hollywood wife mah-jongg fanatic type of human. But that's on the outside. On the inside they could very well be a neurotic mixed-up mess, bordering on delusional, and involved in any sort of bad business. It's shocking, though, when you see that other side.

Wesley had a wary look in his eyes. But he used that special, soft voice of his that was so soothing, where he speaks slowly in those low tones. It comes in handy on our party circuit when he must talk some poor over-wrought hostess down off of some figurative ledge. I like to think of him as the crazed-female whisperer. He said, "Look around here now. This isn't a house. It's a construction site. Of course you can't stay here. It's not even safe."

"Listen," she said, calming her own voice down. She took a breath and spoke more slowly. "I know you think I'm crazy, but I promise you I'm not. It's very complicated. But that doesn't matter now. Now, I just need a place to stay. I'll go to Buster's for the party, but then later, I need someplace safe. Please help me. Please," she said, turning to

83

me, "let me stay with you for a few nights. That's all."

"Stay with *me?*"

What was in that water bottle, anyway? Do I look like the kind of idiot who goes down to see what the noise was in the basement in some horror movie? Do I? I leave the basement door locked and bolted, and I leave any casually met psychos alone. That's just me.

"No one will ever find me at your house, Madeline. It's perfect. We hardly know each other. Our only connection is that you cook for parties and I go to parties. That's nothing. It will work. I'll be safe."

"Look, Quita . . ."

Her eyes pleaded with me. Why is it so hard to just say no?

"I'd like to help you. I would . . ."

I turned to Wesley, who was giving me a very stern look.

"But," I continued, "I just don't know what is going on here. And with a thief still on the loose, I think this has gone way beyond anything I can help with. Please talk to someone."

"Talk to someone? Who? What do you mean?" She pulled her hands through her long blond hair, a gesture of confusion as much as anything else, leaving it more tangled than before.

"Go talk to Buster, or your sister, or your therapist, or the cops."

"The police?" Quita looked baffled, her eyes opening wide. "You want me to go to the cops? They won't listen to me. They won't believe me."

A guarded look came over her.

We stood there for a few moments, in the dark. It was getting chilly.

"So," Quita said, looking down at the ground. "You won't let me stay at your house? Even though I told you I really need your help? Even though I explained how I can't stay at Buster's house tonight."

Honestly. How do I get into these things?

"Can't you check into a hotel?" Wes asked, the voice of reason.

"They'll trace me from my credit cards. I can't do that! I know how they trace people." She looked pretty scared.

"Well, here." I slipped my wallet from the back pocket of my jeans and pulled out several twenties. "Take this."

"What?"

"Go ahead. Check into a hotel somewhere. Don't stay at Buster's after the party tonight if you're worried about it. Tomorrow morning, you'll feel much better."

Quita looked at the money. "Okay. That's it. I'll slip out after the party."

"Right. Tomorrow morning, things won't look so bad. And you can always think it over. Maybe, later, if you are still worried, you can go talk to Buster."

"No!"

"Or the police."

Wesley looked at me. He thinks I'm soft, always helping everyone I meet. But even the nutty ones need help. Maybe especially.

And I started thinking about fate, as I so often do lately. I've always rejected that notion. I've made fun of my friends, like Holly, who think we are fated to do this or that. I believe in self-determination. But maybe we're meant to be here doing what we're doing. And, so, maybe, if Quita McBride was meant to be here, having some kind of breakdown, maybe I was meant to be here, too, helping out a woman who's had a whole lot of bad news lately. But, you know, at a distance.

"Thanks, Madeline. Thank you."

"And we'll see you at the party tonight. So if you want to talk some more . . ."

Quita gave us a smile that was almost convincing, then turned and retreated down the walkway to the curb. She climbed into a two-year-old yellow Cadillac and pulled away into the night.

I looked at Wesley, who was giving me an affectionate once-over.

"Stray dogs . . ."

"Don't tell me this, Wesley. I do not —"

"Stray cats —"

"Wes." I started to laugh.

"Little birdies with broken wings —"

"Stop. Hey. I didn't let her move in with me, okay? I think that showed some kind of enormous restraint on my part."

"You are such a softhearted person." Wes gave me a hug. "I think that's why you hang with Arlo. You're the one with the chocolate chip cookie and a Band-Aid. You think you're so tough. But you aren't, you know."

"Hey, I'm *tough*," I said.

Wesley had no right to bring up my man issues at a time like this. True, my boyfriend and I had been having our difficult moments lately. In the garden of love, as it were, I was definitely the gardener and Arlo the temperamental hothouse orchid. Problem was, lately Arlo had begun to develop a form of relationship blight, and I was getting just the slightest bit tired of the constant lovelife pruning, spraying, and upkeep.

But Wes quickly changed the subject back to our encounter with strangeness. "Quita," he said, "what a trip. She was obviously overdue for her medication."

"What was all of that? Do you believe her? Why was she so freaked out about Catherine Hill? Or was she making all that stuff up? And what is going on with that red book?" I asked.

"Who knows? I don't even want any of it to make sense. What I did see, though," Wes said, talking to me in his low, soothing voice, "was a pretty disturbed woman, for whatever reason. And what's starting to worry your old pal Wesley is — I think you want to fix Quita McBride."

I watched Wes lock up the house on Wetherbee. "This has got to be my favorite part of any evening, Wes — the part where you tell me how uncool I really am. Okay, tell. Why am I so nice to all these assorted nuts?"

Wes, my oldest and kindest friend, put his arm around me. "I'm not trying to criticize, Mad. I just would love to see you be happy. You spend so much of yourself taking care of others."

"I like others," I said. I do.

"Yes. But you could be a little more particular about exactly which 'others' you allow to get close, eh?"

"I did pretty well when I found you, partner."

"Ah, that you did. And one lucky stroke of

88

genius does not mean you shouldn't be a little more careful now."

Careful? Of course. But I'd heard too many curious things, my brain was itching, and I knew I'd never get to sleep again until I figured out what was spooking Quita McBride.

Chapter 7

Despite the tens of traumas and dozens of crises that make up our little lives, for a caterer to stay in business, the party must go on.

Think, for a moment, about mah-jongg. It's not something you probably ponder on a regular basis. But still. Maybe you picture a card table set up in a suburban living room. Four Jewish ladies, their hands busy, the sound of heavy jewelry clacking against the ivory of the tiles. There's noshing. There's laughter. Emily asks Minkie if her daughter, Marcia, is still seeing that cute anesthesiologist. For the past fifty years or so, that's been mah-jongg in America.

But the world of mah-jongg is changing. With the Internet, on-line versions of the old Chinese game have popped up. Suddenly, a new breed of players has discovered the exotic flavor of this "game of one hundred intelligences." Such was the case with our clients in the Sweet and Sour Club.

"That's everything," Holly said.

Holly and the guys had been unloading the truck, taking the food and cases of liquor and decorations up to Buster Dubin's mansion. He lived only two blocks from me. His 1920s Spanish castle was situated in the better part of Whitley Heights, the part that didn't border the Hollywood Freeway, like mine did. Buster, like so many of us, was infatuated with the romance of Old Hollywood.

It was almost seven-thirty, and we had a lot of work to do to be ready by eight. Ray Jackson came down the front steps and met us at the tailgate of Wes's white station wagon.

"I think that's it." Ray leaned against the wrought-iron gate. He was decked out in the same "uniform" all my serving staff wore for informal parties — black pants and white shirts. I believe in self-expression, so there was a fair amount of leeway at casual parties. In Ray's case, he wore black Adidas wind pants and reflective Nikes. His spotless white sleeveless knit shirt exposed dark skin stretched over hard muscles. Ray's shaved head and wide smile made him look more like a well-paid athlete than the just-scraping-by brilliant kid from South Central L.A. that he was. Ray worked many of my parties, earning extra money to help toward a UCLA undergrad degree.

"Are all the tables set up in the Chinatown room?" I asked.

"Yep. Four tables, sixteen chairs, and the buffet and the bar," Ray said. "Hey, check you out, Holly. You're looking fine."

Holly also took liberties interpreting the standard server getup. Her white T-shirt was a tiny thing. With it, she wore low-slung black-linen pajama pants. On her feet were black patent thongs with tiny heels.

Once we were inside Buster Dubin's house, Ray went on to the party room to get things started there. Wes and Holly and I stopped for a minute to talk over who would do what. A fat Buddha sat in the entry, grinning. Even he seemed to sense it was MJ night.

In his exotic decorating style, Buster Dubin didn't just try for a *taste* of the Orient; he indulged in a whole glorious ten-course banquet. Antique bamboo screens sat behind low, black-lacquer tables. An impressive collection of Celedon pottery sat atop ebony chests. Fabulous old silk panels hung on the walls, cream-colored backgrounds featuring scenes of rice fields and cranes taking flight. One wouldn't expect this spare, sophisticated Asian décor to work with the Art Deco Spanish architecture of Dubin's home, but the rich subdued palate of black and cream with accents of pale green was a success. The bro' was not only chillin', as Ray called it, but he had exquisite taste.

How could a guy in his twenties afford authentic antique Chinese art? you may wonder. This is Hollywood, don't forget. There's money here. In Buster's case, the money could have come from his family. His mother was the daughter of some chemicals tycoon, and of course his father was Stu Dubin, who directed *Wyoming Drive* and *West of Here* and had a couple decades of wild popularity before he went out of phase. But I suspected Buster could afford to buy his own carved jade doodads with the money he earned himself.

Buster Dubin didn't direct films, like his famous dad, but instead, started like many do today, by directing music videos. He rose fast. And along the way, he was persuaded to bring his hot visual talents to sell stuff. His commercials instantly connected with the young and the hip and the disillusioned. It was a notoriously hard market to capture with advertising, and therefore a decidedly lucrative demographic. Buster's ad with cows flying won awards. His commercial with computer monitors doing the limbo was a hit. His thirty-second spot with the talking bras was featured on the Super Bowl. Lately, he was making a killing with dot-com commercials, like the one that crowned Mr. Geek Universe for GeneYus.com. His bent sense of humor had found a perfect video home.

"Dolls. Dudes. How's it hangin'?" Buster, in a red-silk blazer, seemed to glide down the curved staircase to greet us in his entry hall. It was a clever parody of the sweeping entrances Hollywood stars of the past must have made, maybe in this very house. He was a handsome guy, late twenties, with tousled hair so dark and shiny it seemed unnatural. It probably was. His sharp jawline and angular chin were covered by one of those five-o'clock-shadow kinds of beards. The perfectly even, grayish black wash of stubble emphasized the rugged lower half of Buster's face, like the precisely pointalized shading you see in comic books.

He kissed me on both cheeks, barely splashing the potent bright pink liquid in his highball glass, and then turned to Wesley with a wicked gleam in his eye. "Wes?" He held his arms out wide. "Kisses?"

Wesley half snorted a laugh, casting a quick eye at the jovial host. "In your dreams, Bus, my boy." And as Wes disappeared down the hallway, we heard him chuckling on his way to survey the party room.

"Ladies! Alone at last."

Holly and I laughed.

"Anyone thirsty?" he asked. "Quita has been experimenting. She's prepared the Singapore Sling." He gestured to his own pink drink. "I've started to party before my guests arrive. I hope you're not shocked."

"Nothing shocks Maddie," Holly replied.

I don't know if I can actually claim that. But I do have a tendency to bounce back rather quickly. Which is a talent, I submit, in our worrisome world. The last couple of days were a perfect example. Look at this morning. Mugged by that chard guy. And look at the odd little scene at Wesley's house with spooky Quita McBride and her tears and her fears. If we were scoring stress points, you might say I have been through rather a lot. And the night was still young, my friends. We hadn't even begun the party yet. So, therefore, I'd have to say finding a host with a drink in his hand preparty was about the least shocking thing I'd seen all day.

"Don't worry," I said to my client. I said these same exact words in this same soothing way thousands of times. It worked like a charm.

Buster visibly brightened. If that was possible.

I said, "We'll have to take a rain check on one of Quita's drinks, though." And I shot a look around. Where was she, anyway?

"Pity. But, then," he whispered, "you probably make one that is infinitely better. Am I right?"

"You may be the judge," I said. "So save some room."

"Tonight's party will be amazing," Holly said. "Did you check your e-mail? Maddie sent out virtual fortune cookies."

"Did you?" Buster looked up from a big gulp of Singapore Sling and smiled, delighted. "Fantastic. I'm going to go upstairs and log on." He looked at his watch. "Guests will be here in half an hour. So, are you guys okay? Is everything set?"

"Oh, it should be terrific," I said. Caterers must be up. "We're having special and most significant Dim Sum. We have the steam cart and Holly will do the honors."

"Excellent." Buster took a closer look at Holly and his gaze drifted south, seeming to focus somewhere near her exposed navel. "Excellent!"

"We have many surprises tonight — some special treats in honor of the New Year. We have coordinated every dish with its auspicious meanings and cross-referenced them to harmonize with the Chinese horoscopes of each of your guests."

"You're kidding." Buster looked astonished.

"Well, okay, we didn't do the horoscopes, but we've got loads of treats in store. And a surprise guest will arrive after dinner. My special New Year's gift to you and your guests."

"You are too hip, Maddie, which is why I love you."

Holly, who was something of a fashion extremist in her own right, couldn't keep her eyes off Buster's amazing jacket.

"You like?" Buster ran his hand over his famous lucky red-silk smoking jacket and grinned a grin that resembled the one on the face of his Buddha. He was quite a character. He showed Holly and me the motto that was embroidered over the red-satin pocket. It read: *The Hand from Hell*.

Holly laughed one startled, Ha! and asked, "Is that the name of a mah-jongg hand?"

She was just starting to learn the game and knew that many a winning hand or special combination of tiles carried a special name. "I've heard of *The Thirteen Wonderful Lanterns*. And *The Great Snake*. And isn't

97

one really lucky combination of tiles called *The Hand from Heaven?"*

"Very good!" Buster said, smiling at her. "You're learning the traditional names. Aren't they groovy? I just love the whole ancient symbolism and the rich Chineseness of MJ. It's awesome."

"But what's *The Hand from Hell,* then?" Holly asked.

"My own invention, actually. My friends and I are always adding new nicknames of our own. We keep improving the game here at the Sweet and Sour Club. We are evil geniuses. What can I say?" He looked down again at the embroidered motto. *The Hand from Hell.* "Sometimes that *Hand from Heaven* for one person can be the *Hand from Hell* to his opponents. Know what I mean?"

"You don't like to lose," I suggested.

Buster Dubin laughed. "Maddie gets it. Life's a bitch, and then you die, right?" He winked at me as Holly giggled. "But every now and then, you can invite your friends over, kick back, play a little MJ, win a few bucks . . . you know? Just have a few smiles." He slipped his arm around Holly's bare midriff, which made me frown just a little.

I knew Quita was here, somewhere, and I don't generally like my staff to appear to be upstaging the party host's girlfriend. It is by just such judicious staff management that I have devised to keep on top of the L.A. catering heap. Angry girlfriends/wives/lovers do not make for repeat business. And some people think the quality of the gourmet cooking is the most important ingredient to catering success. Ha!

"Holly, can you help me in the kitchen?" I picked up my toolbox, filled with my personal collection of cooking implements and gadgets and accoutrements.

"Right-o." Holly slipped from the light grasp of our host.

Just then, in a swish of taffeta, descending down the sweeping staircase came Quita McBride. How long she'd been standing at the top landing, I couldn't say.

"Party time?" Quita asked, swishing pink-tinted liquor in her crystal glass, pale eyes dancing from me to Buster to Holly.

Well, wasn't this interesting? Just a couple of hours ago, Quita McBride had told a heartbreaking story of her wonderful memories of old Dickey at the Wetherbee house, but she was now clearly marking her territory around her man.

For his part, Buster easily seemed to share his huge home with a parade of beautiful women. They moved in, they moved out.

Quita had only been on the scene a few months. Perhaps she had a more permanent arrangement in mind. What is it about men that the more interesting they are the more messed up their private lives seemed to be? Ah, well.

In the looks department, Quita was quite a startling contrast to Buster, with her light hair worn long compared to Buster's short shock of blue-black hair. And she was tanned a bit past the point of the current fashion in our health-conscious city, while Buster was quite fair. As for her long body, which was wrapped in a cream-colored slip dress, it was a knockout. Other than her overample chest, the rest of Quita was so wispy thin, she didn't look entirely of this world, while Buster was powerfully built, although perhaps an inch shorter than Quita. They made an attractive couple.

I watched as Quita stopped about two steps above us and took a sip of her brew.

"Hello, again, Quita."

Leaning over the end of the railing, she said, "Hello, Madeline. How are you?" She held out her glass, still half-filled with the bright drink, in Holly's direction without actually looking at her. "Would you mind?"

"Would you like a refill?" Holly asked, taking it from her.

"Not now, sweetie." Quita slowly turned to her and narrowed her eyes. "Just take it away. I need to be alone with my guy."

We took our cue, quickly making the trip through the large house, arriving at the kitchen.

"She's thinner than . . ." Holly whispered, searching for just the right image.

I tried to help out. ". . . string?" I suggested. We crack ourselves up, sometimes.

"Thread," Holly corrected.

And then, we heard something.

"What is that?" I asked.

Holly turned slowly. We both strained our ears to catch the sound coming from the front of the large house.

"Is that crying?" I asked.

"Shh." Holly said, trying to listen. She opened the kitchen door and the sound improved.

"It sounds like a child's voice — you know, very high-pitched," Holly whispered, as we tried to make out more.

"Could it be Quita?" I looked at Holly. "What is going on out there?"

"You're right." Holly grinned. "She's yelling at him."

I, on the other hand, sighed. Quita McBride was all over the map. First that incredible scene at the Wetherbee house, with

101

the tears and the memories of her dear old departed husband. Then the mysterious stories and her fears and the pleas for help. Now this. The night had barely begun, and already fireworks. I turned to Holly. "Keep your hands inside the roller coaster at all times. I have no idea what is going to happen on the ride tonight."

Chapter 8

Buster Dubin's kitchen was cramped and old-fashioned, reflecting the lifestyle of a bachelor with little use for anything save a refrigerator to hold take-out leftovers and a microwave to reheat them. It was odd to still be able to find such an impressive older home with such a small kitchen. Remodels usually did away with the original narrow sculleries, which had been suitable enough, at the time they were built, for the help. In current times, these homes fall somewhere north of the two-million-dollar range. For those price tags, most had their old walls bumped out and new cooking palaces installed. But this room's only beauty was the amazing artwork on the new floor.

Wes showed up in the kitchen as Holly and I unpacked the last of our ingredients for tonight's Dim Sum delights.

"Did you hear?" Holly asked him.

"Trouble in paradise," Wes said. "It was hard to miss."

"Did you hear what it was about?"

Wes shook his head. "Something about money. I didn't hear his voice at all. Just hers."

I shook my head. "Exit Ms. Quita McBride. But I do hope they won't go breaking up right now before all the guests arrive. I'm not sure what she would do. Her emotion-o-meter is pegged pretty much all the time."

"Remember, she said she couldn't stay here tonight, after the party?" Wes asked.

We talked that over a bit. It had happened before, the hosts having a horrible row just before their big event. Actually, everything has happened before. We get through it.

"Oh, get this. Did I tell you?" Wes asked. "Dubin loves the floor so much, he wants me to help him remodel this entire room."

Wesley had introduced Buster to Erin, an artist-friend who carves intricate designs out of linoleum. She uses a precise, hand-cut inlay technique to make graphic master-pieces using the same old-fashioned colorful flooring material that our grandmas favored. For Buster's kitchen floor, Erin cut a stunning Asian-inspired border of pale green bamboo and set it into a jet-black ground. She adapted the design from a very old Japanese brush painting that Bus had given her.

"Aw," Holly said. "So you're going to rip out this one?" Holly looked down at the art beneath her shoes. "How much did it cost?"

"Seven thousand," Wes said. "But Buster wants Erin to do another one for the new kitchen."

It figured. Wesley was getting a reputation. His house projects were fabulous.

"I can't imagine why he's going to bother with a new kitchen," Holly said. "Buster doesn't cook, and Quita doesn't eat."

"Now, Holly," I said. It's a good rule not to talk about the hosts while you are still in their house. "This is a cool job for Wes."

"That's true," Holly said. "Wes, honey, all your house jobs are whack."

"Well," Wes said, turning to her, trying not to sound old at the ripe age of thirty-seven. "Thank you?"

Holly, our designated pep squad, settled herself at one smidge of counter space and started putting together the Chinese Chicken Salad. This was the time that required the most intense concentration. Thirty minutes and closing. All of our creative spirits were engaged.

Our goal with every party, no matter how small or large, is to provide a unique experience to each jaded palate. Each diner's senses must be flirted with, solicited, tempted, invited, tantalized, enticed, intrigued, seduced, and flat-out propositioned before being brazenly indulged. Delectable aromas from the kitchen must waft through the house, greeting each guest's sensitive nose. The soft seductive sounds of cutlery on porcelain should underscore the interweaving melodies of happy conversation, all of which provide accompaniment to the host's favored musical background. Dishes must harmonize to provide a wide variety of textures and temperatures, flavors and ingredients. And, the eye's delight upon first spying a dish must be equal to the mouth's delight at how the thing actually tastes. Presentation is key.

Even for a relatively mainstream little item like our Chinese Chicken Salad, we enjoy giving it a unique visual twist. For this particular salad, we do a parody of Chinese take-out. I have white take-out cartons made up that are four times the size of a normal one.

Holly took one of these Giganto cartons out of our supply sack and tipped it on its side onto one of our large lacquer platters. The contrast of the white-cardboard box on the shiny black platter was lovely. Buster would get a kick out of it. The whole oversize scale was fun, and I suspected the idea of gourmet caterers creating fresh culinary delights and then putting them into a take-out container would strike our host as appropriately droll. The salad, when it was completely compiled, would be displayed in the tipped-over carton, spilling bountifully out onto the platter in a lovely large mound. To finish, we'd stick a pair of oversize gold chopsticks into the carton and sprinkle the salad with freshly fried wonton strips.

I watched Holly work, but my mind kept wandering. I usually consider myself a great judge of people. But Quita McBride had had me worried about several things. What was up with her? She had acted so strangely when we told her about the theft of the mah-jongg set back at the other house that she had me spooked.

I know a guy, a detective with the LAPD, and I gave him a call. I had to leave a message. I told him I hoped he might swing by and check out Quita McBride.

As soon as I hung up, I regretted having called. I shouldn't have bothered him. It wasn't his problem. Besides, he and I had a weird history. Why did I think I should call?

Angry with myself, I got back to work. The wok was placed over high heat, and the oil was now at the correct temperature for frying. I started placing the wonton strips into the oil.

As the wonton skins sizzled, I ran over some of the timetable items with Wes. "We probably shouldn't start cooking the Dim Sum until the guests are here. And let's not dress the salad until the last minute, either."

"Right." Wes had been absentmindedly shaking a large glass jar that contained the Chinese dressing we'd prepared earlier. By shaking it up, he freshly mixed the peanut and sesame oils with the pickled ginger and other spices. This salad dressing recipe was complex, mingling ingredients with varying tastes. It contained white scallions, Chinese mustard powder, and shallots for heat, honey for sweet, soy sauce for salty, and ginger vinegar for sour, along with the spicy chili oil for fire. It was a recipe we had borrowed from Wolfgang Puck and had changed a little over time.

Wes held up the drink Holly had taken from Quita.

"Ugh," he said, eloquent as always.

"It's Quita's version of a Singapore Sling," Holly said.

He took a tentative tiny sip. "Ack! I'm poisoned."

I looked over at him, arching an eyebrow. Wes was deadly serious about every recipe.

Ray entered the kitchen. "What up?"

"Ray, my man. C'mon over here." Wes waved him to the sink. "I'm going to teach you how to make a real Singapore Sling."

"Excellent. They love that shit in the 'hood." He gave us all a sly grin.

"Naturally." Wes grabbed one of the boxes with our liquor supplies for the party and he and Ray set the bottles up on a table next to the sink.

"Oh, hey. Show me how to make one, too," Holly said.

As Ray moved over and made a space for Holly, Wesley picked up what was left of Quita's colorful concoction and poured it down the drain.

Wes was our resident mixologist. "Probably no mixed drink has been as mistreated as the Sling. The only thing most bartenders know about the Singapore Sling is that it's supposed to be pink."

"Ah." Holly looked on as he rearranged the liquor bottles on the table.

"Singapore Sling," Ray said, smiling. "Pleasing groins."

"What?" Wes said, looking up.

Holly gave Ray a wicked grin. "Interesting fantasy life."

"It's an anagram. *Pleasing groins* is an anagram for *Singapore Sling*. Really." He was all teeth. "Betcha didn't know that, Holly."

She was staring at him. "An anagram, huh? How'd you know that?"

"It's just something my brain does naturally. I got the gift."

"You've got the anagram gift." Holly looked from Ray back to me. "Is he messing with me, Maddie?"

I began to laugh. "I always knew Ray was special."

"Thanks, Madeline." He winked at me and turned back to Holly. "*Pleasing groins,* see? Now you'll have something to chitchat about with the guests tonight while we're serving these fancy drinks."

She burst out laughing.

"As I was saying . . ." Wesley waited for his students to settle down, then continued. "The drink was created in 1915 by a Hainanese-Chinese bartender named Mr. Ngiam Tong Boon. Originally, the Singapore Sling was designed to be a woman's drink, hence the attractive pink color. Tonight we'll prepare an adaptation of the original recipe from Raffles Hotel in Singapore."

"That sounds authentic," Holly said, pushing back her bracelets.

"It is. Now look. It's perfectly simple."

We all looked.

Wesley had set up a line of bottles, garnishes, juices, fruit, barware, and ice. "First fill a shaker with ice."

"Okay," Holly said.

She was wonderful. Although she'd never had formal cook's schooling as I had, or had restaurant kitchen experience as both Wes and I had, Holly was a sponge and was always in a hurry to learn.

"Good," Wes said, checking both his students. "Add six tablespoons of pineapple juice and two tablespoons of gin."

"Which kind of gin?" Ray asked, looking at all the varieties we stock.

"Boodles is good."

Side by side, Holly and Ray mimicked Wes's actions as they built the drinks together. Each of them proceeded to measure the proper ingredients. As Wes instructed, they squeezed two tablespoons of fresh lime juice, and added one tablespoon of Cherry Heering. They measured one tablespoon of grenadine, one-half tablespoon of Benedictine, and then a dash of Triple Sec and three dashes of Angostura bitters.

"Got it?" Wes asked, watching Holly as she finished up counting her dashes. "Now shake for a minute and then strain it into a tall glass filled with ice."

111

Ray and Holly shook their cocktail shakers with one hand while setting out twelve-ounce Collins glasses and filling them with cracked ice with the other.

In unison, they poured out their authentic rouge-toned Singapore Slings.

"Then you garnish with a flag made out of a lemon slice and an orange slice and a cherry on a toothpick, like so . . ." Wes demonstrated, and Ray and Holly did their best to follow.

He looked at their work.

"Wait," Ray said, studying Wes's artwork on a stick. "Now how'd you do that?"

"Never mind. I'll make up a lovely pile of fruit garni for you to use later."

"Thanks, man." Ray twirled his sad skewer of fruit.

"Okay, then. Let's see if they're any good. Bottoms up." Wesley said.

In unison they each took a tentative sip.

"Ah." Wes put down his glass, satisfied with his work. "A taste of the exotic East."

"Ah!" Holly took another gulp, pleased with herself and enjoying the taste of her first authentic Sling.

"Ah . . . shit!" Ray put his glass down with a grimace. "Man, that stuff is nasty. I mean, that stuff is sweet. And it's . . . pink."

You had to laugh.

Ray caught my eye and shook his handsome bald head. "I suggest that this right here is the prime reason why the nation of Singapore will never be a world superpower."

"Wussy drinks?" I asked, giving Ray's cocktail-political thesis some thought.

"Well?" he asked. "Am I wrong?"

We all told him, "no."

With his head for world politics and anagrams, Ray was sure to go far.

"I'll stick with beer, Wesley," Ray said.

"Well, there's simplicity in that," Wes agreed. "And for those at the party who share your simple tastes, there's a case of Tsingtao on ice."

"Hey, I'd better get to squeezing up some couple dozen limes or I'm gonna be killing myself come show time," Ray said.

Wes and Ray discussed where to set up the bar in the party room and they huddled together packing the liquor bottles and accessories back into the cartons. Ray easily lifted two cartons at once. And then Wes turned to me.

"Madeline. I was just thinking, do we have enough cash to pay the staff?"

Ray, who was almost at the door, stopped. "No problem," he said. "We took care of it."

Holly said, "Maddie always has enough

cash to cover the payroll. That's why she's the queen."

It was true, I usually had that stuff wired. Earlier that day I had sent Ray to the bank to pick up the cash we'd need for the party. He brought back a stack of twenties. In fact, I had to talk to him for defacing the bills. He had drawn a tiny frowny face in the corner of each twenty. I showed him my frowny face and he apologized, promising to keep his Bic capped in the future.

I tried to explain. "I had an unexpected expense, Holly."

She looked at me, intrigued.

"I just gave Quita McBride a hundred dollars a little while ago. That's all."

"One hundred and sixty dollars, actually." Wes could be very literal.

"Yes, well, she was a human in need. I just tried to do her a favor. She said she couldn't use her credit cards and she didn't have cash handy and . . . And now I guess I am going to run a little short tonight. Damn. No good deed goes unpunished."

"You're kidding." Holly looked amused. "Quita McBride who could probably buy and sell us, not to mention she's got a rich boyfriend who's our client? You gave Quita a coupla hundred bucks?"

"Didn't Mad tell you about our night?" Wes asked.

Holly looked at me, and her green eyes narrowed. "Maddie."

I hadn't wanted to upset her, so I hadn't mentioned our bizarre evening at the Wetherbee house. Honestly, all I wanted to do was focus on the party ahead.

Just then, my cell phone rang from the bottom of my toolbox. I reached down quickly to catch it before the call was lost.

"Well, aren't you going to tell me?" Holly asked, indignant.

"Toss the salad," I instructed. Despite fumbling with the clasps, and rustling through the mess below, I managed to grab my phone and press the answer button just in the nick of time.

"Hey, Mad. It's Arlo."

Oh. See. Just when you think you are keeping all the grenades in the air, one goes thud, hiss, boom. Hearing Arlo's name didn't used to make me tense up. Things had not been going well between us for a long time.

"You working?" he asked. Arlo never seemed to be able to quite remember what I was doing when.

"Is that Arlo?" Holly asked, looking over at me, mouthing the words.

I nodded.

She pantomimed cutting her throat.

Lucky for me, my friends never try to meddle in my personal life.

"So what do you say we get together later?" he asked.

"I say I've had a rough day."

"Great. Then you'll need a chance to unwind," Arlo steamrollered on.

I added one more item to my mental to-do list, then quickly got off the phone.

Chapter 9

The weekly site of the Sweet and Sour Mah-Jongg Club — the game room at the back of Dubin's house — was dazzling. I stopped at the doorway on my preparty inspection. The room, large and elegant and dripping in high-price-tag Asian fillips, appeared ready to be photographed by *Architectural Digest*. It was a spotless re-creation of a luxe, 1920s Art Deco mah-jongg lounge. The success of the room's decoration was a tribute to Buster Dubin's eye for set design, his sense of whimsy, and his deep pockets.

The ebony-stained hardwood floor was a mirror-polished sea, atop which three exquisite Oriental carpets floated. Exotic dark wood paneling covered the walls and absorbed the soft glow of many hanging Chinese lamps. Scattered in a symmetrical pattern, four matched rosewood card tables awaited the night's amusements. David Bowie's voice sang out from a state-of-the-art digital music system. "China Girl" — what else?

Over in one corner was the bar, a big, flashy roaring twenties antique. It was completely mirrored, including all the intricate Art Deco zigzag details. Reflecting wildly from its many polished surfaces were the bottled and bowled ingredients, which had been set out in readiness for the evening's featured drink. In mirror upon mirror upon mirror, endless reflections of cherry liquor red and pineapple juice yellow dazzled the eye, multiplying our potential Singapore Slings to infinity and beyond.

In addition to the hard liquor, the bar's minirefrigerator was also stocked with Chinese and domestic beers and several current brands of water. Next to the bar, a large buffet table had been laid out to display the gourmet snacks, upon which starving mahjongg players were wont to nibble.

Yes, I know it could be effectively argued that Chinese Chicken Salad was hardly an authentic Asian recipe. But please remember whom we serve. Our party guests were the denizens of L.A., after all, and like all of the city's thin and hip, they were serious salad junkies. No Southern California caterer would go broke pandering to this city's intense cravings for mass quantities of gourmet roughage and bottled water.

I checked out Holly's finished salad, rearranged the golden chopsticks, and admired a few of the other bowls and platters. An abundance of fresh fruit, sliced and beautifully arranged, was heaped on a large ornate Chinese platter. Amid Buster Dubin's valuable Chinese carvings and his astonishing collection of Chinese magic gizmos, the display looked perfect.

This is it for me: this brink of high adventure, this special time of fresh expectation, of careful preparations completed, this greedy anticipation of pleasures to come. I love this time right before the party begins. Everything clean and ready, everything beautiful and expectant.

In this brief pause before show time, I was alone. Ray had stepped outside, no doubt to grab a smoke. Back in the kitchen, Wes was beginning to prepare the Dim Sum with Holly's assistance.

Footsteps echoed up the hallway. I am pretty good at recognizing gaits and footfalls. Call it a little-appreciated talent. So, expecting Wes, I turned.

Lieutenant Chuck Honnett walked into the room.

"I told them I'd find you." He stood in the doorway to the party room and gave me a look that was almost a smile.

My heart did a funny little half gainer with

a twist. I was actually a little annoyed with my heart. I guess that's why they call it an involuntary muscle.

"Honnett." It was not my most original opening.

Remember how I feel about surprises? Hate 'em.

Chuck Honnett seemed to look me over without moving his eyes too much. He saw me as I appear when I'm working a casual party, my hair pulled back into a clip, wearing a pair of slim black pants and a sleeveless white T-shirt. I felt his eyes take in the deep V of my collar.

"Hi," I tried again. "I guess you got my message."

"Yeah. What happened to you out in Santa Monica today?"

"Well, I feel silly asking you to come all the way out here. It's just that there's this woman. Her name is Quita McBride." I rambled on a bit, nervously, and told him about our weird encounter and her insistence she was in some serious kind of trouble.

Honnett stood there, listening to it all. Then he said, "Madeline, technically it's not our jurisdiction, Santa Monica."

"I know. I know. This is silly, right?"

"But I called out there, and they faxed

me the officer's report."

I looked at him, hopefully.

"Sorry to say, they have no leads and nothing new. They did send some of those tile things to be fingerprinted, and I didn't see that they had any matches. But really, I wouldn't be too upset. These things happen. There are people ready to grab anything that looks valuable. It's pretty sad, but there it is."

"Yes. I know that. But this woman, Quita McBride," I said, looking toward the door, worried she'd walk in on us and have a fit that I'd invited a cop to her party. I told him the rest, how she was sure someone would want the red-leather book, Dickey McBride's unpublished novel, that she was looking for.

I looked up and recognized Honnett's expression. Incredulous is the word that came to mind.

"So," I said. "You don't think she's in big trouble."

"No."

"And you don't think she should have some kind of protection?"

"From what?"

"And you think I'm an idiot for giving her money so she could get a decent night's rest."

"No. I think you are a good friend."

"Well, she's not my friend, actually," I said, feeling uncomfortable.

"You're a good person, then." Honnett had blue eyes. Deep, deep blue. "But I'm not sure why you have to get yourself mixed up in stuff all the time."

He stood there, across the party room, looking at me, trying to figure me out. Well, that might take the man quite a while. I stared back. Honnett had the look of a transplanted Texas man, just off the range, with that sort of outdoor skin and long legs that look good in jeans, and the kind of hard body that came from real work, not work-outs.

"So, Maddie. How've you been?"

Honnett and I had a history of botched opportunities and lousy timing. He and I had had a few possibilities, a while ago. We'd flirted up and back with pretty much nothing to show for it. Nothing ever got to the interesting point. Maybe it was because both of us were more comfortable *not* knowing each other better. Now that was a sad little thought.

Or maybe it was because I was going with another guy. Honnett's job and my relationship with Arlo were enough to cool things down. My life is forever on the verge of resembling *One Life to Live* on a bad day.

"I've got to get back to work now," I said, "if you're sure there's nothing that can be done."

"No. The problem you had on Third Street is being handled by Santa Monica, so there's nothing to do there." His eyes squinted. "And your friend, McBride, if you'll pardon me saying this, sounds pretty flaky."

"Yeah. But you know, her husband was a big star. And he died not too long ago. Something may be weird about that."

"There are lots of old stars in this town. Some of them die. We can't go digging one up just because something he owned goes and gets itself snatched and his ex-wife is feeling antsy. Right?"

"And you don't want to just talk to her? She's here, somewhere."

"If it makes you feel better, give her my card. Tell her to call me if she has evidence of any other crime, okay?"

I nodded, taking his card, knowing Quita would never call him.

Honnett's voice changed, softened. "And as for that mugging, you sure you're okay?"

I nodded again.

Honnett said, "Because maybe I should keep an eye on the case, as it develops.

When can you and I get together?"

I took a deep breath. I let it out. "You mean business or you mean pleasure?"

He smiled at me. "You never know. You may think of something that you didn't remember at the time of your original statement. Or maybe we could just talk?"

I felt a sharp little pain, wherever the solar plexus is supposed to be.

"Why don't you come over to my house," I offered. "Do you remember where it is?"

"On Whitley? Of course I do."

"Good."

"What time is this party over?" he asked.

"I'm seeing Arlo tonight." I looked at Honnett, wondering what he could possibly make of me and my muddled relationships. "I'll be home pretty late, I guess."

"I'm working pretty late, too," he said lightly. "Well, I had better go."

This was not good at all.

"Hey. Mad?" Holly bounded into the game room, clearly expecting to find me alone. She recognized Honnett. "Oh, it's you. Hi. I'm sorry. I thought Mad was . . ."

"No problem. I'm going." He looked over at me as he departed. "Be seeing you." And he left.

Holly watched him leave. "He's looking good, isn't he? I mean, for a cop."

I became seized with an impulse to check for dust on the fireplace mantel. I found absolutely none. "Hol, remind me to ask Buster who does his housecleaning. She's exceptionally thoro . . ."

Holly looked at me with her big puppy-dog eyes. I read pity. "Even if you don't want to admit it, there is a perceptible level of hormone residue left in this room."

She makes me laugh. What can I say?

"Look, I know he's a cop and all . . ." she began.

"Yes?"

"On the other hand, Honnett's the kind of a cop who doesn't have to wear a uniform, which you figure makes his whole copness a little easier to take."

On the expensive sound system, Ash's version of "Kung Fu Fighting" was coming to a close. And then, in the brief silence that followed, I heard three muted mellow musical tones coming from the front of the house.

"Ah."

The doorbell meant that our party guests were about to arrive.

Chapter 10

An explosive burst of noise clattered loudly, momentarily drowning out the happy hum of many overlapping conversations. It was the precise click and clack of 144 bone tiles being slapped and shuffled upon the hardwood surface of one of the big room's game tables. Sitting there resplendent in his red-silk jacket, Buster Dubin prepared for his next hand of mah-jongg with his closest cronies. Buster's laugh rose above the percussive din as four pairs of hands spread all the mah-jongg tiles facedown, quickly and efficiently swirling them in random patterns on the table.

Quita sat to Buster's right. Across from Buster was a rounder, sweet-faced woman with a perfect bow mouth. Her name was Verushka Mars. She owned her own special effects business. The fourth player at Buster's table was a pencil-thin young man, Trey Forsythe. He was a sufficiently hot sales rep who could easily afford his mah-jongg losings, and he'd been Buster's best friend since way back in prep school. Trey wore a gold hoop earring and had a small blond beard and was devastatingly handsome, according to Holly. Anyway, all but Quita were the founding members of the Sweet & Sour Club. Alas, Quita's predecessor, Jean Geiger, no longer came to game night.

Effortlessly, a fresh round of Singapore Slings appeared at the In table. Ray set the icy pink drinks down silently on golden coasters bearing the S & S Club insignia, then slipped away, followed by murmurs of "Thanks, man," and "These Slings are gonna get me in trouble."

The party was warming up, and I was satisfied. I, too, have gotten rather hooked on the game of mah-jongg since I've been catering the Club's social nights, and I perched on the corner of a nearby sofa to watch Buster's table set up their wall.

In preparation for the new hand, each player began to build a line. As they gossiped, Verushka and Trey and Buster and Quita reached forward into the array of shuffled, facedown tiles, and selected random pairs, stacking them in neat bundles of twos, and pulling the bundles back until they clacked against the edge of each of their mah-jongg racks. In this way, each player began constructing his or her own row of tiles two high and eighteen across. When these lines were completed, all four players pushed their racks forward, forming a cream-colored square made up of double-high rows of tiles. The wall.

"Buster is still East," Quita said. She gazed at Buster from under heavily made-up lids and pulled the little green umbrella from out of her drink.

East Wind was a favored position in mah-jongg. In every round, each player gets a turn to be East, which gives him or her several scoring advantages. He may keep the East position only so long as he continues to have winning hands. Once another player goes mah-jongg, the Winds shift, as it were, and the player to his right becomes East.

The whole symbolism of this game is rather fascinating.

Buster looked up at me and grinned. "We ever gonna get you to join in the fun, Madeline?"

"Not if you are still playing for a dollar a point."

"Madeline. Darling. You're a rich caterer. You charge exorbitant fees. You can afford to indulge in life's upscale pleasures."

"Honey, leave her alone." Quita took a slow sip of her Sling. "She's not interested in gambling with lunatics like you, she's interested in cooking."

Quita was getting on my nerves.

Then, in a flurry of excitement, a young woman's voice from across the game room called out, "Mah-jongg!" The players at her table erupted into a noisy spatter of conversation.

"If you ever want a private mah-jongg lesson," Buster Dubin continued, looking up at me again, "just give a holler."

"Well," I said, "I do have a question."

Quita looked up at me and watched my exchange with Buster.

"Why do they make such a big thing out of the East Wind?"

"Ah!" Verushka's brightly painted bow-shaped lips curved up. She wore an ash-colored T-shirt with the words MAH-JONGG MAVEN on the front, and the enlightening message, MY MOTHER USED TO PLAY, on the back. Verushka leaned back and smiled even wider. "Buster knows all about the history of the game."

"Well, there are a few theories, actually," Buster said, nodding. "One story that's passed around suggests that the origins of mah-jongg come from as far back as biblical times."

Trey looked up at me with amused eyes.

He did exude a sultry sort of something. I did not normally fall for sultry, so it was lost on me.

Buster rolled the dice, throwing an eight, as he spoke. "Would you like to take a guess, Madeline, which game was played on the Ark? I'm talking THE Ark, by the way — Noah and the gang. What did they play? Mah-jongg!"

I burst out laughing.

"Yep," Buster said, smiling up at me, enjoying my reaction. "Think about it. It's raining . . . it's raining . . . they're floating . . . they're floating . . . forty days and forty nights of nonstop mah-jongg action. What on earth else was there for old Noah and his family and all those *fercockta* animals to do?" Buster looked at Verushka for support.

Trey said dryly, "Sure. It could have happened. After all, they didn't have cable."

Verushka chided Trey, "Don't laugh at Buster, you only encourage him." Then, she looked over at Quita. "North opens the wall."

"Oh. Sorry."

Quita wasn't paying strict attention. After the wall of tiles is formed, there are very specific rules as to where the wall is broken to begin dealing out the tiles. "I don't know why we have to do it this way. Why does East throw the dice and then we count around to see where the wall gets opened up anyway?"

"To preserve a romantic Chinese tradition, my love." Buster took one of her hands in his.

Quita giggled and glanced over at Trey.

"And to prevent cheating," Trey said, looking up at her.

Quita quickly picked up the dice and threw a four.

"Four plus eight is twelve," Trey offered helpfully.

"I know that." Quita laughed and counted, brushing her finger lightly over the tops of the tiles from the left hand side of the wall in front her until she reached "12." She lifted up that pair of tiles and placed them on top of the tiles to the left of the break.

I stood up to check on the other tables of guests. They were all deeply engaged in the tiles and the conversation. At one table, small, colorful gaming chips were exchanged, as the latest winning hand demanded its monetary reward.

"Hey, Madeline. Don't you want to hear about Noah?"

I turned back to my host. "Of course I do. I thought you were concentrating on your game."

"Talk to him. Please." Verushka drawled

the last word out, begging. "Distract him. Keep his mind off the game. He's already stolen $50 from me. I need help!"

I reperched on the edge of the white damask sofa, always delighted to mix and mingle with the guests, when my clients preferred. As this was a long-standing gig of ours, Wes and I had become especially casual with Buster and his regulars at the Sweet and Sour.

"Now listen up." Buster hushed his rowdy friends, including four women sitting at the table beside him. "Madeline asked why the East Wind position is so significant in the game and I was telling her about Noah. *East* had been the prevailing wind during the great storm that caused the Great Flood."

"That's pretty cool."

"And thus —"

"Yes, tell us, Professor," Verushka said, and then took a long swig, draining her pink cocktail. She had quite a thirst for gin.

". . . Thus, the East Wind became the dominant seat in playing the game. This theory would suggest that the game would date back to around 2350 B.C."

"Fascinating," I said.

I admit it. Half the time I say stuff like this just to get a rise out of Quita. Not very nice of me. Must work on this.

132

As each of the players grabbed their tiles, taking turns dealing themselves four tiles at a time, Buster continued. "Another very interesting story suggests that Confucius, the great Chinese philosopher, developed the game about 500 B.C. The appearance of the game in various Chinese provinces coincides with Confucius's travels at the time he was teaching his new doctrines. The three Dragon tiles also coincide with the three cardinal virtues taught by Confucius: Chung the Red, which stands for achievement, Fa the Green for prosperity, and Po the White means sincerity. Confucius was said to be fond of birds, which would explain the name mah-jongg, which means sparrow."

"Strictly translated, mah-jongg means 'hemp bird,' " Trey clarified.

Both Quita and Verushka giggled.

While Buster had been speaking, the foursome grabbed new tiles and picked up others' discarded tiles with a wild and thrilling speed, accompanied by the rhythmic clicking of tiles as they hit the table. In front of each player, a trifolded plastic card displayed the combinations that made up the year's official premium hands.

All of the teasing and kibitzing around the tables suddenly brought back to mind vivid memories. Heather Lieberman, whom I hadn't thought of in years. Childhood sleepovers at my best friend's house. She lived with her grandma in a modest fifties split-level suburban tract home. I was over there all the time in fifth and sixth grade. I remember how we would creep silently along the upstairs hallway in Heather's grandma's house. In the late evenings, we were expected to be up in Heather's yellow room, if not sleeping, then at least in bed, giggling, gossiping, and hiding our laughter under the sunflower comforters. But on Friday nights, we used to make a break for it. We would sneak to the top of the steps, careful not to make the top one squeak, to watch her grandmother play maj with the gals. At ten years old, we were preteen Mata Haris.

I remember those nights with such fondness. Heather and I would hide in the darkness, sitting still in our long Lanz flannel nighties on the top step, just out of eyesight of Rose Lieberman and the mah-jongg ladies. We'd eavesdrop, listening to the older women laugh and mildly swear to the accompaniment of the swift and expert clicking of the tiles. I remembered catching whiffs of Chanel No. 5. I remember the flicker of the Sterno candle, which was lit beneath Rose's polished silver chafing dish, its task to keep warm the cocktail weenies in a thick sweet barbecue sauce. I remember feeling safe among the nearby sounds of adult female camaraderie.

"Dead hand." Verushka pushed back her chair. The others at her table grumbled that Buster would remain East and began, again, to shuffle the tiles.

At the door to the game room, right on schedule, Holly arrived with the Dim Sum cart, ready to begin serving. We had discussed with Dubin earlier the possibility of serving an authentic Chinese banquet, but he resisted. He didn't want to slow down the MJ action with a heavy meal. And we agreed Dim Sum would suit the crowd nicely, despite the unconventional hour. The custom of offering bite-size morsels known as Dim Sum started in teahouses in China as a prelunch thing. But we were rather nonconformist in our food tastes at the Sweet and Sour Club.

Dim Sum was a popular treat, and the players looked up from their hands and chattered with excitement when they spotted Holly and her cart.

Dubin was the sort of man who fully enjoyed himself at his own events. Seated at the game table, he found Holly's exposed waistline was but a foot or so from his nose.

"Do you know," I heard him whispering up to her, "what Dim Sum means?"

Not a thing escaped Quita's notice. She was also listening to this exchange.

"To your heart's delight," she answered.

"Ah." Dubin winked at her.

On Holly's cart, the traditional round metal containers, about five inches in diameter, towered up in neat stacks. A series of small holes, top and bottom, allowed the cart's steam to pass through the tins and keep the fresh Dim Sum piping hot while they were delivered to all the diners.

Tonight, Holly's tiny metal pans were filled with Shrimp Har Gow. These pinkish dumplings, packed four to a tin, contained the freshest plump shrimp wrapped in tender wonton skins so thin they were virtually transparent. Holly was also offering homemade Shu Mei, steamed dumplings made with spicy ground pork. Another stack of tins contained triangular packets of Sticky Rice wrapped in Lotus Leaves. In addition to the Dim Sum, Holly also offered guests a trio of tasty dipping sauces.

As we had figured, the mah-jongg players were ready to take a break in the action. Holly slowly pushed her cart, serving each table, as the S & S clubbers finished up hands in progress and cleared their tables in order to sample the Dim Sum.

Big cities with large Asian populations, like Los Angeles, were full of great choices to eat excellent Dim Sum. Chinatown and the eastern suburb of Monterey Park offered numerous noisy, happy Dim Sum palaces. There, at ABC Seafood or Ocean Star Seafood, women who still spoke heavily accented English pushed tiny Dim Sum carts between the tables, offering freshly cooked treats to each table as they passed by. Tonight, Holly did her best to keep up that fine tradition.

Steam coming from the wheeled cart wafted up as Holly pushed it around the room. Her face had turned slightly red. Her pale hair, I'm afraid, under the onslaught of humidity, had reverted to its natural stick-straightness. Alas, serving Dim Sum is not a glamorous profession.

I winked at Holly. She didn't notice. Instead, she stole a few seconds to blow her bangs back up off her sweaty brow.

As I moved around the room, following Holly's path, serving the dipping sauces and helping Ray pass out plates and chopsticks, I noticed the gamers' reaction to our little "heart's delights." There were comments on this one, and compliments on that one. The

Turnip Cake was admired and sampled, as each of the evening's players listened to the story of its portent of good fortune. All in all, a successful event.

I moved to the back of the room to help clear up some empty metal Dim Sum tins. As I approached a far table, I couldn't help but overhear a conversation between Verushka and a man I hadn't met before. He looked to be in his mid-thirties, which of course meant he was probably closer to forty-five, using Hollywood math.

I guess I had half expected to overhear some additional raves over the evening's cuisine. The man, wearing black everything, bent his head close to Verushka, and said, "Okay. Just get it back to me, right?"

"You know I'm good for it," she said, and then looked up with a start, noticing at last that I was standing there.

My eyes, however, were instantly focused on a twentysomething couple. Kelli, the daughter of that Channel 2 news anchorman, and Bo, the beach volleyball champion who did all those Miller commercials. Their passion was, uh, aflame. They were, in fact, making out with such enthusiasm that I could hardly interrupt to ask them if they'd care for another round of steamed octopus balls. But most of my immodest staring at the beautiful couple in the lip lock was camouflage. I hoped Verushka might decide that I hadn't overheard her conversation, after all.

Party planners have a few too many plates to keep spinning to get really involved in the party guests. We have plenty to worry about and a lot of things to hope for. And added to the hope that the Dim Sum wouldn't get too sticky, and the hope that we'd brought enough Chinese soda, and the hope that Holly wouldn't faint from the heat of her steaming cart before we'd finished the meal service, I now fervently hoped that Verushka wouldn't get angry and suspicious. I hoped she wouldn't feel awkward and embarrassed, wondering if her secret conversation might have been overheard.

But, of course, it had.

Was Verushka having serious money problems, or just a onetime shortfall of cash? The fear in her eyes was not a good sign. Had she gotten in over her head? Had the gambling bug pushed her beyond what she could afford? I couldn't help myself. I swear. I just want everyone to be happy. Is that too much to ask?

Chapter 11

I love to plan. I love to cook. I love to party. But I love the relaxing close of a party almost as much. It was eleven o'clock. Dim Sum had been finished hours ago. Many hot mah-jongg hands had been played. We were almost finished clearing away dessert dishes. Our daringly retro Chinese Fireworks Bombe, an amazing bowl-shaped dessert, had been a showy success. Even Trey, who had a nasty habit of ignoring the food, was impressed. He noticed the auspicious number of seven lit sparklers and gave me a less than cynical smile.

The party was winding down. Coffee drinks had been served and refilled. Some of the guests had begun packing up their personal mah-jongg sets. Others were sitting around, lazily nursing their cappuccinos.

Wes, Ray, and I were finished cleaning up Buster Dubin's small kitchen, and I told Ray to go home, counting out the money I owed him in cash, apologizing for coming up a little short. I told him to come by the next afternoon, Thursday, and I'd have the twenty-five I still owed him.

"No problem." Ray showed a lot of straight, white teeth. "Dubin peeled me a C."

I smiled. The art of tipping is yet another of Buster's many talents. I looked over at Holly, who was semicollapsed on a kitchen chair. "Are you okay, pumpkin?"

Holly was sprawled upon the kitchen table. Without lifting her head from the crook of her bent elbow, upon which it was resting, she attempted to nod. "Dubin gave me a hundred, too. He's a sport."

"You should go home," I said. "Really. You want someone to drive you? Ray goes right by . . ."

"No, I'm fine." Holly hoisted her head up and attempted to steady it in an upright position. "I think Ray has plans for the evening, don't you, Ray?"

"I told Marisa I'd drop her off." Ray grinned at me. "I can take care of Holly, too."

"Marisa Tager?" Wesley stopped polishing a silver cake server and looked over at Ray. "Her dad is worth forty million, Ray. And I thought she was dating that guy who owns the Montrose Microbrewery."

"That right? Hunh. That's not the way I

hear it. But, you know . . ." He gave a daz-zling smile. "I've been wrong before."

Nothing got to Ray. At twenty-two, Ray Jackson was the freaking poster boy for self-confidence. We were, of course, well used to Ray's good-humored bragging.

Holly mumbled, "He serves them Singa-pore Slings, and they follow him anywhere."

I looked at Ray, intrigued. "So you two are going out?"

He'd met a lot of women over the past year, working our parties. He flirted a good deal. But I hadn't remembered ever hearing him say he was seeing any of the party girls he's met on the circuit.

"Now, hey. Did I say that? Anyway, Marisa was telling me her Testarossa didn't sound right when she drove up the hill to-night."

Holly groaned. Her face was back down splat on the kitchen table, so her words were faintly muffled. "He shoots. He scores."

Ray looked nothing but innocent. "I better go help her out."

"You are a true humanitarian, my friend." Wesley saluted him.

Ray slipped out of the kitchen as Wes came over and offered me a cold can of Diet Coke. It was, so far, my only addiction. I was hooked on the combination of mucho caffeine and zero calories. Cold, refreshing, and filled with innumerable tasty artificial colors and chemicals, it was the bubbly antidote to whatever ailed me.

There was a knock at the back door. The black poodle dog, whose tail wagged off the seconds on the wall above the sink, displayed the time: 11:10.

"Must be Lee." I opened the kitchen door and there she stood.

"Hi, Maddie. I hope I am not late." Lee Chen stood on the threshold, carrying a mah-jongg case. She was tiny, the size who spent a lifetime shopping in the "petite" section, down in the extremely low numbers. At a guess, I'd say she had to be in her sixties. Her short, jet-black hair and her smooth skin did not give away her age, but I had known her long enough to hear her tell about her twin granddaughters at Stanford.

I gave her a hug. At five feet five inches, I almost felt tall. "How are you tonight, Lee?"

"I feel wonderful, Maddie dear." Lee Chen was educated in Hong Kong, and her accent was faintly British.

Holly attempted to lift her head, revealing a face that had been steam-cleaned of all makeup. "Hi, Lee."

"Hello there, Holly. Is something wrong? You look very pale."

"She served Dim Sum tonight," I explained. "She'll recover."

"Dim Sum is a special treat." Lee smiled at Holly and turned back to me. "It turned out very well, Maddie?"

"Yes, thanks to a wonderful teacher I had a few years ago."

In fact, I had studied Chinese cooking with Lee Chen. After years of running her own popular restaurant, she taught a master's class in Cantonese cuisine at UCLA Extension for just one quarter, and I was lucky enough to get in.

Lee had an interesting past. She spent much of her childhood in the city of Canton, now called Guangzhou. She was full of stories about her visits with Ling Ah, her mother's sister. In addition to passing down family recipes, Auntie Ling Ah also taught Lee about Confucius. What Lee learned as a girl in her auntie's kitchen became lessons she shared with us. Her course was the most spiritual and serene cooking class I can remember taking.

"You remember what I taught you?" Lee asked me, teasing.

I certainly did. In her classroom, I learned about the ancient traditions. I learned about the "Seven Necessities" of Chinese cuisine, those being rice, tea, oil,

144

salt, soy sauce, vinegar, and firewood.

From Lee I learned that color, aroma, and flavor share equal importance in the preparation of every dish. I found the rituals and traditions fascinating, each stemming from a unique culinary philosophy that had been worked out and passed down for hundreds of years in stunning detail.

I learned that each Chinese entrée combines three to five colors, selected from ingredients that are light green, dark green, red, yellow, white, black, or caramel-colored. I also learned to balance the five flavors — bitter, salt, sour, hot, and sweet. A proper meal, Lee instructed, must be designed to maintain the balance of Yin and Yang forces that are vital to good health in the body, mind, and spirit.

I have always been ambitious in the kitchen. As my final class project, I cooked Buddha Jump over the Wall, an intricate dish that took two days to prepare. Lee Chen's recipe for the insanely complex dish called for twenty-eight ingredients, mercifully not including the fish lips and duck gizzards used in the true Fuzhou version. Lee told us that this robust stew was so alluring that supposedly the Buddha himself, a vegetarian, could not resist it. She was an inspiring teacher.

But cooking was just one of this tiny woman's talents. Growing up in China, where mah-jongg is still a craze, she knew the game well from childhood. As the years passed, she also became a great student of the ancient practice of telling fortunes by reading the tiles. In this capacity, I had brought her to the Sweet and Sour as my New Year's gift to Buster and the gang.

"Shall we start now?" Lee asked, tapping her old mah-jongg case. "Where are your guests, please?"

"They're in the game room, Lee. But you'll see that there are many mah-jongg sets already out."

"Ah, but when we use my tiles, Maddie, the fortunes come out better. You will see."

The surprise introduction of Lee Chen and her humble offer to do mah-jongg tile readings moved the party into a second peak of excitement. One by one, the players sat with Lee at a little table near the fireplace. One by one, she instructed them to shuffle the tiles facedown and select thirteen. Most were very happy with Lee's predictions.

Verushka would hear good news about money soon, Lee foresaw. Verushka, naturally, was happy to hear that. In more startling news, Trey and the Swansons could expect a visit from the stork. This news pleased Max and Greta Swanson silly. They were a cute couple. But the stork news left Trey shaking his tousled blond bachelor head. Oh, well. Can't please 'em all.

Most of the others eagerly listened to predictions of the future with that great L.A. mixture of hope and skepticism. Each took a turn to learn that: a new game-show pilot would be picked up, a Silverlake band would find a label, a new job involving both water and costumes (!) was around the corner, a health problem (having to do with feet) was to be overcome, a canned-fruit voice-over job was a sure thing, a location would send one to Brazil, a bad agent would be lost and a lost Gucci bag was to be found (look in high places), a prestigious preschool would have a last-minute opening for twins, a ski accident was to be averted in Aspen, a new sports car should be ordered in the auspicious color of red, a script needed a quick rewrite, a beach house would have termite damage, beware, and a network would be unfaithful. Well, that last went without saying. By midnight, the only ones whose fortune had yet to be read were the hosts.

Buster had just said good-bye to the last of the guests. Quita watched Trey as he walked out with Verushka. She said,

"Doesn't it look like Verushka's gaining weight?"

That has to be the single most catty comment I'd heard after a party. I was annoyed, but I ignored it. Instead, I called to Buster, "Come on over here, with your lucky red jacket. Your future awaits. Your turn."

"Oh, goodie." Buster loped over, then slouched down in the chair opposite Lee Chen and grinned. He looked across the room and noticed Quita down by the mirrored bar, serving herself another Singapore Sling from a pitcher Ray had left in the bar's minirefrigerator. "Hey, Queets. You haven't had your fortune told."

Quita had been twitchy and bitchy and restless all night. "I know what's coming," she said darkly. She'd also been drinking all night.

"She's in a pleasant mood," Buster said to Wes and me, shuddering. And then he turned back to her. "Come on, Queets. Your fortune is waiting, doll."

"What if it's bad?" Quita didn't budge from her barstool.

"I'm giving up on her," Buster said, turning his attention back to Lee Chen. "She doesn't deserve a good fortune, but I do. I'm all excited here. Let's do it."

Wesley and I had been lounging on two

black-leather club chairs, which had been pulled up near Lee's fortune table, listening to all the predictions made from the tiles. I popped up and asked Lee for perhaps the third time that evening, "May I get you something to drink?"

She smiled up at me. "Thank you, Maddie. Perhaps just a glass of water? Do you have Perrier?"

Even little Chinese ladies have their favorite brand of H_2O.

As I trotted over to the bar, Lee Chen turned her full attention to young Mr. Dubin. "Do you have a specific question? Or perhaps you would like to know the future in general? Which do you like?" As Lee spoke in her soft accent, her fingers were constantly combing through the mah-jongg tiles on the table, gently shuffling and reshuffling the facedown cream-colored rectangles.

Buster picked one up. "This is beautiful. Is it bone or is it ivory?"

"Thank you. It is ivory, very rare." Lee studied the tile Buster had randomly selected. For once, her hands stopped shuffling. The other 143 tiles sat suddenly silent. She looked up.

For a brief moment, the boyish grin slipped from Buster's face. "What, Mrs. Chen. Is it bad?"

"No, no. Something very good. You see! You drew the East Wind, which is a very powerful tile. It means very good luck."

"I love this," he said. "What else?"

"You had good luck tonight. You won a big pot of money, I think."

Quita McBride looked up from the bar. She walked, a little unsteadily, over to join us. "That's an easy guess," Quita said softly. "Look at how the man is gloating. I'd say it was shocking bad manners for the host of the party to take so much money from his friends."

"I don't think it is his fault, Miss," Lee said, laughing. "He cannot avoid fate, you see? He is East Wind, tonight."

"That is so true," Buster said. "I can't help it if I'm lucky."

Quita sat down on Buster's lap and turned to Lee Chen. "So how does all this fortune-telling work?"

"Mah-jongg, you know, is a very old game. Quite old. In China, some women play this game all day long. The men gamble in the mah-jongg halls, and even in public. The tiles, you see, have pictures and numbers engraved on the front to mark the different suits, like these." She quickly turned over a few tiles, and pulled out a tile with six stalks of bamboo, etched in green. "This

150

one here is Six Bamboo, or sometimes in this country you say Six Bam, do you not?"

"Yes," Quita said, watching intently. "My husband taught me to play."

"Oh. This gentleman is your husband?"

"No," Quita said quickly. "Buster and I aren't married. My husband died last year. You've heard of Richard McBride, the actor?"

Little Lee Chen looked up astonished. The name of a big-time movie star has power. It's always been that way.

"Ah," Lee said, her voice recovering, "then you must know about all the tiles. The three main suits are Bamboo, Wan, and Circles."

"We call those Bam, Crack, and Dots," Buster said.

"Yes. And there are also the Flowers and the Four Winds and the Four Seasons and the three colors of Dragons. But, when I tell fortunes, the tiles become an oracle to interpret the future. Each tile in the set has a symbolic meaning all its own."

"Kind of like tarot cards," Quita said.

Lee said, "An oracle requires an interpreter if the meaning of its secrets are to be divined. I am that 'diviner,' you see? It is quite simple."

I had seen Lee Chen give readings of the

tiles once before, and it was fascinating. She must sit in the West position and the party guest sits in the East. She had cautioned me that the table should not be placed in a direct line toward a door, as this is regarded as unsympathetic to the oracle.

Lee looked up at Buster. "Now, you must shuffle the tiles, if you please."

Buster spread his large hands over the facedown tiles and gave them a swish.

"How long should I shuffle?" he asked.

"Until you are satisfied, my dear," Lee answered.

"Well, that could take forever," Quita said. "Buster, I really need you for a minute. We need to talk."

Buster eased her up out of his lap and turned to face the game table. "Not right now, doll," he said, quickly shuffling the tiles in earnest.

"Keep in your mind a question," Lee advised, and smiled modestly. "You do not need to tell me what your question is."

"There," Buster said, and he raised his hands off the tiles in a dramatic gesture. "I'm ready."

"Very good. Now you must push all the tiles to the sides, you see? This will clear an area in the center."

Buster did as she instructed as we watched.

"This," Lee said in her singsong instructor's voice, "is the 'lake.'" She referred to the central area that Buster was clearing. "The tiles you push to the sides must form a circle with no breaks, please."

Wesley leaned over and whispered to me, "You're up next, so pay attention."

I jabbed him.

"Very nice, Mr. Dubin. Next, please select thirteen tiles from the outer circle, any tiles at all, sir, and push these into center of the lake."

Then Lee instructed Buster to reshuffle the thirteen tiles that he'd selected and then to push three tiles toward the West sector of the spread, then three tiles towards the East sector, then three tiles toward the North sector and then three tiles towards the South sector. Finally, he was told to push the one remaining tile toward the center.

We looked on as he completed building the pattern as he was instructed.

North 7-8-9

West 4-5-6   center tile   1-2-3 East

South 10-11-12

"Now, I turn them over in order," she told

153

us, smiling. "And we shall see what fortune has in store for you." She turned over the center tile. "The tile in the center represents the focus of the reading. This is your present problem."

"Funny," Buster said, "it doesn't look like you, Queets."

Quita stood directly behind Buster's chair, brooding. She did not laugh.

Lee Chen studied the tile. It had a small numeral four in green and a squiggly blue Chinese character that meant four on top and a red squiggle that represented the Wan suit. "You see? It is the Four Wan, which represents the Chinese character: *Ch'in*. This character is symbolized by the lute and represents the performing arts. It is a symbol of music."

"You are unreal, Mrs. Chen," Buster said, delighted.

"My god." Quita looked at Buster. "Did you waste your question on the stupid *Warp* music video?" She turned to us, and added, "He's desperate to do it. I don't know why. But they are not coming up with the contract."

Buster gave his girlfriend a pained look. "They want me, Quita. Look at my Four Wan. They just have to come up to my price. But with my East Wind and my Four

Wan, I think it's a done deal."

Then he turned back to Lee. "Please, Mrs. Chen, go on."

She continued to turn over tiles and tell their significance, but just at that moment my cell phone rang. I moved out of range of the reading so I wouldn't disturb them as I answered the call. It was Arlo. He wanted to see how late I was working so we could meet for a late dinner. By the time I returned, five minutes had passed and Buster's reading was nearly done.

I looked down at the table where all of the tiles had, by now, been turned face up.

"I'm sorry I missed everything. How'd it turn out?"

"Not bad." Buster looked up at me, grinning.

"Mr. Dubin is a very lucky man." Lee Chen's eyes held an extra twinkle. "Money he will get, and he will hold on to it, which is most important. Success will be his as well. I saw for him a big project with music —"

"The *Warp* video," Buster interpreted.

"— but there may be a delay. There was only one thing we do not like to see, I am afraid."

"Well." Quita stood up and straightened one of the spaghetti straps on her slim shoulder. "I think this whole thing is a joke."

She looked at her watch and, immediately, some other expression wiped clean the annoyed, pinched look she'd worn throughout most of the late part of the evening. "I've got to go, Buster. We still need to talk."

"Later, honey," he said.

"There is no later," she said, pouting. "I told you I can't stay tonight."

"In a minute. Hang out a while longer, okay?"

Quita stomped out without another word.

Lee Chen watched her go. "That lady is not happy with me, I think."

"What's not so happy about Buster's future?" I asked, although I had a pretty good idea, even without the mah-jongg oracle. "Quita?"

"That we can only guess," Lee said, hiding a smile. "The tiles only tell us that after a brief romance with a duplicitous partner, Mr. Dubin will start over. And here is lucky news again. He will find a very nice new romantic partner."

"Oops," Wes said.

"Actually," I said, "I'm pretty worried about Quita. We talked to her earlier, and she was horribly upset."

Buster didn't look surprised. "You can't let her drag you into her drama, Madeline. Quita has so many wheels turning up here, so many plots" — he tapped his temple — "she doesn't have much time to knock two rational thoughts together."

"I guess," I said. "I think maybe she hasn't gotten over her husband's death yet."

"She was really freaking out," Wes said, remembering like I did how differently Quita had behaved back at the Wetherbee house.

"She's a sweet kid," Buster said, "but she has problems. Hey, who doesn't?" He got up and pulled out the chair opposite Lee. "Come on, now, Maddie. Your turn."

"Don't you think we should be going?" I asked, looking off in the direction Quita had gone.

"No way. She'll keep."

"Come sit down, Madeline," Lee instructed, and so I did.

After a rapid bout of shuffling tiles, and making a lake, I quickly selected thirteen tiles and pulled them into the center. Then, as Lee guided me, I set up the tiles, three apiece in the positions that represented East, West, North, and South, and one in the center.

Lee turned over the tile in the center first.

"Ah. Six Wan. Very interesting."

"What?" I looked down at the tile. It showed the number etched in red in the upper corner and the same Chinese character as the other wan tiles etched in black.

"It means many things. One thing is intelligence."

"Of course." Wes began to laugh. "That's perfect, Mad."

"I love smart women," Buster said. "So why don't I ever date any?" He gave me a goofy look, raising his eyebrows several times, Groucho Marx style, to signify possible future romance.

I laughed and turned back to Lee. "Intelligence. That's a nice compliment, Lee. That's safe. But I forgot to think of a question. So does that botch the reading?"

Lee was intently studying the Six Wan tile. When she realized she'd been addressed she looked up quickly and smiled. "No, no. Nothing is ruined. You may have a general reading, Madeline dear. Listen and learn about the future."

She turned over another tile. Five Wan meant house. I thought perhaps it could be Wesley's new house, but she didn't confirm that. Four Circles meant hard work, but it also meant friendship and it also meant justice.

Wesley smiled at me. "This is just so *you*."

I blushed. These things are fun, but they are not very specific.

"Here's Five Bam, and look, here's another Five Bam. Two children."

"Oh, really?" I had much to think about.

"Soon," Lee said, beaming up at me.

"Not too soon," I said, laughing.

"Ditto," said my business partner, Wes.

Then Lee turned over the tiles that represent relationships. Buster moved in closer, making jokes about taking notes. I must admit, I settled down and paid a little more attention, too.

Lee said, "Here, you have West Wind. This is a very masculine person. A man with strength and power."

"Well, that leaves out your boyfriend, Arlo," Buster said.

Wes chuckled.

Men liked to make such jokes. I ignored them.

"Then another tile here." Lee turned over the next tile. "It is the Eight Circles. Ah." Lee looked deep in thought.

"What is it, Lee? Bad news?"

"Madeline, the Eight Circles is also a man, very masculine. This tile means an authority figure."

"Good grief," I muttered.

"You mean, like her father?" Wes asked.

"It could be a policeman," Lee said, sounding worried. "I hope this is not scaring you, dear Madeline."

"Only just a little, Lee. I know a police fellow, actually. I saw him tonight, as a matter of fact."

"Oh? Then it is all right? Good." Lee went through the rest of the tiles, but I don't think I remember much else she said. I just fixated on her nailing Honnett, right there on the Eight Circles. Jeesh.

"So Madeline, when we add these tiles here to these others, we see stability."

"Stability is okay," I said hopefully.

"Stable, happy work. Stable, happy home. Stable, happy man in life," Lee said, looking over all thirteen exposed tiles. "Stable, happy partners."

"Thank goodness," Wesley said.

"You get married soon to Arlo, Madeline?" Lee asked, after careful thinking.

"No!"

"Well," Lee said with a shy smile, pointing to the two flower tiles, "then what are these two babies doing here?"

We all laughed.

Lee said, "They are only tiles, after all. You like to hear more?"

"Go ahead." I never take this sort of thing seriously. It's just fun to imagine life's possibilities.

"Your man. He is very powerful. A very passionate person. A very affectionate man. It says this quite clearly in the tiles."

I burst out laughing. "Lee Chen!" This was not the type of reading I expected from a grandmother of twin college girls. "Really."

She joined me laughing. "I do not make this up, Maddie. You can see it yourself. Here, here, and here." She pointed out tiles as if I could read their meanings.

"Well, I'm shocked," I said, trying not to smile, kidding my former teacher.

"I do not see why you are so modest, Madeline. You know about the philosopher Kao Tzu, I think."

Buster and I shook our heads, but Wesley looked up, alert. "Kao Tzu. Yes, the famous Warring States-period philosopher."

Wesley.

"Yes," Wes said, "Kao Tzu was a keen observer of human nature."

"Very good," Lee answered. "No reason to be shy about love, Madeline. Kao Tzu said, 'Appetite for food and sex is nature.' "

Well, how was one supposed to refute a Warring States philosopher? And given his philosophy, why would one want to?

It had gotten to be so late, I was anxious to get Lee home and so we left shortly afterward. Wesley left in his own car. And I had one more stop to make. The call I'd received had been from Arlo. He was leaving his office after a typically long night of doing rewrites, and he wanted to meet me for a late dinner.

I stood in the street next to Lee's small black Acura, waiting for her to safely start her car. I heard the engine turn over, but she didn't pull out from the curb. She rolled down her window and called me to come closer.

"Thank you so much, Lee," I said again as I approached. "Your talents are extraordinary."

"You are always welcome, dear Madeline. But I think I must tell you one more thing."

"Oh?"

"I did not want to say this in front of your friends."

"Say what?"

"It is the Six Wan."

"The Six Wan?" I tried to remember. "Wasn't that the center tile? That meant intelligence?"

"Very good memory," she said, always my proud teacher. "But the tiles have many different meanings. I told you. It depends on what the position, what the next tile. And

162

the Six Wan . . ." She frowned.

"Yes?"

"It is also the tile of grave danger."

"Oh."

"I do not want to scare you. I just think you should know this. The Six Wan. It is the tile of greatest warning."

"Warning of what?" I asked. I don't know if it was the chill of the night, or perhaps I was getting tired. I pulled on my leather jacket but felt no warmth.

"Six Wan can mean an accident. I'm sorry, Madeline. I want you to be careful, okay?"

"Okay, Lee. Don't worry about it."

"Goodnight to you. You are going straight home now?"

"No. I'm going out with my boyfriend. Arlo."

"Ah."

Ah, indeed.

Chapter 12

"OH NO!"

"Man oh man."

"Oh my God. It's dead, Madeline. You killed it."

I looked at the small, sleek cell phone, ice tea dripping off its pathetically flipped open flip part. A dark watery stain formed on the pink-linen tablecloth beneath it. The thing was dead all right.

"Oops."

I don't know how it happened, really. I am not clumsy. I am actually pretty damn graceful. But I was holding Arlo's little phone for a second and it slipped and it fell and the Atlantic Ocean of ice tea kinda swallowed it up. It fell straight into his glass. I don't know how that happened.

"Okay, I'm not a technical guy. Granted, okay?" Arlo was getting agitated, as the enormity of his cellular disaster washed over him like a wave of, well, tea. "But I'm pretty sure these things don't work anymore after they have been deliberately dunked in *iced beverages.*

I'm pretty sure that was in the ninety-page Ericsson instruction manual. The phone, Maddie, is dead. It is never coming back."

I handed him my napkin. "Sorry, Arlo, honey. It was a freak accident."

And then I realized. That was *it*. That was Lee Chen's prediction of an accident. It had to be. I smiled myself silly.

Arlo looked at me with suspicion as he gently patted his little gizmo.

He was cute. No one said otherwise. He had that boyish thing down, with shaggy brown hair and a prep-school face. Behind his small wire-rims, Arlo's large, troubled brown eyes met mine.

"It was an accident. I swear," I swore.

Jeesh. Drop a guy's new cellular toy among the ice cubes and it's some deep, sinister plot. He asked me to hold it for a second, and technically, I held it for a second. And then, well past the agreed-upon time limit, it slipped. I wasn't trying to drown the gizmo. Honestly. At least, I don't think I was. Murdering electronics was beneath me.

"Some people believe there are no accidents," Arlo said.

"Then they should talk to my old teacher, Lee Chen."

"What?"

"Never mind, Arlo. Never mind."

"Some people might think you dropped my phone on purpose."

"Yes, and some people believe that Barry Manilow is one of the greatest singers of all time."

Arlo stared at me. Arlo loved Barry Manilow. "And?" His voice had gone up a notch or two. "Your point would be . . . ?"

"I'm simply saying, Arlo, that there is no end to 'what some people believe.' "

Arlo and I were meeting for a late supper at La Scala Presto in Burbank, just a few blocks from his office at Warner Bros. studios. We had yet to order. We'd hardly had a moment to talk. Even at one in the morning, Arlo's job kept him tied to his cell phone, making vital network decisions as to why Jim J. Bullock could not possibly play an alien in the sitcom pilot on which Arlo was consulting. Our menus were still on the table. They, along with the table's linen cloth and the china and silver, were now dripping with tea drops and scattered with beached cubes.

"What a shame." The restaurant hostess was at our side now, surveying the splash zone. "Perhaps the table there?" The restaurant was fairly empty at this time. She indicated a vacant table that was freshly set up.

As we stood, Arlo wrapped the napkin around the tiny wireless phone and patted it gently. As we crossed the room, an upscale trattoria, I looked around. Green ivy leaves were hand-painted onto the white Italian tiles that surrounded the open-hearth pizza oven, and a full-time prep chef at the counter continually chopped the ingredients to their famous Leon Chop Salad, even this late. I noticed the head of prime-time programming at NBC sitting alone in a corner booth. We had catered a large event for him last year. The hours people worked in this industry were cruel. He was absorbed in reading a script and appeared to be the only one in the room who hadn't looked up when I *accidentally* sent Arlo's little phone deep-tea diving. I decided it would be better not to disturb him. I could say hello later.

I sat down and looked over at Arlo. He was pushing and repushing a number of tiny buttons on his cell phone in frustration. Yes. I got it. It didn't work.

I had been telling Arlo about my day between his urgent calls. I told him about what happened in Santa Monica. I told him about the strange conversation at Wesley's Wetherbee house. As I started and restarted my saga, Arlo juggled calls. Momentous decisions re: series minority (Chicano vs. Asian); sofa color (Nile green vs. plum); and rehab program for the star (Sierra Tucson Clinic vs. Betty Ford) were made. And as I tried to tell Arlo about the mah-jongg party, I waited while he received three more calls during which everyone wanted to change those decisions. And then the ice tea incident occurred.

"Dead, dead, dead . . ." Arlo looked me in the eye.

Perhaps I should explain where I'm coming from. I've been going through a lot lately. Heavy things just keep happening. I mean, for a gourmet chef and caterer, admittedly a lighthearted kind of profession, I've been swimming an awful lot, lately, in the deep end of life's little pool. I have observed several serious events recently, some involving death and lives ruined. So watching Arlo make a federal case out of a little mishap with passion fruit ice tea was not playing well. I was becoming less amused, by the minute, with always having to accommodate Arlo's inalienable right as a comedy writer to milk anguish to the tenth power, so long as it got a laugh. If Arlo had a raison d'être it was simply this: the joke must be played out. And, therefore . . .

Arlo picked up the phone, pressing all of

the buttons and shaking it again. "It's really dead, Maddie. Dead and gone."

I put my finger next to my eye, right where I could feel the little headache pinching. "And now what, Arlo? The five stages of grief? First you cry? Can we just order, honey?"

His lip curled. A smile, perhaps?

"Or could you hurry up and move into the denial phase?" I asked sweetly.

He laughed, despite himself. "Don't make fun."

This was Arlo and me. We're not the easiest couple. For one thing, we both work a lot. Maybe too much. We had been squeezing what might pass as a fairly passionate, fairly hilarious relationship around his sitcom's insane production schedule and my never-ending parties. But lately. Well.

Just then, I began to detect the sound of slightly raised voices somewhere in the background. I turned and saw the NBC guy upset on his cell phone. Short and wiry, with rolled-up sleeves, he kept talking as he slammed back his chair, speaking into his receiver in a harsh tone. It didn't look like he had finished eating, but he was pulling out his wallet, saying wait a minute, wait a minute. In a flash of insane and perfect irony, I wondered if the NBC guy was just receiving the unacceptable news from some underling that his newest series producers were insisting on a Latino sidekick with a Nile green sofa.

Nah!

The waitress brought us a pair of dry menus and cast an eye over to the small commotion. "I don't know what it is tonight. Maybe the Santa Anas. People are acting strange. Would you like to order now? Or do you need a few more minutes?"

I told her we'd like to order just as Arlo told her we needed more time. I gazed over to Arlo with intensity.

Under protest he tossed out his usual order. A burger. Well-done. Make that extra-well. Plain. No onions. No tomato. No lettuce. With fries. Actually, it's about the only thing Arlo ever orders. He is a man with rigidly simple tastes in food. Nothing green. Nothing, in fact, of a vegetable nature of any kind. Imagine what the average four-year-old likes and you can safely have Arlo over for dinner.

By the time I looked back over to check on what was up with the NBC guy, he had gone.

"So, anyway, whose party did you do tonight?" Arlo asked.

"Buster Dubin. He's a neighbor of mine.

Remember?" I think I'd explained this to Arlo on at least four occasions.

"What does he do again?" Arlo asked.

"Directs," I said, looking at Arlo, waiting for him to wake up. "Remember? He did the music video for The Julies. And a bunch of big commercials. You know the one for Tattoos.com? That's his."

"Oh, yeah."

"Oh, yeah."

"And isn't his girlfriend that model or something?"

I shook my head. "That was one of his old girlfriends. Lately he's been living with Quita McBride. He kinda goes through women."

"I'd better use the pay phone to call Mark back," Arlo said, checking his watch. "Before the food comes."

"I thought it might be nice if we, like, talked."

"Oh?" Arlo adjusted his glasses. "Okay. If you say so, sweetie. A talk. Shoot."

I resettled in my chair and tried to restart the evening on a better note. "I heard this lovely story yesterday. From my friend, Sophie."

"Is she still the chef at that restaurant in Pasadena?"

"Uh-huh, she's doing great. Did I tell you

she's adopting a baby girl? From China. She just found out they've matched her to a little girl."

"She wants a baby?" Arlo began doing his Rodney Dangerfield schtick, pulling at the collar of his denim shirt, mock nervous. "Um." He cleared his throat. "She didn't go giving you any ideas."

"Arlo. Sophie's ten years older than I am. She's thought about this decision for a long time. Jeez! She would be a perfect mother. But don't worry. I'm not ready. You know that. I don't want to have children anytime in the foreseeable ever. Don't worry."

"Because we're not the kind of people to go and have some of those, are we? We're too young."

I put my finger back on the spot that ached, at my temple.

"Well, I'm almost thirty, Arlo. And you are five years older than I am, so. . . ."

"Exactly. We're mere children ourselves."

I shot him a look.

"We're babies, Mad. And, also, we're focused on other things. We've got our work, obviously. We're busy people. And we've got hobbies."

"Hobbies?"

"Sure." Arlo, apparently jacked up on several barrels of ice tea, got excited making his point. "Loads of very time-intensive hobbies. I enjoy cutting out the crossword puzzle in TV Guide —"

"Because," I said, interrupting, "you're always hoping they'll use your name in one of their puzzles."

"Low blow."

I laughed. "That's not much of a hobby, my friend."

"But it's terribly time-consuming, just the same. And you . . ."

I looked up. Pretty much all I did was work away at my little business with Wesley and Holly.

"What are my hobbies, would you say?" I asked.

"You, Maddie, are teeming with important things that take up all of your time."

"Such as . . . ?"

"Making insane, passionate love to your devastatingly handsome boyfriend."

"Ha."

"And your hair! You are busy all the time shampooing."

"Shampooing." I bit my bottom lip. To laugh at Arlo's award-winning humor was to succumb to his powers, so I made him work a bit for it.

"Yes. You take a lot of time with that hair

of yours, Mad. I've been meaning to talk to you about it, actually."

My hair has the look of a reddish blond mop that's been set on spoolies. And that's its natural state. In fact, it does take a lot of time to brush it out and blow-dry it straight, so I mostly let it go in ringlets. But I knew Arlo's schtick. He liked to disarm me with wit.

"So," he said, in conclusion, "it's really absurd to be thinking about babies."

Our waitress brought us fresh glasses of ice tea and withdrew quickly. Just what this man needed.

"Arlo. Did I say this has anything to do with us? Can you possibly imagine there are other people in the world? And sometimes, just sometimes, there are things that happen to *them*."

"Other people." Arlo sipped his drink. "Now that you mention it, I do believe I've heard of them. So go on about Sophie."

"Thank you. She is very excited about her new daughter. She had just gone to the bookstore and found some great books. One of them is a little folk tale from China. It's called *The Empty Pot*."

Arlo spoke up in a tone of voice that sounded absolutely outraged. "Now wait a darn minute. Sophie wants to be a mom and she's buying books about pot? I think some women were just not meant to be mothers."

"Arlo!"

"I'm joking. I'm joking. Go on already." I think Arlo gets a special charge out of riling me up.

"I wanted to tell you about this story because it really affected me. Okay? So settle down."

"I'm settled." He put on his good-listener face, the one that must have disarmed Mrs. Beven, his fourth-grade teacher, when he was in reality whispering one-liners to the back row, and then chuckling when they got into trouble for laughing.

But this was about the most of Arlo's attention I'd had in a while. With neither one of us at our offices, and his cell phone temporarily out of commission, I began my story. "*The Empty Pot* is a folk tale about an ancient Chinese emperor. The aging emperor gives one flower seed to each child in his kingdom. He tells them, 'In a year's time show me what you have grown, and the flowers will choose my successor.' But what the children don't know is the seeds they get from the emperor are incapable of germinating."

"Now that's downright cruel, Madeline.

175

Are you sure this emperor didn't work at Disney?"

"Arlo. It was a test." I crossed my legs and noticed my tight black pants got his attention. Whatever it took. I continued the story. "Naturally, all the children were horribly disappointed when their flowers didn't grow. They didn't want to show the emperor they had failed. Now, what would you have done in that situation?"

"Okay. No brainer. I'd have gone to the florist with my Kung Fu MasterCard and charged something impressive. *Voilà*. The best flowers would win. And basically, you'd be bowing and calling me Your Highness tonight. Because bottom line, I have always been the kind of guy who wins. I'm a winner."

"Of course you are." I didn't have the energy to roll my eyes. "However, in this story, Ping is chosen to be the next emperor because he is the only one who has the courage to come before the ruler with an empty pot."

"That's it? He wins with an empty pot? Now *that* I don't buy. He might have had more courage than the rest of those other wimps, but so what? That doesn't show leadership ability. What do you think Bill Gates would say if one of his managers brought him an empty pot? I'll tell you what he'd say: You're fired. Let's face it, Ping was a nice guy, salt of the earth, yadda, yadda, but he didn't get the job done."

I looked at Arlo. "His honesty was the most important quality."

"Yes, I get the story, Mad. But I disagree, honey. Honesty sounds nice and everything, but it just does not play in our modern world. Results are what matter. If the emperor wanted flowers, then it's the guy who brings him flowers that gets the job done. Anything else is just excuses."

"Arlo!"

The waitress brought our late supper. Arlo took a look at his bun and made a sour face. "I thought I said no sesame seeds. Could you take this back?"

She looked down at the plate, and said, "Oh." She squinted up at Arlo and looked like she was about to say something. Instead, she just turned around with his plate. It was at that moment I pushed my chair back.

"Mad? Hey! Where are you going?"

I grabbed my purse from the floor and stood up. I took one long last look at Arlo. I took it all in. His familiar funny handsome face. His tousled hair. His mouth. His wide shoulders beneath his designer blue-denim shirt. His slim waist, zipped into expensive jeans. His long, slender fingers with their nibbled fingernails. His Rolex. His "I ♥ El Lay" key ring with the keys to his Porsche. His dead cell phone.

I turned and walked away.

"Hey, Mad. What's going on? Madeline!" Arlo had raised his voice a notch, getting the attention of just about everyone in the semifilled room.

I had made it about ten feet before I stopped and turned. "I just realized something. I've been with the wrong guy. I don't need a guy with an Emmy and an ulcer. I need someone who can bring me an empty pot."

"Madeline. That's nuts."

"Not to me." I walked back to our table, flushing hot. I stood there, looking down upon him. Seeing him now. "Arlo. I want different things than you do, that's all. I don't know what took me so long to realize it. I just need something else."

"You want kids? Is that it? You think you want a baby?"

"NO! I don't want a baby!" I shouted. "I want honesty. That's what that story was about, you moron! I want a little freaking honesty from the man I love."

I looked up and realized everyone in the place had just clammed up, watching Arlo and me. Our waitress stood off to one side, holding the plate with Arlo's hamburger and its new, de-seeded bun.

"I want an honest man, Arlo. I am in serious need of an honest individual who can eat a freaking hamburger with the works."

"Mad. What exactly is going on here? First you drown my cell phone, then you insult my burger. Are you trying to tell me something?" Arlo looked more upset than I can remember seeing him.

"We're over, Arlo. We're past tense. Get it now? We are done." I turned and started to run.

"Wait. Are you saying you're breaking up with me?"

And as I ran out the front door, as it slowly closed on its hinge behind me, I could hear a chorus of "YES!" ring out from the dozen of our disturbed fellow diners who all, apparently, got the message of *The Empty Pot*.

Out on Riverside Drive, I took a deep breath of cool air. Okay, I could have managed that in a more dignified way. But damn. I felt good. A few cars cruised by on Riverside, but the street was generally empty. During the day, this street sees a lot of traffic. Its shops bustle. Its restaurants hum. But at night, everyone leaves their jobs in the nearby studios and heads home to the furthestmost burbs and hangs with their families. I heard the sound of an engine turning over from somewhere, but otherwise the street was pretty quiet. The Media District of Burbank kind of rolls up by nine, and the hubbub on its main drag dies down.

Still all pumped up from dumping Arlo, I took a deep breath and exhaled three years of my romantic life. Looking back at the doors to La Scala Presto, I knew Arlo was not going to follow me out, was not going to come rushing to stop me on the sidewalk, was not going to beg me to talk about it. Don't get me wrong. I knew that beneath his shock, he was terribly hurt. On the other hand, the waitress had just delivered his hamburger.

The pitiful thing was, I understood his logic. Just like I knew he would be crying tonight, later, in private. I understood him, loved him, flaws and all. But the realization that I had never been half-so-well understood by Arlo in return hit me now, hard as a fist, choking me up all of a sudden. Blinking back tears, I turned to walk around the block to where I'd left my car. I'd parked it on Yucca up at the next corner.

That's when I first saw her — a tiny thing,

only just old enough to walk, dressed in miniature black leggings. I waited to see her mom coming after her. This intersection at Riverside and Yucca was a fairly busy one. Even with the early-morning light traffic, I expected such an unsteady tot to have an adult by the hand.

The little black flare-legged pants got to me. I looked down at my own clothes. I had come straight from the Sweet and Sour Club party. I was still dressed in white V-neck tank top and black flare-leg pants.

The little girl tottered all the way to the corner, and I was beginning to feel a tiny ripple of alarm shoot up the back of my neck. The child, perhaps twelve months old, looked over to where I stood, sixty feet up the sidewalk.

"Hi!" I started walking toward her and she stood stock-still, big almond-shaped eyes fastened on mine.

What was she doing out here at night, anyway? Don't babies go to sleep earlier than this? Shouldn't she have a parent looking after her? As I slowly came closer she looked back down the side street, toward the spot beyond my vision where I presumed her adult must have been standing. I was just about to reach her at the corner and get a look down the side street. I felt like yelling a little at the idiot who would leave a baby alone so long on a major street corner.

The child had big, very dark eyes. Her deep bangs covered her forehead like thick, shiny fringe. As I approached, she backed up a few faltering steps, almost backing off the curb.

"Wait there, honey," I said, in that sing-song cartoon voice people use to talk to babies, an octave above normal speech. "Wait, wait, wait . . ." I crooned to her, as she teetered on the edge of the foot-high sidewalk curb.

Just when I needed it most, it became clear that I was lacking a vital rescue skill. I just don't have that squeaky-voice thing down. Without friends who have babies, I've never practiced. Who knew it would be such a drawback? Shit!

"Wait there . . ."

The child took one more baby step backward. In an instant she tumbled down into the street.

"NO!"

I watched her fall, heard her cry out, and then I looked up. An F-150, big and dark maroon, was just entering into the intersection. But, instead of driving straight in its lane, it began veering toward the curb. The truck crossed through the intersection, heading toward the fallen child. I processed all this in an instant. Man, he was going to pull it right up along the curbside, and crush her. I jumped down onto the asphalt, screaming and waving my arms. The truck's brakes screeched. The baby wailed. I admit it — my pulse racing — I kept screaming, making eye contact with the man behind the wheel, reaching down for the little girl. Not quite clearing the intersection, the nose of the pickup truck came to a stop only a few feet from us as I scooped up the baby.

I was not processing input precisely. I didn't think, oh my God, we were almost run over, instead I marveled at how light and how warm she was. Holding her to me safely, I jumped back up onto the sidewalk. But immediately, I was jolted by sound. I heard the explosive crunch of metal. The pickup truck, which had stopped in the intersection, had just been hit hard. Rear-ended. With the powerful momentum of the Corolla that smacked into it, the truck jumped forward, propelled curbward, coming at us again.

I hung on to the crying child and turned, moving as fast as I could away from the new threat. The impact of the collision had enough force to ram the truck to the curb and, in another second, lift it up and onto the sidewalk, just a few feet from us. I backed up as far as I could go — holding a crying, wriggling baby in my arms — pinned up against the stucco wall of the corner picture-frame shop. I could do nothing more than watch, horrified. The pickup truck came straight at us, still out of control. The driver, a man in his sixties, gave me frantic eyes from behind the windshield. He put up one hand in front of his face, unable to watch as he hit us. I turned away, shielding the crying baby with my body, but not before I saw his ring. On his pinky, a chunky golden ring. That's what I had forgotten!

The F-150, I realized, had not struck me. I turned around to look. There, on the sidewalk, the maroon pickup had suddenly lurched to a stop, its front bumper only ten inches from my knee.

Chapter 13

Sometimes you have to believe in fate.

You don't want to, of course. You want to be modern and cynical and scientific — that is, if, like me, you'd been raised by rational, unromantic parents in the Midwestern suburbs. As life goes on, if things occasionally seem odd and even a bit overly coincidental, you don't wig out and go all Mulder. You remind yourself about laws of probability and mathematics and odds. You want to believe in randomness, in one-out-of-a-bazillion chances, in luck. But then sometimes, maybe when you are least expecting it, like when you are standing on some odd Burbank street corner, hugging a little girl you hadn't known existed only moments earlier, some unsettling "fateful" thoughts may come to mind. At such a moment, you might start to lose a bit of your Scully cool.

What if?

What if, say, I had not gone out to dinner? What if I had not dropped a particular object (blue Ericsson X12) into a particular drink (large, full, just Sweet 'n Low'd)? What if I had not told Arlo good-bye, and walked out before tasting my Leon Chop Salad with chicken, what then? Was every choice, every decision, and every act leading to that one moment at the curb? Does all the stuff, both good and bad, that happens to us in our seemingly random lives nudge us in a very specific direction?

The baby I was holding in my arms began to settle down. My heart was still pumping hard. My hair felt damp with perspiration. My ankle throbbed from where I'd nicked it early this morning. I must have scraped it again when I jumped back onto the side-walk.

Around us, I began to notice a lot of noise. The driver of the truck seemed to be yelling how sorry he was. There were people coming out of a couple of restaurants on the block, attracted by the nause-ating crunch of fenders. Voices shouted, "Are you all right?"

I put the child down. Unaccustomed as I was to such intimate baby contact, I didn't want to intrude on her space. But as soon as I put her down she put her hands up, looking at me.

"Caroline! Oh my God. Oh my God." The NBC guy pushed through the little

186

throng. He looked out of his mind. Truly.

"Is she yours?" I realized my throat hurt. From screaming probably.

"Oh my God." The NBC guy picked up his daughter. "She was asleep in her car seat. I didn't want to wake her, you know? I was only going for a quick salad. Oh my God. My wife is working late, so I . . . I just thought the baby would be more comfortable with her seat belt loose. She's only fourteen months."

"You left her in your car?"

"She was sleeping, and I was only gone fifteen minutes. I didn't want to wake her. How did she open the car door?" He held his daughter gently. He kissed the fine black hair on the top of her head. She looked comfortable now, and unconcerned.

"Where were you?" I asked, astonished at his stupidity. "She could have been . . ." Well, there was really no reason to point out the obvious. Besides, I saw something on that foolish NBC guy's face that one rarely observes. I saw him get it.

"I came out here. I checked on her. But then I had to finish a call."

"You what?" I asked.

He looked at me, frantic. "It was an idiotic call. I was mad and getting loud, you know. I didn't want to wake her up. I just walked around the block to finish it. When I came back around the corner, I heard the noise over here. I had no idea Caroline was involved. How could I have known she would . . . ?" There were tears in his eyes. ". . . that she wouldn't be safe?"

"Well, she's okay," I said, feeling the energy sap out of my limbs. "She's okay now." People do dumb things. It happens. And who ever expects such danger waits on a quiet night like this?

"I know you," he said, as the sound of a police siren wailed in the distance, growing louder. "You did a party. You're . . ." He shook his head.

"Madeline Bean."

"Yes." He looked at me again and then he looked at the smashed truck perched awkwardly up on the sidewalk. "I will never forget this."

I felt a little weak. I looked for Arlo among the small crowd, but he wasn't there.

"I'll never forget this," the father said. "Never. I'm . . . Can I do something for you? I mean to thank you?"

"Why don't you take a little time off work?" I suggested.

The baby began to close her eyes, her head heavy on his shoulder. He shifted her in his arms so she'd be in a more comfortable position.

"I'm going to quit."

"You are?"

"I have never been so sure of any decision in my life."

I nodded and told him, good for you, but I knew. It was only the fear talking. He had made a mistake that almost couldn't be taken back. But in time, in a few hours or a few days, he'd remember his other fears — the payments due on his BMW and his mortgage and his MasterCard. He'd be overcome again with the fear that the network's new pilots were crap, or that the fall season would tank and someone would figure out that programming executives like him were just gamblers, guessing and playing for time.

And yet. Wait. I was beginning to see past my pat, cynical side, wasn't I? I was. And, I figure, if you're going to turn to the freaky side and start believing in fate, you have to remain open to the entire woven entity that is life.

If it was fate that drove me to break up with Arlo at exactly the moment in time that would propel me to that one particular street corner whereupon a child's life was teetering, then wasn't it equally possible —

probable, really — that the father of that child was meant to learn this sickening lesson at just this moment in his life?

I watched the shaky NBC guy cradle his daughter. I had to have hope. I had to hope he would wise up. I had to hope this fateful "hand from hell" would slap him awake, here in the middle of the night. Perhaps now he'd realize that he owed more to this little one than he did to the American viewing public. He owed her an entire lifetime of caring and tending. I hoped he'd retain, at the very least, the vivid memory of how much she needed him.

Which is why, friends and neighbors, I do not long for babies. Having children is a shattering responsibility. I bit my lip, knowing I wasn't ready to take it on, wondering if I ever would be.

In this mood, I started home. I had frankly had enough of this day. More than enough. Lee Chen's warning of an accident. How do you explain that? On the other hand, what about her predictions of stability? Of happy me and happy Arlo in our happy home with our two happy babies?

I pulled into my little cul-de-sac, weary and sad. But, I soon realized, not alone.

Out on the steps that lead up to my front door, someone sat and waited. In the dim light, I couldn't be sure. But perhaps Arlo, after all, had decided . . .

As I pulled into my driveway, my headlights swung two arcs of white light across the tile-and-stucco steps.

Chuck Honnett was sitting there at 2 a.m., waiting.

For me.

Chapter 14

"This is not a good time, Honnett." I sat myself down next to him on the step, settling my purse on the step below.

"Too late for you? I thought you were the tough girl. Nothing is too late for Madeline Bean. What happened to that?"

"That is a very good question." I didn't look at him. Sitting together on the step in the chill air, our sides touching, the warmth of his body felt good.

"Rough night?" he asked, checking me out. "You kinda lost your zip."

"You have that keen detective talent for observation working, don't you?" I said. "I have indeed lost my zip. Please don't let it get out, though. Bad for business."

"What's the matter?" Honnett's voice got husky. He usually sounded more, I don't know — cynical.

"I'm tired, maybe," I said, trying to get my voice to sound lighter. "My birthday's coming, did you know that?"

"You're feeling old?" He began to laugh.

"You're like a puppy. What are you turning? Thirty? I don't even own jeans anymore from back when I was thirty."

"Yeah, it does sort of cheer me up to hang out with an old guy like you," I said, beginning to smile. I looked up at him. Big mistake. Honnett looked especially good in street lamplight. Wouldn't you know?

"I'm trying to cheer you up, here. Is it working?" He kind of whispered. My tiny street was deserted, and we were sitting so close together, I had no problem hearing him. "Look, we can do this another time," he said. "I'm just going off duty now, anyway. Not a whole lot of progress on your mah-jongg-snatching, but you expected that. I'll call you tomorrow."

He stood up, but I couldn't.

"Hey, are you okay?"

"I think," I said.

"Are you crying?"

When I didn't answer him right away, he sat back down and put his arm around me, rustling it around the shoulder of my bulky black-leather jacket.

"This is not the best time for you to have dropped by, I'm afraid." I smoothed my face with both hands, wiping away the tears that kept coming.

"What's the matter?"

"Nothing," I said. Tears came harder. "Everything."

Honnett said, "Look, you want to go inside? Maybe I could make you a cup of tea?"

Oh, boy. The first time I had cried in as long as I could remember, and I find myself with a man who doesn't go running away in a panic. I was in a very dangerous place.

"You don't have to do this," I said. But I had also discovered I had no tissues in my purse. I had to go upstairs.

He followed me up to the landing at my front door and waited, patiently, as I fumbled in my bag to find my key ring. As we moved through the house, we left the lights off. I went upstairs, and he came along, making small talk.

"I don't think I've been upstairs before. This where you live?"

I use my downstairs for our catering business, but the three bedrooms upstairs had been converted into my private apartment. The former master bedroom was now my living room. I walked in and found the box of Kleenex.

Honnett came into the room, leaving the lights off. I think he realized I didn't want to be seen like this, falling apart. He walked over to the little fireplace in the corner and knelt, checking it out, moving his hand lightly over the tiles.

"Are these Batchelder?"

My house was built at a time when the famed tile-maker was doing relief tiles in colors popular with the Arts and Crafts movement, like gold and moss green. My fireplace surround was covered in a rare shade of matte blue. I was mildly surprised a guy like Chuck Honnett would know anything about ceramic artists of the early twentieth century.

"Would you like me to make a fire?" he asked.

See, everything he said seemed to make me cry more. I don't have to explain, do I, that Arlo didn't know anything about building a fire. That if you couldn't turn a little metal key in the wall, Arlo was worthless. I thought about that some more as Honnett started arranging a few logs.

"I broke up with Arlo tonight. Remember him?"

"Sure. The rich kid."

I laughed. I don't know if it was hearing Arlo called "rich" or a "kid." So, Honnett thought I dated rich guys. Is that why he'd fought the attraction all these months? And the age thing again. Honnett was forty-three, I guessed, and he had told me once before he thought he was too old for me.

"That all you're gonna say?" I asked, looking at him as he lit a match and touched it to the crumpled newspaper in the grate.

"Well, from the look of you tonight, I'd have to say you aren't all that happy about losing him."

"I didn't lose him, Honnett. I walked out on him, and I'm glad I did it."

There are two wonderful wing chairs in my small upstairs living room, but he didn't choose to sit in either of them. The cushions on the down-filled sofa sank as he joined me there. "So, tell me about it."

I turned to him, made eye contact, and spoke. "I thought I loved him, Honnett. I think I still do." Tears. "When I started dating Arlo, I was getting pretty successful. The business was taking off. Wes and I had turned a corner, and I could see it. And Arlo was just as ambitious. We were the same that way."

"Oh, I think not," Honnett said, reaching up to touch my hair, pushing it back off of my wet face.

I leaned against him and talked. I told him about how I'd been drawn to Arlo in those days. Arlo liked that I had my own career. He liked that I wasn't an actress because he was always fighting with actresses at work. As he grew more successful and wealthier, he liked that I was self-supporting and didn't ask him for money like his family did. He liked that I didn't object to his long hours. I think, over time, one of the only strengths we had was that we didn't object to each other's weirdnesses and hang-ups and obsessions.

"We were willing to leave each other alone."

"Not the best setup for a couple," Honnett said, "if the most they have in common is they leave each other alone."

"True."

"Didn't he love how funny you are?" Honnett asked, his hand stroking my hair.

"Arlo was the funny one."

"Didn't he love how strong you are?"

I looked at Honnett then. I reached out and touched his face. I kissed him. I needed to be held. I wanted to be touched.

He pushed my hair back and kissed me.

"Arlo was scared I wanted to marry him. He was scared I was turning thirty and I'd force him to marry me and have children. He never wants to have babies," I said, pushing Honnett back, taking a breath.

"What's wrong with him?" Honnett asked softly. "What can a man have against children? Is he too cynical to have any human feelings?"

"He works from such a skewed perspective all the time, writing jokes, being smarter and tougher and funnier than everyone all the time, to stay on top. I felt like when I was with him, I got smarter and funnier, too."

"Well, there's nothing wrong with that." Honnett looked at me, waiting as I talked it out.

"I got hard, though, too. I got cynical. I think the worst of people. I suspect the darker motives, not the best."

"Well, so do I, Madeline. That's my job," Honnett said.

"I know. I'm worried that's why I may be attracted to you so much."

"You are?" Honnett cracked a smile. "Finally, we're talking about me. Hot damn."

"Don't distract me, please. I'm thinking it all over. I think being tough and cynical has helped me become better at business."

"Yes. And seeing things from a distance, it helps you get to the truth."

"Yes." I sat back, considering the price I pay for those benefits. I have lost, I realized, that idiotic inner child everyone in L.A. is always rattling on about. I felt tears well up again. What was happening? First I go all weak on the idea of fate, and now I was crying over my inner child.

"I think . . ." I grabbed another tissue. ". . . I think I've been living in Los Angeles too long."

Honnett smiled. "Just recognizing that, Madeline, is like your armor against it."

"I want to be different. I want to be freer." I wadded up the tissue and threw it into the wastebasket.

"Then do it."

"It doesn't just go away. I still think I see everyone's ulterior motives and moves."

"For instance . . . ?" He looked over at me, and pushed one of my unruly curls back off my forehead, again.

"For instance. What do you get for being such a decent guy tonight? What is your reward?"

"Well." He looked at me again. "That fine questioning mind of yours is what would have made you a pretty good cop." And then he smiled. "I think, if you are okay now, I had better get going."

And in that moment, I knew I wanted him to stay.

I was in the shower the next morning when I thought I heard the phone ring. I stood under the oversize chrome showerhead, the old-fashioned kind that made me feel like I was rinsing shampoo out of my hair in a steamy hot downpour.

There was a tap at the bathroom door, and then I heard it open.

"Hey," Honnett's voice called from the doorway. "That call was for me," he said. "I'm afraid I have to go out now. It's work or I wouldn't leave like this."

"Oh." I turned off the water. "Would you mind handing me a towel?"

I heard Honnett, who must have been up and showered and dressed before six o'clock, enter the foggy room and step across to the tub. He drew back the shower curtain and looked at me.

"Yes?" I asked.

"I wanted to see what you looked like wet."

So, yes, there was more kissing and so on. In fact, there was all that. What is it about tantalizing and distracting a serious, hard-working man, that makes it sexier?

"I had better let you get to work," I said. But of course, I said it when there was no chance in hell that he would move off of me, not right then, not for a while longer.

At one point he said, "I've thought about this."

"Really? You mean standing in the shower?"

"Not exactly. Just with you."

I would forever think of my bathtub a little differently after that morning.

Sometime, too soon after that, we heard the phone ringing again, down the hall from my bedroom.

"I'm sorry. I thought it would be best to give the desk your number. I should get it."

"Go right ahead."

I rinsed off and then wrapped a big white towel around myself and began the long process of towel-drying my hair. Ten minutes later Honnett returned. His face looked serious. His eyes were steady. "Maddie."

"I don't even know what your schedule is," I said, seeing him there. "Are you —"

"Um, Maddie. Come out here for a minute, okay?"

I let him lead me to my bedroom, which is the smallest of the three upstairs rooms. The bed was neatly made, so I knew I wasn't with Arlo anymore.

"What?" I looked at the bed, which just about filled my tiny room, and smiled. "I thought you had to go to work."

"I do. Please, sit down for a minute. There's something I have to tell you."

I sat down, not knowing what to expect. Now, the old Madeline Bean would have become worried, suspicious. That other Maddie would suspect the sorry, I can't have a relationship with you letdown talk. I'm afraid a lot of that old Maddie was still in charge.

"What is it? What's wrong?"

"That last call. It was the watch commander. There's been a death. I have to go."

That was it? So he wasn't letting me down easy? I felt relief, and then, shocked at myself, guilt.

"Madeline, listen. It's some bad news. I wish I didn't have to tell you this, especially this morning. You know the victim."

"What? No."

This was my punishment for one night of self-indulgence. This was why we shouldn't break up with our boyfriends who are pretty decent to us and go instantly to bed with some cop. "Who is it?"

"The woman at the party last night. Quita McBride. She fell down the steps to that big house up on the hill where you catered the party."

Chapter 15

"Madeline? You here?"

Holly's voice echoed down the hall. I had heard the key in the lock. It was just after eleven on Thursday morning, her usual start time. Holly's desk is set up out in the large entry hall, and I heard her bustling about out there, getting settled for the day.

She wandered into my office a few minutes later. I was sitting behind the double partners desk, the one I share with Wesley. In the original old house, Wes's and my office had been the dining room. But now, it is filled with a scatter of file cabinets and bookcases. On the walls are framed photos and invitations from some of the more dramatic parties we've done.

Yes, there are pictures of Wes and me with Jim Carrey and with Cameron Diaz and with Regis Philbin. In L.A., there's not a Kinko's or Petco or an optometrist or proctologist or a preschool or funeral home that doesn't have a few celeb photos on the wall.

"Oh. You're here." Holly's bright voice sort of cut through the silence.

I looked up.

"What's going on?" Holly lowered her long, lanky self into the khaki-colored club chair, waiting. "Hey, Mad. Is something wrong?"

I shook my head no. I'd been sitting there all morning. I'd meant to get a start on the billing. I'd even pulled open a file drawer, I think. I looked at my desk and noticed that my computer wasn't turned on. Ah, well.

"Maddie, honey, you are scaring me. What happened? Where's Wesley?"

"I don't know. I called and left a message for him. He's probably at the Wetherbee house, and his cell phone must be off."

"Something is wrong. What happened last night after I left Buster's party?"

"What happened?" I repeated, trying to think how I could explain. "I told Honnett there was something wrong. I told him I was worried. And he told me to just forget about it, Holly. He didn't think there was any real threat."

Holly drummed her long, slender fingers on the section of her baggy white capri pants that covered her knee. "I need to hear the whole thing," she said. "And then we can freak together, okay?"

I told her about the night before. At some point in the story, between the part where I broke up with Arlo Zar and the part where I saved some stranger's baby, Wesley joined us. He sat in his desk chair and didn't say a word.

"So you saved weird Curt Newton from NBC's baby girl?" Wes said, shaking his head in wonder. Both he and Holly made no comment on the part of the tale where I walked out on Arlo at La Scala Presto. I suppose they were a little gun-shy. They had been through a lot of on again/off again with us over the past six months. I realized I had taken Arlo back several times too many. They just didn't realize that we were now completely off. Instead they were going over the part with the truck crashing on the sidewalk inches from me. "So you must have been pretty scared."

"It was weird," I said, answering Wesley. "What was I doing out there on that street corner? And then that little girl. She shouldn't have been there either. What can it all mean?"

"Freak coincidence," Wesley said, thinking about it.

"Or destiny," Holly suggested.

I rubbed my head, not wanting to admit that I was getting to be more like Holly each day. "So . . . you two have nothing to say about me leaving Arlo after all this time?"

"Well, we've kinda been expecting it, Mad," Holly said.

"And you do go up and back," Wes said.

"Not this time," I answered. And I told them about Honnett. All of it.

"Holy Moley." Holly looked over at Wes and then back to me. "What about all that junk you always say to me? You always tell me, don't jump in. You always say, leave a cooling-off period. You always say, take it slow. Oh, Maddie."

"I know." I put my hands up to my forehead. "I know. I was looking for something. I . . ."

"It's a different thing, Hol," Wes said. "*You* always jump into impetuous romantic things. That's *you*. You're the one who needs to cool down. But Madeline's different. She is usually so sensible. She stays in her relationships too long. I mean, look at how long she's been taking care of Arlo. Maybe she just needed to be spontaneous."

As they sat there, talking about me, figuring me out, I wondered what I could say. In the light of day, how could I ever explain what happened? How, the night before, I'd succumbed to the moment, seduced by the luxurious idea of fate. I had a glimpse of myself as I was becoming, on the turning point of my next decade. And I was scared, okay.

"Look," I said. "My birthday's coming. I can't waste any more time with Arlo. I mean, if I ever do discover what my needs are, he sure as hell isn't the guy who can handle them."

"Amen to that," Holly said, sounding impressed.

"So, I've had enough. And maybe I got a little too crazy with it all. I felt so free. I stopped thinking about doing the right thing."

"You are always putting everyone else's needs before your own," Wes said.

"I know you both will laugh at me, but I finally thought I could put my cynical old soul to sleep, for a minute there." I looked from Wesley to Holly. "I mean, I cried last night. Now when have either of you seen me cry?"

"You must have been a wreck after the Arlo thing, and then that car accident thing," Holly said.

"Yes, but it was okay, Hol. I needed to cry. I felt like I awoke something inside of me that I've been missing."

"Like you awoke your *inner child*, Madeline," Holly proclaimed.

"Yes. Well." I felt suddenly squirmy. "I

was hoping to avoid mentioning that disgusting concept, but maybe so."

Wesley fought back a smile. He was such a thoughtful soul.

Holly said, matter of fact, "You got in touch with your inner child and let her out. Amazing. But then Honnett was around, and who knew your inner child was starving for affection and had such amazingly poor impulse control?"

"Please. Don't remind me." I shivered.

"Well, so what's everyone so glum about?" Wes asked. "Honnett's not a terrible guy. I hope."

I smiled at Wes. "It's not that, Wesley. There's more."

They both looked at me.

"I should have been paying better attention to everyone else's needs after all. I picked a hell of a night to start getting selfish."

"Why?"

"Because Quita McBride was asking for help last night. Remember, Wes? At the Wetherbee house? She was going on about being scared, and she asked me to help her. And I said no. I thought she was nuts, which she may have been, but I said no, here's some money."

"Everyone asks you to help them,

Maddie," Holly said, dismissing it. "You can't help everyone."

"Well, she seemed fine at the party later," Wes said, looking at me, worried. "Don't you think she may have been overly dramatic, Mad?"

"I don't know. I just don't know. Because even though I warned Honnett that Quita was scared and I warned him something might be going on with her, he did nothing to help. He said there was nothing the police could do."

"So?" Holly looked worried too.

"So she fell down the stairs outside Buster Dubin's house sometime in the middle of the night."

"Oh no," Holly said.

"She's hurt?" Wes asked, upset.

"She's dead, actually. She died. Quita McBride, who was begging me to let her stay here at my house. But I didn't want her here. I thought she was nuts. I gave her a few dollars, and now she's dead."

"Maddie, this isn't your fault. You can't think that." Holly reached for a Kleenex and blew her nose. I noticed a tear was wiped as well. "So this is what you were obsessing about when I came in. Oh no."

I couldn't get my head around it. I couldn't. I had been sitting here most of the time since Honnett had left, trying to imagine that Quita McBride was no longer living.

"What happened?" Wes asked.

"Sometime, in the middle of the night, outside of Buster's house, Quita McBride fell or was pushed down the front steps. No one knows which. Isn't that horrible?"

"Bizarre and horrible," Wes said.

"Honnett told me about it this morning, when they called him to go to the scene. There were no witnesses. The only one home at the time seems to have been Buster."

I thought of Buster with the glint of fun in his eye. Whatever had happened, his life was going to be hell now. Everyone knew he and Quita had not been getting along well.

"You know she might have slipped," Holly said. "She was drinking a lot. Maybe she slipped."

"Maybe." I shook my head. "But I really wish I had listened to her earlier, instead of telling her to go to the party and not to worry. I really wish I had listened."

"Do they know what time it happened?"

I shook my head. "But I can pretty well guess where I was when she fell. I was pretty much involved with my inner child all last night and on into this morning."

"Madeline." Wesley called my name sharply. "Do you think this is somehow your fault, sweetie? Because it isn't. She was a troubled woman, no doubt, but you tried to help Quita. You gave her good advice. You gave her money. You can't take care of everyone. Don't do this to yourself. And anyway, it could have been an accident."

"It could, Maddie," Holly said.

"It seems like an obscene coincidence, I know," Wes said. "But coincidences happen."

I looked at him sadly.

I knew in my heart that my dear friends meant well. I knew they were worried about me. Anyone could see that I'd had quite an emotional day and night. But I was sure there was more I could do. I had to do it really. Because I was convinced that the death of Quita McBride was tied to the mah-jongg set that had been found and then stolen. Or tied to the missing red book she had wanted so badly.

I was sure whatever had frightened her there at the Wetherbee house was tied to it. Maybe, even, the death of old Dickey McBride was part of what happened to Quita. Perhaps, I was afraid even to think it, Buster Dubin was involved as well.

I knew I would have to find out. I couldn't

help myself. I always needed to know. I needed to know a lot more before I could begin to forgive myself for casually writing off a woman I hadn't liked very much.

One night of inner child indulgence, and now I was overwhelmed by the sting of consequences. I guess I didn't feel that hot about what I had been doing with Honnett on the night Quita McBride fell to her death.

Chapter 16

"Was it murder?"

Chuck Honnett sat across from me at a small table at Louise's on Los Feliz Boulevard. It was Friday at two in the afternoon, late for lunch.

I hadn't heard from him since he'd left my house early the previous morning, going off to investigate the death of Quita McBride. It was probably a good thing, too, because I'd needed some time to sort it all out and finally settle down.

"Was it murder?" I repeated.

"There weren't any marks on the body, other than what you'd expect after she tumbled down a steep flight of stairs. She broke her neck, looks like. We'll get more details after the weekend."

"Oh."

"The boyfriend, Buster Dubin, gave us nothing. He said Quita McBride left the party, and that's the last he saw of her. The last to leave, he said, were you and Wes and a Mrs. Chen. He said Quita didn't come back before he went to bed at two. He was alone, so there's no corroboration. Dubin said he didn't know where she was going, which I think is bull, but I couldn't shake anything more out of him. So, basically he saw nothing, and he heard nothing."

"And so he said nothing." I finished the old Chinese proverb.

Honnett looked at me.

"Evil, I'm talking about."

"Yeah, aren't we both. We'll work on the neighbors and talk to friends, see if we can catch Dubin lying. Maybe I should write this down, Madeline. You left the house when?"

"Around twelve-forty-five," I said. "I don't know if Quita was still there. She'd left the game room about fifteen minutes earlier. And I told you before, she had been acting weird. She told me she was going to spend the night in a hotel."

"Did she tell you which one?" Honnett asked.

"No."

"I'll look into it. If she checked in somewhere and then came back to Dubin's house, we can trace her through credit cards."

I shook my head. "I lent her some cash. She would have used cash."

214

Honnett looked up. "It's a long shot anyway," he said. "She probably never left the house."

"So you don't know anything," I said.

"I've talked with several of the party guests already. I'll talk to the rest of them today and tomorrow, if I can. They haven't told us much. The neighbors have been a little more helpful. Time of death seems to be near 3:00 a.m. A neighbor heard some noise at five minutes past. Woke him up. Sounded like trash cans falling. Her body was found among four large plastic trash bins down at the end of the driveway by the street. That fits with the time we get from the coroner."

"How did she die, Honnett? Exactly," I asked.

"I'd have to guess until the autopsy report comes back."

"Guess, then."

He looked at me. "She fell down the steps and hit her head. A lethal head injury. Blunt trauma. They'll likely find an intracranial bleed, which is bleeding in and around the brain with or without a fracture of the skull. This sort of death happens every day, Maddie. Especially when someone is 'under the influence.' Death can be instantaneous or it may take minutes, or hours, or even days."

"Will the coroner be able to tell you if Quita was pushed?" I asked.

"A shove would not leave any marks that the coroner could identify."

"I see," I said, not happy. We didn't know a thing that would make Quita's death any clearer, and we probably wouldn't. "Who found her? Buster?"

"Another neighbor. A jogger who was up at five. He ran by there early, but didn't see anything. Then he changed clothes and was going out to work at seven-thirty. His driveway was near the knocked-over trash cans and he got out of his car to straighten them out. That's when he found her. He called it in."

I thought it over and went back to the thing that was nagging at me. "What was Quita doing on the stairs at three in the morning?" I shook my head trying to put the pieces together.

"You didn't see her leave," Honnett repeated.

"No." I thought back. I remembered standing in the street, talking to Lee Chen in her little black Acura, saying good-bye. I remembered getting in my big black Grand Wagoneer, on the way to my fateful meeting with Arlo. I remembered starting my car, my

216

headlights coming on, illuminating the yellow Cadillac parked in front of me at the curb. "Honnett, I remember now. Quita's car was still parked at the curb when I left."

"You're sure?"

"My old cooking teacher Lee Chen and I were the last to leave."

"Can you write down Mrs. Chen's name and address for me?"

Honnett was taking my statement. Wasn't that romantic? He and I had skirted around anything more personal, and it felt strange to look at him and remember the last time we were together.

"Did Quita have her purse with her when she was found?"

Honnett checked back a few pages in his notebook. "Yes. The body had become tangled in the shoulder strap. It had her identification." Honnett looked up at me. "You wondering about that cash you lent her?"

"Was it still in her purse?"

Honnett read his notes quickly. "There was seven dollars and change in her wallet."

"I wonder what happened to the eight twenties I gave her earlier."

The waiter came to our table and delivered a pizza, putting it on one of those wire stands that held it up off the table. Honnett served himself three slices, but I wasn't hungry. I sipped a Diet Coke, wondering what to make of us now.

Honnett was polite, professional, maybe even friendly. But nothing more. I could almost believe our evening together had never happened.

"This must be hard for you, Honnett. Interviewing a woman you've been . . . you know, I don't know what to call it."

He met my eyes. "I guess you're angry with me."

So he was a good detective, after all. "Maybe."

Honnett let out a breath slowly. "Because I didn't call you?"

I let it just hang there.

"Or because I have this job to do? Because I'm a cop? I remember you telling me once that you don't care for cops, right?"

"How about," I said, "because you didn't take me seriously? Quita was scared. I knew she was in trouble, no matter how crazy she was acting. And what did you do about it?"

"Look. I know you feel bad."

We sat there looking at one another.

"Look, Maddie, no one is happy that a young woman fell down a flight of stairs and died, but things like that are known to happen. Hell, she'd been drinking all night. She was wearing those crazy shoes. The steps were steep. It was late."

"She was scared," I said.

"I know. I'm working on it. Neighbors saw lights on upstairs all night, so Dubin was probably awake. Some friends have told us Dubin and Quita were about to break up. That still doesn't mean the guy pushed her with intent to kill her. If we don't find a witness or some major forensic evidence, what can we do?"

"I don't believe this is about Buster at all," I said. "He could never do something like hurting Quita. There's something else going on."

"Tell me what you think."

"Someone stole that mah-jongg set. That's got to be the key. Someone wanted that old book that was inside. I think Quita was lying. I'll bet it wasn't any novel. But whatever that book was, it's the key to this thing. When she found out it had disappeared she came unglued."

Honnett looked at me, and just to appease me he wrote down a few notes.

"You still don't believe me."

"First off, this is not about me and you. Okay? This is about logic. Explain what you think it was that was so important about that missing book that it could have gotten Quita killed."

"I don't know. Maybe she knew something, and it was dangerous. Or maybe this whole mess has something to do with Dickey McBride." I grasped at a stray straw. "Quita mentioned Catherine Hill was friends with Dickey McBride."

"I knew that," Honnett said, trying to lighten the tone of our meeting. "See, I pay attention to old Hollywood gossip. Are you surprised?"

"In fact, I am," I said.

"I like to go to the movies. Do you?"

"Of course," I answered.

"Want to catch a movie with me sometime?"

I had to smile. "Possibly. I don't know. I'm confused right now."

"Well, it's just a movie, Madeline. Think it over."

"So, are you going to question Catherine Hill?"

"It would make you happy if I did, right?"

"It makes sense to me."

Honnett sighed.

"Well, why not?" I asked, getting more frustrated.

"We have nothing to go on here. Hill has about fifty years of experience dealing with people who come at her with questions. She won't tell me anything, that's why."

"You don't strike me as a guy who lacks confidence in his job skills, Honnett."

"There are limits to this job."

"I've always said so. But if she knows about Dickey McBride's red book . . ."

"Chances are Catherine Hill knows nothing at all about the book or about Mrs. McBride and her unfortunate death. Chances are, even knowing nothing, she'll shine me on. Because people like her are into privacy. But let's just suppose for a minute that she does know something that has a bearing on our investigation. And let's suppose it's information she considers incriminating, whatever that might be. What are the chances she's going to tell me that information?"

Following the rules, burdened by the laws, he couldn't get any real information that way.

"I see."

He stood up, and said, "I'll call you when I hear anything."

"You can call me before that, too, you know."

"Aren't you coming?"

"I think I'll stay and finish my Diet Coke," I said. And figure out just how I could go about meeting the multi-Oscar-winning leading lady, Catherine Hill.

Chapter 17

The Wetherbee house was a work in progress.
Wesley and I sat out on the large grassy lawn
in back of the house in the shade of a California live oak. Two workmen walked in and
out of the open French doors bringing out a
chandelier and other lighting fixtures,
bringing in pails and drop cloths. With the
demolition nearly finished, they were getting
a start on replastering.

The garden table was made of heavy
white-painted iron, and its round glass top
was covered with blueprints and computer
printouts showing the layout of the house.
Wes was connected to the Internet by wireless modem, and his laptop computer sat
close by, atop the pile of renderings. All this
was part of the fun of planning his remodeling project. He'd been working and re-
working the plans for the master bathroom
as we talked, playing with a pencil, tapping
the eraser end against his straight teeth.

Birds sang brightly as the late-afternoon
sun moved through the branches above,

casting slowly shifting shadows over the paperwork and us and onto the old patio tiles beneath our feet. A leaf, curled and golden, fell onto the blueprint Wesley was studying, and he smoothed it away.

"So you won't do anything dangerous, right?" he asked me.

"No, of course not. I'm not stupid. And anyway, if it turns out that Quita's fall was an accident, there *is* no danger, right?"

"Right." Wes looked at me with concern. "But you don't think it was an accident."

"You know, I wish I did."

Wes leaned over and patted the top of my head.

"I'd feel better," I said, "if I could be sure."

"Of course you would." He was never enthusiastic about my little investigations, but I had faced a few problems in the past and gotten through them all right.

"This is going to be useful." I touched the edge of Dickey McBride's antique rosewood mah-jongg case. It was back with us since the Santa Monica police had found too many smudged fingerprints on it and none they could identify. They hadn't seemed surprised. In all, their manner had not encouraged our expectation, either, that they might continue pursuing this crime with anything mimicking vigilance.

"So how are you going to get in touch with Catherine Hill?" Wes asked. "I'm assuming she's not in the phone book."

I had this plan. It seemed to me that I would have more success talking to Catherine Hill, privately, than the police ever would if they tried to question her officially. And that was assuming the cops were interested in Catherine Hill. Which they weren't.

But first, I had to figure out how to reach her. I knew she had a big house in Bel Air, but short of going out to Westwood and buying a Map to the Stars' Homes from one of those boys on a street corner, I was stumped as how to talk to her.

"Remember Six Degrees of Kevin Bacon?" Wes asked, starting to erase another line on his plan.

"The game? Of course."

Several years ago, a bunch of college boys with too much time on their hands and a bottle of Southern Comfort came up with the game Six Degrees of Kevin Bacon. The game is a rather inspired, if loony joke based on the John Guare play and movie *Six Degrees of Separation*, which suggests that we are all connected by six or fewer stages of acquaintance.

In other words, if I were in line at my neighborhood Mayfair market and I ran into my hairstylist friend, Germaine, and I invited her to see an Orson Welles film retrospective, we'd hardly be through checkout before she mentioned that she does Loni Anderson's hair, and that Loni was in *Munchie Strikes Back* in 1994 with Dom DeLuise, and did I know that Dom was in *The History of the World: Part I* with Orson Welles in 1981, so did I think she should call and invite Loni to come with?

In that case, I believe it was only four degrees of separation between me and the illustrious Orson Welles, but you get the general idea. Those wacky and inventive college boys must have noticed how nicely Kevin Bacon could substitute for "Separation" in the meter of the phrase. It seems it was all they needed to hypothesize that Kevin might also be the center of the universe, at least when it comes to connecting actors. What makes their Kevin Bacon joke actually work as a game is the fact that Bacon has been in a significant number of ensemble films, from *Diner* to *Apollo 13*. And if you use Bacon as an end point, you can link him in six degrees or less to almost any other performer.

And the whole thing caught on like

gangbusters. For those who don't have the entire filmography of the Western World memorized, the Internet comes to the rescue. It now has several websites that help you make the proper links. For instance, by consulting the Oracle of Bacon website, which is run by the University of Virginia of all exalted places, you'd learn that Julia Louis-Dreyfus of TV's *Seinfeld* takes all six steps to make a chain. She was in *Christmas Vacation* with Randy Quaid, who was in *Major League II* with Tom Berenger, who was in *Shattered* with Greta Scacchi, who was in *Presumed Innocent* with Harrison Ford, who was in *Raiders of the Lost Ark* with Karen Allen, who was in *Animal House* with Kevin Bacon.

A very amusing game, you might be saying to yourself. But what in heaven's name does all this have to do with us? Well. As it turns out . . . *we* know Kevin Bacon. And if we were lucky, we could just use the Oracle of Bacon to quickly discover how closely we could get a link between Kevin Bacon and Catherine Hill. Then all I'd have to do is trace backwards.

"Should I try it?" Wes asked, tapping his keyboard.

"Of course. Everybody cut footloose," I said.

226

Wesley was already on it. He'd entered Catherine's name into the screen, and a few seconds later he smiled.

"It's a good one. Catherine Hill was in *Rhapsody* in 1954 with Vittorio Gassman and Vittorio Gassman was in *Sleepers* in 1996 with Kevin Bacon."

"So," I said, pulling out my cell phone, "all I have to do is ask Kevin to call Gassman and explain I need to talk to Catherine Hill."

"Right," Wes said. "However, if Vittorio Gassman is still alive and if he lives anywhere we can reach him, we have to wonder if the phone number he may have for Catherine Hill is still current after almost fifty years."

"True." I began to rethink. I would hate to bother a celebrity client just to run into an eventual dead end anyway. "Besides, I need some up-to-the-minute scoopage on Ms. Hill. This won't do."

"Wow," Wes said, looking back at his computer screen.

"What?"

"Did you know Kevin Bacon is only two links away from Bob Barker?" He looked up from his screen. "Sorry, Mad. I got carried away."

I knew he was dying to tell me. "Go on."

"Bob Barker was in *Happy Gilmore* in 1996 with Andrew Johnston who . . ."

A male voice with a Spanish accent interrupted us. "Mr. Wesley?"

It was one of the men who were working on the house. Wesley put down the laptop and went over to talk to him. After a few seconds, Wes turned to me. "We've got visitors. I'll go see who it is."

Who had come to call? Maybe Honnett, I thought, and felt my pulse pick up with a jolt. Maybe he'd tracked me down and was coming with some big, important news. It was unlikely, but still . . .

Maybe Arlo, I thought, jolting in another direction. Ah, what about that? It had been a couple of days since I'd walked out on him at the restaurant. It was strange he hadn't called. But maybe he'd decided to stop by and see me in person. That was stressful.

By the time Wesley came back outside, I'd had a little too much time left on my own. In those few minutes, I'd managed to run through several disturbing possibilities about who might be coming to call. I was, by that time, staring at the open French doors with more intensity than I normally would have. And, still, I had not expected to see the group he ushered forth — the regulars from the Sweet and Sour Club.

Buster Dubin, dressed in baggy gray shorts and an oversize Hawaiian shirt, looked an awful lot like his regular fun-loving self, just perhaps a shade more subdued. Trey and Verushka were with him. They lumbered over the shaggy grass, calling out "hellos" and eventually settling, at Wesley's urging, in the chairs around the patio table.

I'd brought over a pitcher of lemonade and supplies from my house and started pouring glasses of fresh-squeezed lemonade all around. I can't help it. Really.

"You know about what happened to Quita, right?" Buster asked after thanking me for the drink.

"It's horrible," Verushka said. "It's hard to believe, isn't it? She's dead."

"I will miss her," Trey said solemnly. The wind gently ruffled his pale blond hair.

"We all will," Buster said. "She was a lousy mah-jongg player, but she was a sweet girl."

"Say," I said, "do any of you remember how she did that night? Did she win or lose a lot?"

No one spoke for a minute. "She stayed pretty even," Trey said. "Didn't she?" He turned to Verushka.

"I think she was down, but then she had a

megalucky hand at the end," she confirmed.

"Really," Buster said, "for Quita that was a winning night."

Verushka sent Buster a questioning look, but didn't say anything.

"Do you guys have any reason to think Quita's death might not have been an accident?" I asked.

Wesley looked at me. Dead buffalo times made him edgy as a cat. In fact, he looked like he would rather be cleaning out cesspools.

"Why?" Verushka asked quickly. "Is that what the police think?"

I shrugged. "She just seemed so disturbed," I said. "Didn't any of you notice?"

"She seemed pretty wasted to me," Verushka said, looking over at Buster. "Quita was Buster's girlfriend, and we loved her, of course — but she was hard to really get to know."

"How did you meet her?" I asked Buster.

"Trey brought her over to the Sweet and Sour Club," Buster answered.

"Right," Trey said, sipping his lemonade. "She played MJ."

Buster looked over at me. "I wonder if I could talk to you? I called your office, and Holly said you were with Wes. We took a chance we'd find you here."

"We're like his escort service," Verushka said, clowning. "We're all attached at the hip, and my hip is, like, my biggest part." She laughed loudly.

"Can I have a moment with you, Madeline?" Buster asked.

We took the flagstone path through the rose garden and entered the French doors into the large empty living room. From another room we could hear the sound of a radio tuned to a Spanish language station. The plasterers had finished in this room and it smelled like damp cement. We settled ourselves on the long wooden step that leads up from the sunken living room into the entry hall.

"What can I do for you, Buster?" I'd selected a spot on the dusty hardwood about eighteen inches away from him, farther than I would normally have chosen to be seated from a friend. He was the same man with whom I'd goofed around two nights before. And yet it was different now. The shocking death of Quita McBride at Buster's house had rubbed off on him, raising uncomfortable questions. I was glad the crew was noisily at work in the room next door.

"I need a favor," Buster said.

I looked at him carefully.

"Your fortune-teller was right," he said,

smiling. "Mrs. Chen is hot. I got that gig I wanted. The music video."

"*Warp?*" I remembered the rock group Quita had mentioned at the party.

"Right. Yes. The shoot is in Europe."

"Congratulations."

"Thanks. Yeah. Copenhagen and then France. It could be a blast. Trey never talks about his chicks, but I want him to come with and bring his girl. And I may take a babe along. Have you ever been to Denmark, Madeline?"

It wasn't taking Buster long to jump back into his fun, fun life. I chuckled at the bad taste of it all. Sometimes gallows humor is all that's left.

A workman stepped lightly past us on the step, carrying a bucket of white goo. We waited until he passed.

"Look, Mad, I heard that you are friends with a homicide detective."

Remember that cynical side of me that I had been trying to give a proper burial? Imagine it rising from the psyche graveyard. "Who told you that?"

"Well, word gets out. Whitley Heights is like St. Mary Knee."

"St. Mary Mead," I corrected. Holly, I thought to myself. She told everything to everyone.

"I have to leave the country, Mad. For this gig. It's only two weeks, and I'm coming back to edit here in Burbank. So I need this cop with a hair up his butt to agree to let me leave."

"If you are under suspicion, Buster, nothing I say would help. If anything, it could hurt."

"Let's play truth or dare, Maddie." Buster gave me a sly grin.

"I know that game," I said, amused. "All it can do is lead to trouble, right? Why would anyone play that?"

"I'm not trying to flee from justice. I'm directing a big shoot in Europe. Well, let's say I dare you to talk to your cop friend for me."

"Okay," I said, "and if I accept your dare, what do I get?"

"You get the truth. Ask me any question you want to."

I looked at Buster Dubin, his jet-black hair and his permanent five-o'clock shadow and his dancing eyes.

He said, "You know you want to ask me something."

My heart began pounding in an odd way. I became aware of the sound. I had to know. "Okay. I'll talk to Honnett."

"Excellent." Buster smiled up at me and

edged a little closer on the step. "So now it's your turn. What do you want to know? And remember, I am a fairly eligible bachelor, I always win at MJ, and I have made a fortune on the stock market."

So Buster expected me to ask him advice? I was afraid he was in for a shock. I wanted the truth about something a lot more important to me than his sex life, or how many tech shares he was holding.

"Truth," I said, looking him in the eyes. "What really happened after I left your house?"

"After you left?" He stared at me.

"This is your game," I said.

"Quita and I had a fight."

Oh, man.

Buster told me more. "Quita was a good kid, really. But, you know, she could be demanding as hell, and lately she was getting all weird. You know, she had never seemed happy. It was like she always had some other thing on her mind. And over the past week, Quita had been getting more and more spooky. I told her she didn't have to leave right away. She could take as long as she needed to move her things."

"So you broke up with her that night?"

"Look, it's not like I was breaking her heart, okay? I'm pretty sure she was seeing someone else. I get a bad rap for going through a lot of very beautiful women, but I'm not really so difficult to please. A lot of times the chick leaves me."

Yeah, I thought. Right.

"Now look at you, there," he said, smiling. "You don't believe me. And that is terribly sweet. It is. But I guess I just wasn't famous enough or pretty enough to keep Quita's attention. I am just a humble guy who directs TV ads. I wasn't what she wanted as a steady follow-up to Mr. Movie Star Man."

"Maybe she was really in love with Dickey McBride, then," I said.

"She was fond of the old dude. She was impressed as hell to be Mrs. Big Name Star. You know that type. The fame game. She was into it. No, what you're saying makes sense. I think she liked Dickey okay."

I thought it over while a radio in the other room played a slow, sad Spanish song. "Did she ever tell you how he died?'

"She said he had a heart attack one night," Buster said. "She was there, if you know what I mean."

"That's the rumor I had heard, too." I nibbled my thumb. "So tell me this, Buster. When you were breaking up with Quita, what time was it?"

"Just after you all left the house. It must

have been about one o'clock. Quita said she couldn't stay with me," he said.

I looked over at him in his bright green-and-aqua Hawaiian shirt and nodded. "Tell me the rest of it. After you and Quita argued that night, what then?"

"She left. She took off. It was like one-thirty or two."

"But you didn't go straight to sleep, right?" I asked.

"Not right away. I worked on the storyboards for the new video, then I played my N64 for a while. That was it. I swear. I never saw Quita again."

"So," Buster said, making a lame joke, "I guess your cop friend won't let me leave the country now, anyway," Buster said. "You have to tell him all this, don't you?"

I nodded. "See? I told you this was a ridiculous game."

He laughed. "If Quita slipped out there, it wasn't my fault. I figured all this will sound a lot better coming from you. Sorry to get you mixed up in the middle."

He had a conscience at least. He wanted to get out from under his little lie.

But I had a lot more questions to ask a lot more people. And when I got the answers, it might just clear up what happened to Quita that night.

"I'll take your message to my cop friend," I said. "He'll come back and terrorize you, though."

"That's cool. And maybe when it's all over, I can take you to Copenhagen."

Chapter 18

The staccato on/off hissing of automatic sprinklers sounded like some hopped-up percussionist was laying down a light rhythm track for the dazzlingly bright day in the community of Bel Air. You'll find this uppest-of-upscale L.A. neighborhoods is home to an older generation of money, that which is most often found in the pocketbooks of old movie stars, businessmen, and former Republican presidents. Bel Air folk have special needs. They crave a private driveway upon which to park the Rolls, lots of leafy trees under which to shade the latest face-lift, and thousands of square feet in which to display their highly insured collections.

This concentration of ultraplush homes creates a booming industry of day workers. Mansion upon mansion require a never-ending supply of workers to wash, polish, mow, trim, add chlorine, buff, fertilize, launder, wax, vacuum, sweep, blow-dry, press, cook, deliver, replant, clean, paint, fold, and dust.

As it turned out, getting Catherine Hill's address was not a big trick. I called a caterer friend whose company does weddings for the old movie crowd and he had it on an invitation Rolodex. He was rather a dear about it. The inside information I had really been hoping for was a little harder to acquire. But that turned up, too, in the end.

Alba, the lovely woman from El Salvador who comes to my house three days a week is a godsend in more ways than her obvious skill with the Dustbuster. I remembered her cousin Maria worked for a family in Bel Air on Bellagio Road. So that's where we started and Alba got on the phone.

Her cousin Maria works with Rosa from Guatemala, and it turned out that Rosa's sister-in-law Lillian was the nanny for Catherine Hill's grandchildren. Imagine that. Lillian had the phone number for Sonia who worked days for Miss Catherine Hill. In L.A., we can play the Six Degrees game both upstairs and downstairs.

With just a few phone calls, I was speaking to Sonia, a sweet-voiced young woman with a light Spanish accent. She answered my question, telling me what time on Friday would be my best bet.

I timed my trip accordingly. I checked my watch as I drove up Bellagio Road. On either side were estates that would sell today in the two-to-ten range. That's millions. Hidden behind tall fences and large hedges were the homes that once belonged to Ray Milland and Gene Roddenberry, Franchot Tone and Jim Backus, John Forsythe and Alfred Hitchcock.

On the 11500 block, I pulled my vintage Grand Wagoneer up to a pair of tall, wrought-iron gates. They barred a long brickwork drive that led up to Catherine Hill's massive property.

I sat there in my car for a while, taking in the sounds and sights of the street. It was quiet, save the ubiquitous on/off hissing of the sprinklers. I pressed the speaker button on the gate and after a minute, a voice greeted me.

"Who is there, please?"

I was startled and thrilled at the voice. Instead of some anonymous employee, the voice that came from the speaker was completely familiar, smooth and girlish, with just a trace of a British accent.

Catherine Hill had starred in so many movies over so many years that a Buddhist priest from Mars might be the only individual in the galaxy not to recognize it instantly.

"Hello, Miss Hill. My name is Madeline

Bean. I have a gift to deliver."

"Yes?" she said sweetly. "From where?"

"My friend just bought Dickey McBride's home. We found Mr. McBride's old mah-jongg set. I understand he had wanted you to have it."

"Dickey's mah-jongg tiles? What a kick. Can you drive in, Miss Bean? I'll buzz you."

The trick, here, in case any of you are going to try to charm your way into a celebrity's compound is 1) don't sound like a stalker, and 2) bring something the celebrity really, really wants.

The large automatic gate slowly swung open, and I drove onto Miss Catherine Hill's property. It was a narrow drive, lined with precisely trimmed hedges. I followed the drive up a gentle grade to the portico, a two-story-high structure with enormous Tara-like white columns, and left my Jeep parked to one side.

The large front door was open when I pulled up and standing in the doorway was Catherine Hill herself. She was dressed in a turquoise green muumuu, and even more interesting, her world-famous head was wrapped in a gold turban. In case you haven't seen her in the tabloids lately, Ms. Hill has ascended about a half dozen dress sizes since she ran almost naked to the sea in

Fiji Princess in 1948. A muumuu covers a multitude of sins.

"Miss Beall, is it? How lovely of you to come over. Did you say you knew Dickey, my dear?" Her brightly colored lips stretched over perfect, white-capped teeth into a brilliant smile. Her face was just as I remembered it from all her many movies. Only older. Much, much older. But even with all her hair tucked up under the gold hair wrap, it was still clear to see why she had once been known as the Big Screen's most intoxicating beauty.

I walked up two steps and met her on her front landing.

"Miss Hill, it's a great honor to meet you. I am a huge fan of yours."

I should point out that this is THE required Hollywood greeting when meeting any form of celebrity. This greeting has no actual meaning whatsoever — just like "hello" in other parts of the country. It's simply the appropriate polite greeting in this town, no matter whom you might meet, whether it be Jesse "The Body" Ventura, or the woman who years ago played the second Von Trapp daughter in *The Sound of Music*, or Snoop Doggy Dogg or the guy who does the voices on *Pinky and the Brain*. Without this greeting, most Hollywood insiders would be put momentarily ill at ease, and wonder how your mother raised you.

"I'm sorry I didn't call first to set up an appointment, but then I didn't have your phone number . . ."

"No, of course not. How could you? It's impossible to get my phone number. It's not only unlisted, it practically doesn't exist." Her dancing voice dipped and then returned in that pleasant musical way she had. I was mesmerized. The same charming voice that said, "I'll always love you, Frank, but I can never forgive you," on-screen to Gary Cooper, was now addressing me.

Catherine Hill smiled. "Finding my house, on the other hand, is never a problem. Just follow any tour bus up the street. They point this place out once every fifteen minutes without fail."

"Oh dear," I said with a trace of dismay in my voice, bonding a bit with the superstar movie queen of old over the sad lack of privacy one in her position must bear. Well, I mean . . . I could imagine it would be tough, couldn't I? I had empathy.

"Please, come in," she said sweetly. Throughout our little chitchat on the front steps, I knew she had been checking me out. What variety of stranger was I? A mental case who might cause injury? A rabid fan? A souvenir hunter who would dig up a plant or steal one of her little porcelain poodles? An Herbalife saleswoman?

I had dressed in my "good" clothes, ones that have labels people like Catherine Hill would recognize. Thanks to Wesley's mother I had a small supply of such outfits. Mrs. Westcott is a clotheshorse and just my size. For years she has sent me last season's wardrobe whether I could use it or not. To make a good impression on Catherine Hill, I wore a St. John knit suit in navy blue and white.

The star opened her front door wider to me. "Oh! Dear child. What have you brought me?"

My hands were full. I had carried from the car Dickey's old mah-jongg case and I was also rolling a professional food cooler.

"These are for you."

"Oh, goody," she squealed, sounding just like a five-year-old girl. "Gifties! Can I get Sonia to help you with any of that?"

"Please don't bother. I'm fine." I followed Catherine Hill into the darkened coolness of the house. Although the daytime temperature outside was about eighty-five, Catherine Hill kept her eleven thousand square feet of living space at a permanent sixty-eight degrees. She brought me into her large entry hall, which was a magnificent circular room, painted a deep persimmon pink.

Ms. Hill turned and looked at me brightly, her smile in place.

"It's so nice of you to invite me in. Actually, I'm a professional chef, but I'm afraid we've never met."

"Ah, yes?"

"My partner and I plan special events and cater parties. We did the breakfast for the pope last year."

"Oh, yes? Really!" Catherine Hill gushed with a pretty smile.

I detected a bit of real warming up behind the professionally warm exterior.

"You must know Keely Bartolli? She does all my parties. Has for years."

"Yes, of course I do. She's wonderful. We've done a few parties together."

"Have you? Isn't she marvelous?"

One connection made. I was still proving myself.

"And then," Catherine Hill said, frowning, "poor, poor Vivian Duncan. She did two of my weddings. You must know Vivian."

"Oh, yes. Sadly, I was actually helping Vivian Duncan with a wedding when . . ." I didn't feel I should finish. After all,

Catherine Hill and I and everyone knew about Vivian's unfortunate last party. At the time, it had been impossible to turn on a television set and not hear: "Woman found dead at wedding, film at eleven." We both shook our heads.

"Yes." Miss Catherine Hill gave me a rather penetrating look with her deep turquoise eyes. "I thought I recognized your name." She had known who I was all along. Of course. Fame was the game she played best.

At close range, Catherine Hill looked somewhat better and yet somewhat worse than she had in the bright outdoor light. Age could not be denied. Her famous sharp chin was now only sharpish, and set in a rounder face. The profile of her famous heart-shaped face was still strikingly heart-shaped, only now the silhouette was subtly softened with years. She must have been close to seventy-five, but she looked at least ten years younger than that. In her heyday, in the fifties and sixties, she was described as having the loveliest lips on the Silver Screen. Now, their strong shape owed much to the curvy outline that was penciled in. In all, her strong beauty was still evident, if paying its dues to time.

"Come into the little parlor," she said,

cheerful as ever, leading the way. "Let's look at what you brought me."

Down the hall she turned to the left and we entered a chintz-covered den. The walls were padded and upholstered in an English print featuring big puffy pink hydrangea blooms amid green leaves. In fact, an entire English country garden bursting with flowers of all sorts covered each and every cushion and pad and sofa and window. I set the rosewood case down upon a small black tole tray table, while settling my caterer's case in a corner beside a love seat.

I hadn't quite realized how petite Miss Hill would be. On the screen she had seemed tall and slim and in perfect proportion. In the bright chintz room, I realized she might only be five feet tall. And while her figure had filled out over the years, her hands and feet were quite small and dainty. She turned to me, and so naturally I stopped staring.

"Now this is from Dickey, did you say, darling?" She glinted her turquoise greens up at me.

"Yes. Would you like to hear a strange story?" I asked.

"My dear child, I live for it." She sat herself down in the center of one hydrangea-covered love seat and I took it for granted she wouldn't mind if I sat down as well. I chose a feminine-shaped wing chair with a forties feel to it, covered in a riot of violets.

Catherine Hill checked her wrist, on which tinkled a dozen little diamond bracelets and bangles and a small Cartier watch. "Oh, pooh!" She looked up. "I am expecting guests in about fifteen minutes. If they should come early, I'll have to greet them, you see."

"Of course." I only had a short time, and I had many questions.

"So . . ." Miss Hill looked at me with interest. "You and Dickey were friends. Good friends, I imagine?"

"No. Oh, no. I never actually met Mr. McBride."

"No?" Catherine Hill let out a loud, boyish laugh. "Well that's probably a very lucky thing for you, my dear. Dickey was a dirty old man. He was scandalous."

"Oh, really?"

"Truly. He was quite a rascal, our Dickey. He invented scandal. That man had quite an appetite for young ladies, I'm sure you have heard."

"Well, yes I have. All those wives and models, of course. But I didn't ever meet him, and I thought the stories were mostly gossip."

"You are a very pretty girl, my dear. Very pretty with all that strawberry blond hair and those big hazel eyes and your slim figure. Do you act?"

"Me? No. Never."

"Good for you." Catherine Hill showed me her legendary dimples. "You are too smart for that nonsense."

Now, what was the polite response to that? I simply skipped it and went on.

"Here's the odd thing . . . the thing that brings me here today in a way. Through my work, I met Dickey McBride's wife. I didn't get to know her very well."

"Which wife was that?" Catherine Hill pecked at this new topic of gossip like a bird finding a fresh juicy worm. "Was it Emilette? Emilette was a foolish woman, I always thought."

"No. Her name was Quita."

Catherine Hill looked at me blankly. The name did not seem to register.

"Quita McBride . . ." I said, trying to make things clearer, and failing. ". . . um, I don't know her other name."

Catherine Hill did not seem to know her. "I assume this was the girl whom darling Dickey was schtupping at the time he died?"

I looked at her wide-eyed.

"You hadn't heard that rumor?" Catherine

Hill looked extremely happy, just as I'd hoped. She loved to be the one to tell. "Frankly, I believe it. That's just the way Dickey would have liked to go out. I just don't remember if I ever met that last girl. They didn't have a big wedding. That I know. It must have been wedding number five or six for Dickey. I told him, after the fourth, just have something simple. That's what I did. Otherwise," she said, confiding in me, "it's just not in good taste."

I nodded. Heck, I should have been taking notes. These were the etiquette tips one so rarely finds in the pages of Emily Post.

"If there had been a wedding," Catherine Hill went on, "I'd have certainly been invited. It was our tradition, you see. We'd known each other for ages. Eons, actually. I like to say I'm the only beautiful woman in Hollywood that Dickey never slept with!" She laughed with glee, truly enjoying herself. I chuckled, too, careful to be polite.

"I attended four of Dickey's weddings and remember each one. Vivian Duncan planned some of them. Beautiful parties, beautiful. And of course I sent the rascal a disgustingly expensive gift for each one. I didn't mind, but it was always the girl who kept the gift. After a while, I simply had had enough. I mean, I still own every wedding gift Dickey ever bought for me."

I remembered that Catherine Hill had been married at least five times herself, and two of those husbands, she'd managed to marry twice. That's a lot of chatchkas.

"I told him. After that Emilette character took the lovely pair of sterling George II candelabras in the divorce settlement, I told Dickey enough was enough. If he couldn't resist the urge to marry any more of them, he simply had to make it clear that he would have custody of Cath Hill's wedding gift!" She laughed loudly.

"You," I said, staring at her with admiration, "have led an amazing life."

She beamed.

"I know you don't have a lot of time . . ."

"Nonsense. We're having such fun."

"I want to tell you about what I brought for you."

She looked at the mah-jongg case with some interest, opening one of the latches and pulling a drawer. "Yes, Dickey's maj set. I remember it. Now how did you get it, again? From this new wife person?"

"I have a partner. His name is Wesley Westcott."

"In your catering company?"

"Yes. But he also buys houses and restores them. He just bought Dickey's old house, as a matter of fact. The one up on Wetherbee."

"Wetherbee. Yes. Marvelous house up in the hills. Dickey had it for years. It was rather a wreck, actually, so I'm sure your friend is having a jolly time cleaning it all up." Her eyes twinkled. "And so?"

Cut to the chase, she was telling me. I cut. "He found this mah-jongg set as he was renovating. We heard that Dickey had wanted you to have it."

"Ah, Dickey, Dickey, Dickey. He was a sentimental old fool, you know. But he was also a ferocious gambler. He taught me to play mah-jongg — did you know that? We were doing a picture together in Hong Kong. *Flower of Love*. There was simply nothing to do there, and we were all dying of boredom. I was married to Todd Stiller, then, and Todd insisted on staying home and working, so I was all alone. Dickey was married to Dee Dee, I think, and she wasn't there either. So we were bored. Dickey found a little friend, of course. He was incorrigible . . . is that the word I mean? You know Dickey."

I felt at this point I did.

"She taught him to play mah-jongg, and he came back to the set and taught me and the crew. We played every break. I couldn't even remember my lines half the time.

Watch that film and see if I'm not stumbling all over the words. We were much too happy sitting around playing maj."

She smiled at the sweet memory of how truly difficult she once had been. I could only imagine some poor beleaguered director on a foreign location shoot with his prima donna of a leading lady refusing to come to the set because she wanted to finish her mah-jongg hand.

"The game is simply everywhere over there. They gamble in the streets. They gamble in those mah-jongg parlors, filled with smoke and Chinese men and drugs I wouldn't wonder. It can be very addictive. Do you play?"

I shook my head.

"Oh, you really should. It is too much fun. It really is."

"It's coming back into style," I said. "I'm trying to learn, but I don't have much time to play."

"Oh, I'll teach you. But don't bet big money, okay? Over the past forty years, I've lost more money to that old scalawag McBride. He was a cheat, I always said. But we couldn't catch him."

"He cheated at mah-jongg?" I had to laugh. It was hard enough for me to imagine this big-time movie star lothario playing mah-jongg with the girls, but cheating? That was funny.

"You know, dear one, your timing couldn't be better. All the maj girls are coming over in a few minutes. It's our old group — Dickey was a regular until a few years ago. They'll be tickled to find out that Dickey wanted us to have his old set of tiles."

"You're playing today?" I asked, sounding genuinely surprised. Hey, maybe I should consider acting. "So, you do recognize the set?"

"Oh, of course, sweetie." She pulled open the little drawers and opened the top of the box. "It was Dickey's pride and joy, this set. We always figured he used these tiles to put a hex on us. We could never win. But it's almost impossible to cheat at mah-jongg, you know. The Chinese invented the game back when Confucius was a pup, and they know how to prevent cheaters, dear."

"I didn't know that."

She smiled. "So we couldn't imagine how Dickey was winning all the time."

"I wonder if you would mind signing a letter? It just states that I turned this mah-jongg set over to you, see — right here? In case there is ever any question."

She smiled her biggest smile. "Want an

autograph, do you? This is a treat. I'd be happy to sign, honey. Do you have a pen?"

"Oh, dear. You know? I changed purses and I don't think. . . ." Which wasn't exactly true, but I wanted to ask some more questions and I needed a little more time to build up to it. In fact, I'd brought the letter in case I needed to stall.

The doorbell rang.

"That must be my maj buddies. And I'm sure you're too busy to stay today."

"No, not really," I said. "I'd love to."

I heard the soft footsteps of a housekeeper who walked past us on her way up the hall to answer the door.

"Well, then. That's fine," she said.

"But, I wonder if you might have a pen so you could . . ." I touched the letter. "I'm sorry to bother you . . ."

"Oh, surely I can. I'll be back in a minute. I'll go find one."

She swished out of the room leaving me momentarily alone. I stood up and started looking around the room. The paintings on the wall were original oil paintings in the style of the French Impressionists. For a moment I wondered if they might be originals. I studied one very, very closely. Oh my God! Bel Freakin' Air.

Chapter 19

"Ahem."

I jumped.

At the doorway to the chintz parlor stood a woman with steel gray hair clipped very short, just like a man's. She wore a gray pantsuit, which perfectly matched her hair. Her sharp jaw and slender nose reflected a sense of beauty past, and I figured the woman to be in her mid-sixties.

"Yoo-hoo?" She made it a question. "Where's Cath?"

I noticed her staring at my hand. I quickly pulled it back from the small, perfect Renoir. Her gaze moved down to the low tray table and rested on the antique mah-jongg chest.

"Holy Toledo. Is that Dickey's?" she asked.

"Rosalie, doll." Catherine Hill floated into the room in a swirl of green-silk fabric and a waft of Joy perfume. "Rosalie. Look what turned up on my doorstep."

She was talking about the mah-jongg set, not me.

"Yes, I saw."

Catherine Hill's lovely voice went quite deep with what sounded like sorrow. She patted the rosewood case lightly. "We miss you, Dickey boy."

"And you have a visitor?" The woman looked at me with open curiosity.

Catherine cooed. "Madeline Beall, this is Rosalie Apple."

"Nice to meet you, Beall."

"It's Bean, actually. Madeline Bean. Nice to meet you."

"Bean?" Rosalie's face took on a pained expression. "Oh, poor thing. Have you thought of changing it, dear?"

I shook my head.

"You should. I know names."

"She really does," Catherine Hill said, as she focused on the bottom of the letter I'd brought. She signed her name in large, loopy script.

A doorbell rang softly from afar, but neither woman moved a muscle to go and answer it. There was staff on call to perform that chore.

"You have heard of Rosalie Apple, of course," Catherine Hill stated firmly.

I smiled, without a clue.

"Rosalie is my personal manager. Has been for years and years and years. The best."

"Thank you, Cath. I'm putting that blurb on my tombstone."

"Rosalie was also Dickey's manager, for a time. But . . ."

"But!" Rosalie snorted.

". . . but that didn't work out. This was years ago, and even though Dickey left Rosalie, they remained the very best of friends, right up to the end of Dickey's life."

Rosalie Apple nodded. "I am the one who first called him 'Dickey.' That name made him accessible. America's favorite young man. He came to me as Richard Lipinski. Imagine that!"

This was almost better than I could have hoped for. I, the little fly on the wall, was being treated to all these insider memories of one of the biggest names in old-time Hollywood.

I carefully chose my words. "This lovely old mah-jongg set of his has been through a lot. Would you like to know the strange story of where it was found?"

"What fun." Catherine Hill sat down, tucking one short, plump leg under, getting comfy on the leaf-print sofa.

"Do you remember the last time either of you saw it?"

"Let's see," Catherine Hill said. "I think I remember that last time that Dickey brought it to one of our games. It must have been five years ago, at the very least. He started seeing that new girl around then, I think."

"What was she called, again?" Rosalie asked.

"Quita," Catherine answered.

"Quita McBride," Rosalie repeated. "Now that's a name."

"Actually, it's a very sad story," I said. "She fell the other night, and I'm afraid she died." I watched both women for reactions.

Catherine said. "In that accident? It was on the news."

I nodded.

"I hadn't heard that," Rosalie said, startled. "She was very young, wasn't she? I'm sure she was. Oh, dear."

Catherine continued as if Rosalie had never interrupted. "After they met, Dickey stopped coming to our games regularly. Remember that, Rosalie? When Dickey stopped bringing his antique Chinese set?"

"I never remember anything anymore," Rosalie said. She wore a pair of reading glasses on a golden chain around her neck and she pulled them up onto her nose and looked more closely at Dickey McBride's old mah-jongg case. "I have a terrible memory, you know that. It could have been five years or ten years, don't ask me."

"Well, that's rather interesting," I said. "My partner bought Mr. McBride's old house up on Wetherbee Drive. It turns out that this mah-jongg set was hidden behind one of the walls. It had been plastered up in an old fireplace."

"You're joking," Rosalie said.

"Fancy that," said Catherine Hill.

"But this is the part that gets really odd . . ."

Both women leaned forward. I wasn't sure it was because of the suspense of my story or just the fact that their hearing wasn't as good as it once was. I spoke up a little more clearly, just in case.

"Just the other day, a man came along from out of nowhere. He knocked me down and grabbed this mah-jongg set and ran."

"Oh, good heavens!" Rosalie said, clutching the front of her gray blazer.

"Terrible! The street crime these days. It's the homeless! No one does a thing about them." Catherine Hill shook her head sadly and turned to her old friend with an added comment, "I simply won't go out on the streets anymore. And neither should you."

"Luckily," I said, "they recovered this lovely old antique mah-jongg set. I wondered if you know if this set has any value?"

Rosalie looked surprised. "I don't think you could get very much for an old Chinese mah-jongg set, do you, Cath? It doesn't have all the tiles we use in the American version. It's rather pretty, of course. But as to real value, I don't know."

"Maybe a few hundred dollars?" Catherine said, guessing.

"It is a shame this man got away," I continued. "A few other items that he took are still missing . . . a book bound in red leather and a . . ."

But I was not to get a chance to finish my thought, for just then we were interrupted by the arrival of two more women.

"Hello, Rosalie! Hello, Cath!"

Catherine Hill turned her gold-turbaned head, instantly bestowing all her attention on the newcomers. "Darlings. Come in and meet someone."

Damn.

I had been leading up to the red book all along.

The new arrivals brought with them clouds of yet two more strong perfumes. As they kissed the air and traded greetings, their sweet scents mingled and I had a few seconds to look them over.

One I recognized instantly as Silver Screen star Eva James, still blond, still slender, with skin pulled so tightly over her celebrated cheekbones that her facial expression was now rather permanently set in a look of startled amusement. She'd been a huge star in the days of the giant MGM musicals, and I felt myself flush.

Beside her stood a buxom woman wearing a wildly printed big shirt. She also had a familiar face, but in this case it was an extremely wrinkled one. I had to stare for a minute, but then it struck me. Oh, my goodness. It was Helen Howerton. She'd done hundreds of B movies, all of them forgettable, but rose to fame playing the faithful secretary on that old fifties TV series, *Mike Heller, Private Eye*. Her shiny lacquered hair was a shade of bottle black that was startling against her pale wrinkled face. It looked like a hard-shell beehive with a tiny flip at the ends.

Amid the tumult and the laughter, the subject of Dickey McBride and the theft of the mah-jongg case had been dropped cold.

Instead, Catherine Hill began introductions once again. Everyone seemed eager to check out the new girl. It was a heady feeling. Inside this movie star's castle, clucked over by her movie-star friends, I'd suddenly become the center of attention.

"Girls! Girls! You must meet Madeline Beall."

My guardian angel can always be counted on to kick a little sand of reality into my starry eyes.

And no, I didn't correct Catherine Hill again. I didn't want to annoy her, frankly. She was too up. I was Catherine Hill's toy du jour, and she loved to see all the fuss I generated. As she introduced each woman, she reeled off an abbreviated bio of each.

Eva James, slender to the point where she might have proved useful to med students cramming for their skeletal anatomy exams, was, Catherine announced in mellifluous tones, ". . . an Oscar-winner for *Two on the Town*."

"I loved that movie," I piped up in a pretty gush.

This is required, as I'm sure you remember from the previous lecture. Needless to say, one neither needs to have loved the specified movie, nor even have seen it to gush thus. However, in the case of *Two on the Town*, I had and I did. This was one of the real kicks of meeting genuine Hollywood royalty. All the de riguer little niceties were startlingly sincere.

"That," Catherine continued, "was the first time Eva had costarred with Donald O'Connor and, we always tell her this — Eva stole the picture."

Rosalie picked up the tale. "Donald never forgave Eva and wouldn't costar with her again until Louie Mayer made him."

The four women giggled.

"Oh girls," Eva said, shushing them. But you could tell Eva James was pleased. She stood, smiling her tight-skinned smile, and demurred. "This is old news: 1959." And then Eva turned to me, and added, "I was only nineteen at the time."

Rosalie Apple brushed her hand through her short gray hair and said, "Let's not give the dates, dear. We all can add."

Indeed we could. By that math, when Eva James starred as a showgirl in *High Kicks of 1943*, she would have only been *three*.

And then Catherine Hill turned to introduce Helen Howerton. "Helen, here, is what is known as a fabulous utility player."

"Well, Cath, really. I starred in *Mike Heller* for twelve years." Helen straightened her silk blouse, with its mad pattern of mice and cheese. I detected just a hint of touchiness.

"Yes, of course you did. You are a big TV

star, darling, which everyone knows, but I'm talking about the really marvelous work you did in pictures dear."

"Three Emmys," Helen added to herself, "and seven nominations."

"Yes, dear. Yes. But what I was going to say was that you were simply the best sidekick the Big Screen ever had."

Miss Howerton had played the good-buddy roll in countless movies, including the very popular *Heavenly Girls* films. Catherine and Helen had played American girls at a Catholic boarding school in Paris, always in some new fix. Cath Hill was always the lead, the young ingenue, while Helen played her poker-playing, freckled, thrill-seeking sidekick.

"I recently rented *The Heavenly Girls in the Forbidden City*, actually."

All eyes turned to me.

"It was fantastic." Required.

They smiled.

"Well, isn't that old mah-jongg case familiar!" Helen said, giving her black beehive hairdo one gentle pat.

"Isn't that Dickey's?" Eva asked.

Amid the loud exclamations, Catherine Hill spoke softly. "Dickey cherished this set, and he wanted me to have it after he was gone." That theatrical trick of lowering her voice to a whisper was effective. I swear, I could be picking up dozens of acting tips if I was ever so inclined, just watching all these elderly divas peck at one another.

Eva James, blond and cool, looked at me with open curiosity. "Don't tell me this is Dickey's last wife. Not how I remembered her at all. Or had he gotten a newer one that I hadn't been aware of?" Her hand went to her throat and caressed a strand of pearls that were large enough to be gumballs.

Catherine Hill shouted above the clamor of the other ladies as they set to squabbling and correcting one another and chastising the new ones. "No, no. Now let's not go picking on poor Dickey again. He was my oldest friend. We started at MGM together when we were just kids. He was a charmer, which was why everyone loved him. He was gorgeous, too."

Hot dog. We were back to talking about McBride.

"Yes," Catherine continued, "he was a rake and a scoundrel, but he was also our friend. We played mah-jongg together for close to forty years. And no one here should throw stones."

"We always had fun gambling with Dickey," said Helen, the early TV star, "even if he did take my money. What do I care, ducks? I get residuals forever." She gave me a big wink with one false-eyelashed, elderly eye. "Eva never liked losing, though, did you?"

"Nonsense. Dickey was great fun." The tall, thin, blond former song-and-dance star shook her head, setting her drop diamond earrings to swinging. "Dickey and I were practically engaged at one time. I got a ring out of him, anyway."

"Enough chitchat," Rosalie said. "Let's play mah-jongg. The sooner we play, the sooner we eat, and I'm starving."

"Yes, me too," said Helen.

Rosalie eyed Catherine. "What is it going to be today, Cath? Deli?"

"Rosalie," Catherine said, playing the hurt hostess to nice effect, "you love deli. We always have deli. It's a tradition."

"It's cheap," Rosalie countered.

"Excuse me," I said. Time to speak up if I wanted to stay in the game. "Look, why don't I make lunch? I'd really love to cook for you."

The group stopped squabbling and turned their attention to me.

I had moved to Plan B.

Like the X-Men or Wonder Woman or Kreskin, I have a special power. No one refuses the free services of a gourmet caterer. I hope I don't seem immodest, but food is primal stuff. I can use my powers for good or evil. I choose good. And I still felt there was something these ladies could tell me about Dickey McBride and his red bound book that might be useful.

"Would you let me cook for you?"

"Now this is more like it," Eva said, smoothing a ring-covered hand back over her blond bob. "What a relief. Cath orders the same damn deli platter from Nate and Al's every damn time."

There, settled.

Had Honnett tried to question these women about the red book, not only would he get nowhere, but I very much doubted any of them would even admit knowing McBride. The interrogation tools of a cop were limited. It was like trying to tap open the shell of a soft-cooked egg by wielding a sledgehammer. Honnett himself admitted he'd never get anything.

But my tools were of an entirely different sort.

Catherine Hill gave me a rather shrewd look. "Well, Madeline. What a lovely idea. Quite nice. We eat lunch in one hour."

"Great."

"But do tell us," Helen Howerton said, "what's for lunch?"

The group quieted down, waiting.

"How about a Wild Cherry Fettuccine with shredded duck and wilted mustard greens?"

"Oh!" Catherine Hill's eyes lit up. "Oh! Someone may have to wake up Minnie for this feast."

"Divine!" Catherine's manager, Rosalie Apple, stood up and clapped her hands in happiness.

I was encouraged and went on. "To start, a salad of hearts of romaine with roasted corn and avocado and a garlic-lime vinaigrette."

"Yum!" Eva James stood up on her long, if elderly, dancer's legs and joined the applause.

"Lovely," chimed in *Mike Heller*'s gal Friday, Helen Howerton, joining the others in an ovation to food, glorious, food.

And so, with such a ridiculously easy bribe, I was able to stay at the party. I only hoped I could string the courses out long enough to find out more about Dickey McBride and the book I felt was the root of so much that had yet to be explained. With enough good food, and enough time, I was determined to get one of these old movie queens to cough up a memory that would finally make sense of it all.

Chapter 20

"Five bam. Mah-jongg. Ha!"

The last ivory tile clacked down hard on top of Eva James's red-plastic tray. At that point, she pushed several other groups of tiles from the lower edge of the tray up on top, exposing her winning hand.

"That stinks," Rosalie Apple said, folding her arms over her gray blazer. "I was looking for one lousy three dot. And Eva had all four."

"Be a big girl, honey," Helen Howerton said. She lightly patted her hardcoat black hair to make sure, perhaps, it was still shellacked down. "Eva won. Pay up."

I stood at the door to the billiards room. The women were seated at the far end of the long room at a mahogany game table, swearing and moaning at the money that they now owed Eva. They passed around the little circular plastic coins that represented winnings. These colorful gaming chips had holes in the center, which were kept on pegs at the end of each woman's tray.

"Lunch is ready whenever you like," I announced.

"Hallelujah." Rosalie yelled, scraping back her chair. "We're all saved."

One by one, the elderly mah-jongg divas picked up their drinks and ashtrays and reading glasses, and whatever, and made their way out of the billiards room and down the long hall to the rear of the house. The luncheon had been set up in Catherine Hill's formal dining room with its lush view of the grounds in back.

While I had been busy in the kitchen, Catherine's maid, Sonia, had joined me. I considered Sonia my sister in crime, of course. Sonia had been the one who gave me the heads-up about the proper day and time I could expect to find the mah-jonggers at the house. And as I stir-fried the shredded duck and finished off the soup, Sonia stuck by my side in Catherine Hill's amazing kitchen. She insisted on helping, and I enjoyed her company. I had suggested she set the dining room table for four, not wanting to be too forward.

As soon as the group arrived in the dining room, they crowed and hooted and brayed in delight. Well, that's how it sounded to me, like a barnyard of elderly farm animals at feeding time. I was immensely pleased. I enjoy cooking, but I also enjoy getting a big reaction.

The savory aroma of the freshly prepared Wild Cherry Fettuccine was hard to resist.

"Look at this!"

"I need a refill on Tommy Collins!"

"How beautiful, Beall. It looks too pretty to eat!"

As they were getting settled in their seats at one end of the mammoth burl walnut dining table, I stepped forward.

"I prepared a West Indian Calabaza Soup," I said, and removed the lid of a splendid Royal Doulton soup tureen. Steam curled up.

"What is that, Beall?" Rosalie Apple had taken a strange liking to me, and it evidently had something to do with my new nickname.

"Please, sit down with us, Madeline," Catherine Hill said. "Sonia, bring a place setting for Madeline."

I sat down as instructed. "It's a fresh tomato-and-calamari soup."

"Ah."

"And there's a risotto cake that floats in it, you see." I served a bowlful to the hostess as her guests looked on greedily.

"Well, this sure beats the hell out of corned beef and tongue sandwiches on rye,"

Eva said, crossing her long dancer's legs beneath the table.

The bright afternoon light filtered through creamy French lace curtains at the tall windows. Beyond, I caught glimpses of a pool, a pool house, gardens, and stone paths winding among tall trees. If only Wesley could have been here. He'd have loved it.

The five of us sat clustered at one end of a stunning French antique dining table that could seat sixteen. The room became quiet, as is often the case when guests make serious the effort to get spoon or fork to mouth. I enjoy the quieting down as almost nothing else. Success.

"So you came bearing gifts," Rosalie said, looking up at me and catching my eye. Her short-cropped gray hair gave her a businesslike appearance, unlike the three actresses she sat with. "So what's the catch?"

"My word. That's blunt," Helen said, sipping at her spoonful of Calabaza soup.

Catherine Hill, in her golden turban, and blond Eva were the two biggest names in the room, and they both turned to see how I would answer.

"I am looking for information, ladies."

"Oh, dear," said Helen, crestfallen. "You're not with the *Enquirer*, are you?"

Catherine Hill set down her forkful of

fettuccine. "I had better not eat any more of this delicious bribe, then, until I know what I am expected to reveal."

"No, it's nothing about any of you. I'm not a reporter, but I could use your help."

"You're an actress?" Rosalie asked, crestfallen.

"No, not that. But I could use a personal favor. It has to do with Quita McBride, the one who died. The police are treating her death as an accident. She had been drinking, and then she fell down stairs. But I am worried."

"Why?"

"I think she was troubled about something. It may have had to do with a book she was looking for. She said Dickey McBride had been writing a novel."

"Dickey couldn't write a to-do list, let alone a novel," Rosalie said.

The other women continued to eat, but paid careful attention to my story.

"The sad part is, Wesley and I actually found a book."

"You did?" Helen looked intrigued. I wondered if her old gal Friday role to *Mike Heller, Private Eye* was kicking in on a subconscious level.

"Yes. It was hidden in Dickey's old mahjongg case. But, unfortunately we lost it.

The mugger dropped the mah-jongg case but took that book."

"How mysterious," Eva said.

"That last evening I talked to Quita, she talked about you, Miss Hill, and your mah-jongg group, and she said that Dickey wanted you to have the set when we got it back from the police. That's why I brought it to you today. I was wondering if any of you know anything at all about that book?"

They looked at one another, but no one seemed to know anything.

I was finished here. I'd charmed and gushed. I'd wheedled and gossiped. I'd brought gifts and cooked, and then out-and-out begged. But I had nothing at all to show for it.

"I'm sorry, Madeline," Catherine Hill said, picking her fork up again. "We don't have the answers you are looking for. I hope you are not too disappointed."

"Thanks for listening," I said.

"You look so upset, my dear," Eva James said as she finished another Tom Collins.

"If you'll excuse me, I'll go get the dessert," I said.

"Dessert. How splendid!" Catherine beamed at her guests. "I knew we'd have fun today. My horoscope said so."

As they talked and teased each other, I

went back through the butler's pantry, the little room which led to the large blue-and-white tiled kitchen. The sound of a lawn mower droned from outside. I peeked out between the white plantation shutters that covered the butler's pantry's one small window. In the intense afternoon sunlight, I could see the tractor mower moving across the side yard. The gardener was driving away, but as he turned to come back again, the sun glinted off of the man's hand. The flare caught my attention, just as I was turning away.

There, on the mower driver's hand, there must have been a piece of jewelry that just caught the light as he turned. The gold ring. I looked at the man as he worked his way across the lawn toward the house. He couldn't see me, behind the shutters, but I saw him. The guy driving across Catherine Hill's lawn was the chard man.

I forgot to breathe. The chard man. Here. What was going on?

I realized there was one method of getting information I had been a little too ladylike to try. I moved away from the window and tiptoed back to the door to the dining room.

". . . brilliant chef. I think we were quite lucky." That was Eva James, probably praising the lunch. I frowned and listened.

"Yes, and she didn't press us about Dickey's book. Thank heavens."

Oh my God.

"If she knows about that, does she know about the payments?" That had been Rosalie Apple's voice. I tried to quiet my breathing, and in my sudden excitement, I became superconscious of myself, scared I'd accidentally bang against the door.

"This is too dangerous. What if she suspects?" Helen was speaking.

"She'd be even more suspicious if we tried to keep her away. And what was I supposed to do? She just showed up here with Dickey's mah-jongg set. I had to let her in."

"But she knows about the book." That was Eva.

"She knows nothing."

"And you have it here, Cath? Is it safe?"

My stomach felt queasy with anxiety. They had all been lying to me. All this time. And the book. Here?

"It's in a safe place. Trust Mama," Catherine Hill said. "All your secrets are submerged."

"We all have secrets, Catherine. I'm sure there are things about you in Dickey's diary."

"Everyone has secrets. Dickey taught me that. Even her."

"Yes, we all put up the money. We should burn the book together."

"I can understand why you would want to burn it, Rosalie. Dickey wasn't a fool. He kept financial records, dear. And your book-keeping was not . . ."

"Enough, Cath! She'll be back any minute. I wish she'd just leave us alone."

"What?" Catherine Hill sounded aghast. "Play your parts, my dears. I, for one, would be very disappointed to miss dessert."

On either side of the narrow butler's pantry, glass-front cabinets reached to the ceiling. They displayed enormous collections of fine china and crystal. As I waited silently in the small room, I began to feel suffocated by Catherine Hill's wealth and possessions. Eavesdropping made me feel anxious, sick, and nauseous. There was a pause in the conversation on the other side of the door, and then Catherine Hill's voice spoke up.

"Did you hear about Bella? Her daughter had another baby."

"No!" several voices responded.

The conversation had moved on. I had too many unanswered questions. What money had they all paid? And had these old women sent the gardener AKA chard man to steal that red book? They must have. I was unable to form one cogent thought.

"This is her fifth," Eva's voice was saying, "and that's just too many children . . ."

The women continued to prattle on about their friend's grandchildren, so I left my awkward lurking spot. Quickly, I walked across to the opposite door, the one that led into the kitchen, and shoved it open. Sonia looked up at me, startled. She was eating lunch while standing at the black-granite countertop.

"Oh, Miss Madeline," she said, smiling shyly. "This is delicious. Thank you for making a plate with the duck for me."

"Do you like it? I'm so glad."

But while I made the proper small talk with Sonia, my mind was racing. I had to find that book. It was here, somewhere. I had to think.

I should do the right thing, I told myself. I should call the police. The red book was stolen property and thanks to Santa Monica Bike Patrol Officer Stubb, we had the police reports to prove it. I could call Honnett. He could get a search warrant and then . . .

But, no. He hadn't cared much about recovering that book of McBride's. And, even if he was convinced, it wasn't so easy in this star-sensitive town to get a warrant to search a celebrity's palace, let alone search the mansion of old Hollywood's "most intoxicating beauty." Catherine Hill had more power in Los Angeles than any police detective. She'd block it somehow. Or she'd destroy the book before they could serve the warrant.

I opened the brushed-aluminum door of the large Sub-Zero and picked up the heavy cut-crystal bowl containing my Tiramisu. I'd prepared it that morning and had just popped it into Hill's refrigerator an hour earlier to chill.

Where would the book be, I wondered? I shook the dessert slightly to test the firmness of the custard. If I were an old red book, where would I . . . ? Catherine Hill had said something about all their secrets being "submerged." Could she be hiding the book out in the pool area? That made no sense at all. I thought about it as I turned.

Silent, standing just behind me, was Eva James.

"Dear, I'm just going to give you a little hint," she said to me while handing her empty Collins glass to Sonia. The young woman got up immediately to prepare a fresh one.

"Yes?" I stood there, my breath coming a little heavily, holding the chilled bowl of Tiramisu.

"That book that you are interested in . . ."

"Yes?" I put the bowl down on the counter.

"Dickey had many affairs. Some ended badly, of course. I remember a girl named Jade, I think. Dickey was engaged to her back in the old days. Now what was her name . . ." Eva thought about it. "It might have been Jade something or other. And then, the first name might not have been Jade, at all."

Now what was all this about? Was she just blowing smoke? I had enough to keep straight without being thrown off the scent by Eva James and her story of some old affair.

"You should ask Cath. She knew all about that affair. Cath was working with Dickey at the time. In the Orient, I think. Was that *East Meets West*? No, it was another one. The one where Cath sang. Oh, Lord, that was awful. God love her, they had to dub over every damn note. Marni Nixon did it. She did all of the singing in those days. But not for me, of course. Honey, God gave me a throat, and I sang like a bird."

I tried to get Eva back on track. "And that's when Dickey McBride was having a hot romance with a woman whose name might or might not have been Jade? Okay."

Good try, Eva. I think not. I smiled pleasantly. "Well, thanks. That might help."

Sonia quietly returned with Eva James's fresh drink and set it down on the counter. Just then, Catherine Hill entered the kitchen, her famous face floating above that large turquoise muumuu. She looked concerned. "So here you are."

If food has power, dessert has the most. I was counting on it. I had a plan.

"It's time," I said, "for Tiramisu."

"Yes?" Catherine perked up immediately. "Oh, goody."

And then, into the kitchen walked an amazingly fragile old lady, the size of an elf. Her snow-white hair wisped down around her small head from a gold turban. She was dressed exactly like Catherine Hill, down to the gold ballet slippers and flowing turquoise shift.

"Is it time for dessert?" she asked.

"Mama? Are you up from your nap, dear? Meet our new friend, Madeline. She's a very clever cook. She made the girls a marvelous lunch."

"Is that dessert?" the tiny old woman asked again.

How totally bizarre. Mother and daughter, dressed as twins.

"Sonia," Catherine called out. "Let's set

another plate for Mama at the table." She turned to her mother. "Mama, go get a seat, honey." Catherine spoke loudly into her mother's hearing aid.

The old woman smiled, revealing a little too much of her toothless gums, her head bobbing without a pause. Sonia led Mama through the butler's pantry and on to the dining room.

"Mama's ninety-three. Doesn't she look fabulous?" Catherine asked.

"She's amazing."

"The girls call her minimom." She laughed loudly. "Get it?"

I had no trouble getting the nickname, and then I had an idea.

"She lives here with you?"

"Oh, yes. She had an entire wing upstairs, but she began to get tired climbing all the stairs up to it. We had to give her Sonia's room, but then Sonia lives out now, so it's worked just fine."

"How nice," I said. And I was amazed at how sincere I sounded, when inside I was raging.

"And doll," Catherine said to me, as we walked together toward the dining room, "I wouldn't believe everything you hear from Eva James. That lush has been sipping Tommy Collins since ten-thirty this morning."

After I made sure the old gals were seated and dessert was served and lavishly praised, I rushed back through the kitchen. I remembered what Catherine Hill had said to her friends when they wanted to know where the book was being kept. She had said, "It's in a safe place. Trust Mama."

Trust Mama.

At the time she said it, I'd thought Catherine Hill was saying "trust me." But that was before I met Mama.

I found a door just off the kitchen and turned the knob. A bedroom, just as I had expected. This was the location of the maid's room in every old house I'd ever worked in, right off the kitchen, perfectly situated for the help. And now, I knew, it was Mama's.

I slipped into the room and shut the door behind me. The room wasn't large, but it was pretty, decorated in a soft shade of peach and neatly kept. The heavy peach damask bedspread showed only the slight indentation made, I was sure, by the body of a napping woman who could only weigh eighty pounds.

Where would they hide the book? I pulled up the peach dust ruffle and checked under the bed, I tried opening a few dresser drawers. No dice. I walked across the small room and entered the adjoining bathroom. It, too, was decorated in the same shade of peach. The sink and the toilet and the tub, everything the same. The little room was perfectly clean. On the sink was a glass holding Mama's dentures.

Their secrets. Their secrets were submerged. What did that remind me of? It was a line. A line from a movie. It was a line in one of Catherine Hill's movies, but which one? I thought it out. I had rented a bunch of old films not long ago. Holly and I stayed up late watching them. Yes! *Heavenly Girls in the Forbidden City.* Teenaged Helen Howerton was hiding teenaged Catherine Hill's diary from the nuns. And where did she hide it?

The toilet. I picked up the heavy peach porcelain top and moved it slightly ajar.

Astounding. There, taped to the inside of the tank, submerged in cold water, was a large clear plastic storage bag, the kind famous for its airtight seal. Catherine Hill watched those commercials.

I pulled the bag out of the tank and dried it using one of Mama's fluffy peach terrycloth bath towels. Inside the bag I could clearly see the prize.

With one quick unzip, I had my hands on Dickey McBride's red-leather book. I was high with my triumph. Here, too, in fact, was even the silver case that held the dragon dagger. I had lied, eavesdropped, and prowled, but I was victorious.

Unfortunately, I didn't have another second to enjoy the thrill of espionage. For at that moment, I heard a noise. I looked up. The knob on the door to the little peach bathroom was turning.

Quick, before even the shock wave of fear reached my heart, I rezipped the plastic bag, and stuffed the entire package into the back of my short designer skirt, down between the waistband and my back.

The door began to open.

I spun and sat down, fully clothed, on the toilet, praying the book wouldn't fall in.

When the door swung wide, there stood minimom.

I glared at her with an intensity that required no acting on my part, *whatsoever.* I hissed, "Excuse me, this room is being used."

She stopped and stared, extremely alarmed. Her old eyes caught the completely unexpected sight of a young woman, me, using her loo. She gasped with such force, I feared for her heart. Her toothless mouth formed in a wobbly "O." Catherine Hill's ancient mother sucked in air until I wondered if she would ever remember to exhale.

But unfortunately, her befuddlement was so great, she simply couldn't manage to move.

"I'll be right out," I said, "if I could just have a little privacy." I had snaked one of my hands behind me and used it to hold on to the book, which was snug and stiff against the small of my back, and quite uncomfortable. I realized the porcelain top to the toilet tank was just ajar. Hell, if minimom stood there gasping much longer, she just might notice.

"Oh." She found her voice at any rate. "Oh, my."

Just *leave*.

"How embarrassing," she said, still rattled and trying to find her way. "I . . . you see . . . I forgot my teeth."

I eyed the contents of the glass that stood on the sink.

"I need my teeth," she said, "and I didn't know . . ."

"I'll be right out," I said, my voice singing a cheery if insistent note. "Honest. Right away. In two shakes. Just give me a minute alone, please."

If I sat there any longer, surely she'd notice that I had not really assumed the proper position, my skirt was in place and I wasn't using the facility as anything more than an odd chair.

"Oh," she said, finally reacting. "Must I go out and wait?"

"Would you please?" I asked, finding a smile somewhere and pasting it on.

"Of course. Why, of course." Minimom doddered her way out, slowly, very slowly closing the door behind her.

In an instant, I readjusted the tank, flushed the toilet for verisimilitude, and stood straight up, checking to see that my short navy blue suit jacket would cover the back of my skirt where the bulky package was hidden. It would just have to do.

I pulled open the door. The old woman was about to leave her bedroom. No, no. I couldn't have her tell her daughter that she'd found me in her bathroom. Even if the poor old dear hadn't yet realized how physically close I had been to their hidden secrets, Catherine Hill would guess my motives in a half a second.

"Minnie," I said loudly, mindful of her hearing aid.

"Wha . . . ?" She stopped and slowly turned back. She saw me and smiled. "Take your time, young lady. Wash your hands. Do whatever you need to do. I will go —"

"No, no, no, no!" I rushed over to her and turned her around, faced her back toward her own little bathroom. "Your dentures . . . remember?"

"Oh." She looked startled, raising her hand to her sunken mouth. "Oh, yes. Thank you, dear." And without another thought, she headed back toward her bathroom.

I eased myself out the door of her room, back into the kitchen. How much time would little mama take to put in her choppers and get back to the gang? How long until she told of the terrible faux pas, walking in on a young lady in the john. I knew I didn't have much time to get out of there.

"Miss Madeline," Sonia called, catching sight of me.

"I'm in a hurry. Thanks for your help, Sonia." I grabbed my purse and moved across the kitchen, fast. I had to get to the front door before any of Catherine Hill's friends suspected I had found Dickey McBride's red book.

"You're leaving?" Sonia's voice trailed after me, but I was already down the main hall and almost into the entry. I pulled open the front door, glancing back inside the house, afraid someone would jump out and stop me.

But that was ridiculous. These were old ladies, after all. It was only my guilty conscience imagining forceful pursuers, expecting to be caught. My hormones on overload, I was just overreacting to the urgent need to make a quick getaway.

I sprinted down the steps.

But I was not alone. There, standing right between me and my car was the chard guy.

Okay, so my heart was already pumping pretty fast. It got a jolt, just the same.

"You!" He looked at me, as startled and uncomfortable, if possible, as I was.

"Yes," I said, smiling brightly. "I remember you. You remember me. Very good. Now —" I reached for the handle of my black Grand Wagoneer.

The man was about my height, but powerfully built and tense. He wouldn't budge, blocking my way, breathing through his mouth. His face was stern. No doubt he was trying to work it all out.

"Don't worry. I won't tell anyone anything. I've got to go."

"You wait," he said, pointing at me with the garden tool in his hand.

I looked at it closely, as it was only inches from my face. Oh, good. A trowel.

"Can't wait," I said, as lightly as I could. I wondered how many hours had passed since

I left little mama in the peach powder room. "Must go. Now."

"No." The chard man squinted and pointed the trowel more forcefully my way.

I could run. I could abandon my car and just run. But then there was the eight-foot-high electric fence. And the gate down at the end of the drive. It was locked. I would never get out before he called his boss.

"See here," I said, feeling the plastic bag that I'd stuck in my waistband beginning to slip down. The book. Slipping. The time. Ticking. This was getting out of control.

"You come with me," chard man said. He didn't have what you would call a friendly voice.

"No," I said, aware that the zipper bag had now really and truly slipped another inch. The bad news was the book was now slipping down behind me at an alarmingly quick rate of speed. The good news: I had somehow luckily managed to stick the zipped package inside the waistband of my underwear as well as my skirt, and the damn bag wasn't likely to slip much further.

Unless . . .

I realized with a rising trill of panic, how gravity works. How heavy the package felt now that it was no longer wedged between my back and the tight waist of my suit skirt.

What if the weight of the small red-leather book and the silver dagger case was stronger than the elastic that held up my damn panties? I had a momentary out-of-body awareness; the vivid flash of me, standing near the steps of Catherine Hill's mansion, threatened with a garden implement, with my silk underwear falling down around my ankles and the red book sitting on the pavement for chard man to find.

"Catherine and I made up," I said, talking faster. "She and I just had lunch. You've seen my car here, haven't you? We are just fine. But if I don't get the new *Soap Opera Digest* I promised her right away, I'm afraid she'll be cross with me. I must run this errand, and fast."

"You're getting her a magazine?" he asked, still upset. But I had gotten his attention. He earned his living making the grande dame inside the mansion happy.

"She said to be back in ten minutes and it's already been . . ." I looked at my watch, crossing my legs as subtly as I could. Hell. It had been ten minutes already. Minimom was probably right this very minute telling her upsetting tale about finding that young lady cook in her peach bathroom. I looked at the front door, sure it would open immediately, my panic real.

"She wants it right away?" he said, connecting the real fear on my face to the fear he must live with on a daily basis — of the consequences of not pleasing the boss lady.

"Could you just hit the gate button for me, and I'll run down to Sunset? I'll be back in a few minutes, and maybe Miss Hill won't be mad at me." Hey, we were on the same team, see?

He put his tool down and moved across to one of the front pillars and I saw the button that released the remote control gate. Mustn't displease the boss.

"So . . ." he said, about to punch the gate release.

I scrambled into my car, hastily sliding in and safely sitting down on Dickey McBride's secret book before it had a chance to fall to the ground.

"You are not here about that day in the market?" he said, his face still worried as his finger pressed the gate release.

As the gate at the bottom of the driveway slowly retracted, I said, "Not at all. Think nothing of it." I turned my key in the ignition. The gate that barred access to the street was opening slowly, but it was not open nearly enough, yet, for the large Grand Wagoneer to escape.

I put it into drive and punched the gas, pulling my SUV all the way down to the wrought-iron bars, willing it to move more quickly on its track. I checked my rearview mirror, heart still thumping. I was almost out. Almost out.

In the rearview I could see the front door of the large house opening. Holy shit.

Yes, in the mirror I clearly saw Catherine Hill, gold turban flashing, striding out her front door.

"Come on," I said, urging the gate to open faster. I only needed a few inches more to squeak through and I'd be free. "Come on."

My eyes flicked back to the scene behind. Catherine was turning to push the remote control button, to stop the gate. To stop me. She almost reached it. Chard man was running down the drive toward me. Through my closed windows, I could hear him, his voice yelling, "Hey, stop. Stop!" I locked my doors.

He was halfway down the drive, closing on me, waving his arms. With my eyes glued to the rearview mirror, I stepped on the accelerator. I didn't even look to see if I was going to clear the opening gate. And then, like a flash, I was out. Down Bellagio with the pillared prison rapidly disappearing behind me. Out of the ten-million-dollar zoo cage and barreling down the street.

Just a crazed, run-amok party animal on the loose, escaped with my little book of secrets.

Chapter 21

Back at home, several hours later, I felt the need to be outside. The January night was mild and cool, probably mid-fifties, but I was running a little hot. I needed to clear my head after spending the last hours of the afternoon indoors reading the red book.

In the little courtyard behind my house, a high retaining wall was literally all that separated me from the Hollywood Freeway. The city-built cinder-block wall was covered now with sprays of bougainvillea vines and white twinkle lights. A steady hum of unseen freeway traffic droned like a passing jet. I had become so accustomed to living with this neighbor that I almost didn't notice the rush of noise as I entertained a late-night guest. We had to sit close together, Honnett and I, in order to hear each other clearly.

I had called Honnett to tell him the news. I needed to tell him about the red book and what it meant. But our positions were difficult, as always. He needed rules. I needed answers. And there were other things that would be left unsaid.

"Maddie, don't do this to me. I'm a cop."

I looked up at Honnett. He was rubbing his eyebrows like that would help ease us out of the trouble he was sure I'd gotten into.

"Listen. It was all right, I think."

"Really?"

We were sitting in the cold on a patio bench. I think neither of us was ready to be alone together inside my warm and cozy house with all its memories and temptations. It was almost ten o'clock. I had discovered what the blasted red book really was. I'd just spent the late afternoon with Wes reading Dickey McBride's diary.

"I didn't break any laws, so relax," I said. "I was in the little bathroom off of the maid's room. When the door opened, I tucked the book behind my back, into my waistband."

"Madeline. C'mon." Honnett looked really sore.

"Look, Honnett. It was my book! Well, it was Wesley's, and I was acting for him. It was stolen property, anyway, and I was reclaiming it."

"It doesn't work that way. Don't you realize what you did? Taking that damn book compromises any use it might have as evidence."

"The hell with that. You think I care about some case you're never going to make, anyway? Let's be real. This isn't some drug dealer you're trying to put away. This is Catherine Hill we're talking about. You told me she was untouchable."

"No. Not untouchable. I told you we wouldn't want to bother her for some petty —"

"Exactly," I cut in. "And what's the crime? Possessing a ratty old book, with almost no value, written by an old friend of hers? Don't make me laugh. No one would have given you a warrant." I shook my head in frustration, but tried to calm down. "Listen. There was no way to do this straight. If I'd left the book there, you think it would have still been there when Cath Hill finally decided to permit a search?" I didn't wait for him to answer. "Anyway, I was there. I lucked out. I found the damn book. But man, Honnett. I was practically shocked out of my socks when little Mama opened the bathroom door."

"What did she say?" Honnett asked.

I sighed. Finally, he was listening.

After all, I found Dickey McBride's diary. I got it back. What was done was done. The implications of how highly I had disappointed him and how unwilling he was to help me would be ashes we could poke through some other day.

"She understood. I had to pee."

"Nice detail, Bean. Less graphic, please," he said, going back to rubbing his eyebrows.

"And the cool thing was, I made it out of there. It felt electrifying, you know? Like very powerful. I think I drove seventy-five all the way home."

"Don't tell me this, Mad. I'll worry about you. I mean it."

I smiled. "There I was, wasting my time all afternoon, chatting politely and flattering those old movie sweethearts, and cooking for them, and what did that get me?"

"I'm impressed. It got you inside the house."

"Yes. But I got nothing."

He put his arm around me, casually. I liked it there just fine. I think he was figuring he might as well accept what I'd done.

"It wasn't until I starting working smarter, not harder, that I found out anything at all."

"Please, Maddie. Don't give me all the details, okay? Seriously."

"Okay. But Wesley and I read McBride's diary. It was all handwritten, which was not so easy to read. There were plenty of references that were so obscure we couldn't figure them out. Lots of dates and initials. But we marked two passages that could be important."

"So what do you think happened?" Honnett asked. "Are you saying these old movie stars were behind the mugging in Santa Monica?"

"Of course they were. Aren't you paying attention here? I saw the freaking chard guy riding the freaking power mower over Cath Hill's freaking Marathon II sod! It was him. He was even wearing the gold ring I remembered. And then later . . ." I stopped. After all, didn't Honnett just say he couldn't handle all the details? I tried a different tack.

"Let me try to explain. After Wes found the mah-jongg set hidden behind the wall at Wetherbee, the only person he called was Quita McBride. He told her he was busy all day, meeting me in the morning in Santa Monica, yadda yadda, working on the house. He offered to bring the maj set to her at the Sweet and Sour Club party that night. Wes was being his good-guy self, figuring he should return stuff that must have belonged to McBride."

"I get that."

"But Quita asked to meet him earlier that

night at the Wetherbee house, so she could pick it up privately."

"Does this make sense to you, Maddie? Because it sure doesn't make any sense to me."

"Look," I said again, facing him. "At that point, Quita was the only one who knew Wesley had found Dickey McBride's mah-jongg set. She probably knew that her husband used the case as a hiding place for his journal. Let's say Quita suspected the journal had some pretty hot stuff on Dickey's old movie crowd. I think she called Catherine Hill and offered to sell the journal to her, sight unseen. Quita was acting desperate for cash. So that makes sense."

"Okay. And you're saying Catherine Hill and her friends were scared of that diary. They had secrets from years ago, and they were afraid that maybe McBride wrote them down. The ladies were panicked that little Quita would shake them down. So, Catherine Hill decided to steal the book before Quita could blackmail them."

"Right. Don't you see? Once Quita had that book in her hands and had a chance to read the secrets in Dickey's journal, what would keep her from being a permanent pain to Catherine and Rosalie and Eva and who-all? Quita could keep draining them for cash forever."

"Yes, I see that, but . . ."

"I think Catherine Hill wasn't about to let that happen. I talked this over with Wes. He remembers telling Quita that he wanted me to look at the mah-jongg set. He told Quita we were meeting at the Farmer's Market. I bet she told Catherine Hill about it, too. And I bet Catherine Hill sent her handyman to grab it before Quita got a look."

"You have an amazing mind," Honnett said. He didn't look happy about it, though.

"Thank you. And when I think about it from Quita's side, it makes sense, too. It's the only way to explain the crazy way she had been acting all night. When she met us at the Wetherbee house, she didn't care that Wes and I had lost the mah-jongg case. She only wanted to hear about the red book. And she panicked when she realized it was gone. She had been counting on a big payoff from Catherine Hill. Without the book, she couldn't come up with the cash, and that scared her."

"Yes. I see that."

"It all fits. Those old women were scared of the book. When I was hiding in the pantry, I heard them talking, Honnett. I'm sure I'm right about this."

"Don't keep telling me about your illegal activities, Maddie. If you care for me at all."

I looked at him. The first personal comment of the evening. "Honnett, come on. I checked it all out with Paul. You remember Paul?"

"That lawyer you hang out with." He did not sound terribly impressed.

"Paul is the best lawyer on the planet. And he specializes in alternative law — you know, how to slip through the cracks and not get caught."

"A fine friend. Everyone should have one like Paul."

"Paul told me I don't have anything to worry about. First, I was invited into Catherine Hill's house as a guest. I didn't break in."

"Yes. Good."

"Second, I was preparing lunch with Catherine Hill's permission. No law against a caterer doing that. Believe me. And there's no law that Paul is aware of that prohibits a caterer from spending a little time in the butler's pantry."

"True."

"And third, I don't believe there are any laws against using the bathroom when you've been invited into someone's home."

"Yeah, okay."

"I didn't crack open any safes. I didn't pry open any locks. I simply took a little peek into the toilet tank . . ."

Honnett raised one eyebrow. It looked good on him.

". . . to make sure the ballcock was in operating condition . . . because . . ."

"Because . . ." Honnett said, finishing my explanation, ". . . you are extremely careful about plumbing."

I laughed. "True."

"There is so much about you I never knew." Honnett smiled.

"True again."

"But then, see, we get to the nasty part. You stole private property from Miss Hill's house."

"No, no, no." I shook my head. "Here's the last point: Four, I was so lucky! I found a lost object at a new friend's house."

"You are so lucky." He looked at me.

"Okay, yes I am. But, after all that work, don't you want to hear about what I read in Dickey McBride's diary?"

"I suppose I do. But you won't like my reaction."

"Why not?" I turned to look up at him.

He reached up and gently pushed my hair back, touching my face. "Because whatever it is you read, it's not going to take away your pain, Maddie. Some old man movie star's diary will never tell us why, just a couple of nights ago, that poor drunk girl tripped and fell down the stairs and died. You may never know why."

"But I still have to keep trying. I have to. Have a little faith, Lieutenant."

I sat there and looked at him. He looked at me right back. We had been sitting for about an hour on my padded patio furniture out in the cold night air. I hadn't noticed how cold it was, but now, I felt a shiver. I thought it might be too cold to stay outside.

"So tell me what you learned," he said.

"The diary covers about ten years, from 1946–1956," I said, happy at last that he would finally listen. McBride only kept occasional entries, marking dates and setting down information using a casual style of shorthand. He mentioned many, many women. I was disgusted to report he had a sort of rating system. Stars. I suppose in McBride's line of work, he was used to reviews.

One of the entries that got my attention was dated March 1952. "Rose is lying. She can't find records." And the next month, there was another mention of Rose. "Studio agrees to audit. Rose is raging mad." And another entry, three months later. "Showed Rose ledger. Embezz?"

Honnett looked at me. "Who's Rose, then?"

"Well, today I met Rosalie Apple. She had been McBride's manager at one time, and he fired her. This was all a long time ago. I'm guessing Rose was his nickname for Rosalie. I'll have to check on the dates and things. I'm guessing there were irregularities with royalty payments. As McBride's manager, Rosalie Apple got all his checks. Perhaps she kept more than her ten percent."

"This was years ago. McBride never pressed charges. Do you expect me to go after some old lady without any evidence?"

"Do you always have to ruin my buzz, Honnett? No one is asking you to arrest anyone. Jeesh."

He smiled at me, trying to relax a little. "It's hard enough for two people to get together without all of their personal garbage getting in the way, you know? On top of that, you go dragging all sorts of professional crap into the mix."

"Calm down, Bubba," I said, and gave him a peck on the cheek. "We'll be fine. We will. Just don't come busting down so hard on my good day's work."

He took my hand. "Sorry about that."

My goodness. The man said he was sorry, and it hadn't killed him. I was beginning to have hope.

"You said there were two things in that red book you got excited about. What was the second one?"

"Well, back at the house today, Eva James told me some odd story about a girl named Jade. She told me Dickey had an affair with this Jade back on a movie location in China. At the time, I was sure she was just trying to lead me off the track. But then, when Wes and I were reading Dickey's diary, we found some passages about Jade."

I filled Honnett in. The dates were back in 1947. They were datelined "Hong Kong." Dickey talked about Jade teaching him mah-jongg. He posted his winnings, taking quite a bit of cash off that film crew over the six months they were shooting *Flower of Love*. One entry read: "Jade my soul mate." It was unusual in that it was one of the only affectionate things he'd written over the entire ten years and dozens of women the journal covered. Even more startling, there was an entry, in 1948, where Jade's name appeared again. It read: "Jade arrives LAX. Daughter?"

"What was that?" Honnett asked. "That's a bombshell. You think McBride had a child with this woman Jade?"

"I think so."

"But this all happened years ago, Maddie. Whoever this Jade was, how does it figure into this mess today?"

"You mean, fit in with Quita McBride's death?" I looked at him. "I will always regret what happened to her, Honnett. Somehow, not having liked her much makes it all worse. I will always regret it."

Honnett pulled me toward him, our faces close. "I'm sorry if I hurt you . . . if doing my job, being the guy I am . . . if that let you down. Don't you know that? But in the same situation, I'd respond the same way. Because there is nothing I could have done that would have made this thing turn out any differently."

"I know you think that," I said, "I know . . . but maybe if you and I hadn't been so distracted that night . . ."

He let go of me.

What had I said?

He stood up.

"Honnett?"

"I've got to go anyway. It's damn cold out here . . . don't you feel it? You really ought to go inside and warm up."

"Right."

"Thanks for filling me in," he said.

"What?" I asked. "Are you leaving? For good?"

I was getting that unmistakable sinking feeling that I was splitting up with my second man this week.

He smiled at me, but it wasn't an altogether happy smile.

I stood up, too, and went over to him. "Will you call me?"

"I know you're busy trying to find your answers, Maddie. I hope they are there for you."

"So . . ." How had I allowed everything to get so damn heavy and mawkish? Everyone knows a new boyfriend prefers things light and romantic. I had definitely been thrown off my game. It was probably too late, now, to reverse the damage.

"So . . . you're tired of hearing about movie stars and their love affairs? Man, the *National Enquirer* would go broke if everyone were like you."

"And," Honnett said, grinning, "that would be a bad thing?"

"So, are we still going to see that movie we talked about?" I asked.

"Sure," he said. "Why don't you call me when you have some free time."

I put my arms around his waist and pulled him toward me. Leaning forward, going up on my toes to reach him, I gave him a slow kiss. I knew Honnett and I were not going to have a chance at any sort of real relationship until I got this whole Quita McBride thing out of my system. I just wanted to mark my place. I just wanted him to still want me when it was all over.

Chapter 22

I pushed aside the blue-and-white pineapple-pattern quilt and stretched. On Saturdays, I usually wake up late and spend the day cooking and prepping for whatever party we are catering that night. But not this Saturday. The "couples" baby shower we had planned for a pair of expectant parents in Pasadena was called off because their twin daughters arrived a month earlier than expected. Things happen for a reason, I thought to myself again. I had too much on my mind to cook today.

I went through my shower-and-dress routine, sweeping my hair back in a low ponytail, putting on my favorite jeans and a black sweater. I knew I should use the free day to plow through the snowdrift of correspondence and invoices and menus that covered my desk downstairs. I was falling behind on orders. Last week, Wes and I had made a list of items we needed and others we wanted to try from specialty growers. For instance, I had promised to order a dozen bulbs of

311

Metechi garlic. Each bulb of this fireball-hot variety is the size of an artichoke and with its purple stripes, beautiful enough to put on a pedestal in an art museum. Last week, I couldn't wait to get some in from Texas so we could try their potent flavor in our garlic mashed potatoes. That's the sort of thing I should be taking care of. Instead, I was thinking about Quita McBride and her fatal accident.

If I was right about Catherine Hill and her old cronies, they had sent their guy to grab the mah-jongg set from Wesley at the Farmer's Market, but figuring that out and finding the red book had brought me no closer to understanding what had happened to Quita McBride.

I found my black clogs and stepped into them.

Those old movie stars. They took a stupid risk. I had read McBride's diary with Wesley, and then again later last night. There was simply nothing in it that was worthy of theft, much less murder. The tepid long-ago scandals that were mentioned would hardly shock anyone today. Dickey's diary was from the forties, with a marked forties-era sensibility. It hinted darkly at infidelities of the day. It noted rumors of certain celebrities' closeted homosexuality, and detailed petty studio betrayals, all among figures whose glory days were half a century ago, and most of whom had now been dead for years. In to-day's culture, most of these scandals would be thought of as staggeringly boring.

I shook my head. Only the puffy egos of women like Catherine Hill and Eva James and Helen Howerton could lead them to imagine that their old secrets were news. All that fuss and all that bother and nobody cared anymore what they did.

But there was something else that was not quite right. Even with all these answers, I now began to realize I hadn't been asking the right questions. Catherine Hill might have sent someone to grab the book, but she wouldn't have harmed Quita. Once Catherine got her hands on McBride's diary, Quita would no longer have been a threat. After all, Quita hadn't even seen the book yet.

I roamed around downstairs in the kitchen, putting on the teakettle, getting a big white mug, rooting around for some soothing carbohydrates to nibble with my tea as I thought it all over.

Had Quita's death been an accident? Then why had she seemed so terrified when we saw her? Why had she begged me for help? What had she been afraid of? It still didn't add up.

The pine farm table near the back of my kitchen had ten chairs around it, but I picked my usual spot at the end.

I had to start over. Eliminate the mystery of that damn book and what was left? The key to Quita's state of mind seemed to have been money. Her plan had been to sell Dickey's book. But what if Catherine Hill had something to hold over Quita. What if they were trading secrets? I tried to remember exactly what I had overheard at Hill's house. She had said, "Everyone has secrets. Dickey taught me that. Even her."

I looked down at the thin slice of apple-blackberry pie. Not, perhaps, a traditional breakfast, but decent enough, I rationalized. It contained fruit and grains and if I just added a dab of ice cream, I'd have dairy. I went to the freezer.

Buster should know why Quita was so hyped-up for money. Maybe the others who were at the mah-jongg party with her, like Verushka or Trey, knew what was up with Quita that night.

I looked down and realized I wasn't hungry after all, so I cleared my dishes and rinsed them off. Then I grabbed my bag and keys. It was time to go visit Buster Dubin and, this time, ask the right questions.

Outside, it appeared to be a typically bright day, this one perhaps clearer than most. Rose parade weather. The temperature was mild. Late January was a nice time of year to come visit our side of the continent. The postcard palm trees that lined my street looked like they were ready for their close-ups. I walked the two blocks to Buster's house in a few minutes.

His large white stucco home was set on the hillside, up a steep flight of steps. I stopped. Over the past six months, I'd run up and down those steps a hundred times. But I looked at those fourteen steps now and felt the heat of tears rush up behind my eyelids.

A soft breeze picked up a tendril of hair and set it gently down. I could feel the heat of the sun warming my back and arms. It was a beautiful day. And I was alive to feel it.

I took the steps slowly, checking them out as I went up. There was no indication that a young woman had slipped here. There was no blood or broken railing. Everything was peaceful. Two blocks from the freeway, this part of Whitley Heights was much quieter than mine. Birds perched on an overhead wire sang sweetly, oblivious to the recent calamity.

I rang Buster Dubin's doorbell and waited.

To my surprise, Trey answered the door. "Hey. Madeline. What's up? You looking for Bus?"

"Yes. Is he home?"

"Sure, come on in," he said. "We're sitting out back, drinking Bloody Marys. We have a pitcher."

I stepped in and was greeted by Buster's gold-leaf Buddha, smiling benevolently from his place of honor in the entry. The fellow seemed to be the only one who was sanguine enough in the face of such disturbing events to hang on to his grin.

I followed Trey through the darkened house.

"I thought you were traveling out of town this week," I said, just making conversation. I remembered Trey was a sales rep with manufacturing accounts in Indonesia and the Far East.

"Right. Well we're *not supposed to leave*," he said, whispering the last part in mock menace. He sounded rueful. "They scared us shitless, the cops. They were pretty uncool."

Ah. Honnett had been there. I hoped Buster wouldn't hold it against me. At least he hadn't been arrested.

Trey walked through his friend's house barefoot. He wore a rumpled black T-shirt with the sleeves cut off and a pair of drawstring pants. As we stepped outside into the dappled sunlight, I noticed Trey's normally tawny skin had a slightly grayish cast.

Buster looked up from reading the paper. "Maddie? Hey." He jumped up and kissed my cheek and then pulled over a third over-size teak patio chair to the table. "How cool is this?"

Trey poured himself another Bloody Mary and offered one to me.

"No, thanks. I'm just here for a minute."

"I'm glad you stopped by," Buster said. "I've been meaning to call you. We're going to cancel the Sweet and Sour Club for a while."

"I sort of figured," I said. "It would be strange."

"Everyone is freaking about Quita's accident," Trey said. He sucked down a third of his Bloody Mary and added as an afterthought, "Verushka is a total wreck."

Buster nodded. "She's been out of it, lately. She's got business problems, doesn't she?" Buster asked Trey.

"She's always got business problems. Everything works out," Trey, the philosopher, said.

"Are you talking about Verushka's model-making business?" I asked.

"Right," Buster said. "She's got about eight thousand square feet out in Culver City. Have you seen it?"

I shook my head.

"Oh, man, you should. It's a very retro concept she's got, very very cool. They create miniature models for special effects. It's almost a lost art. They have to train a whole new group of craftspeople to get it going."

Verushka had gotten some publicity when the new company started up. She was working with two master model-builders in a motion-picture special-effects technique that had been used since the days of the silents. By playing with scale on film, the exact miniatures that her craftspeople constructed became life-size on the screen. Now that computer animation had taken over, almost no one was doing miniatures anymore. For one thing, the time-intensive craft was phenomenally expensive compared to the cost of using today's computers. But Verushka and her partners figured there were an awful lot of a hundred-million-dollar film budgets out there. And a lot of big-spending, spoiled directors. There was something irresistible about working with perfect replicas.

"I think she's nuts to invest in a business that's so medieval," Trey said, sucking on a sliver of ice cube.

"CG is fine . . ." Buster, the director, said and the two of them started arguing about computer-generated images on film.

I tuned out and thought about Verushka. If she was working today, I would go out to Culver City and pay her a visit. Maybe she had some idea of what had been bothering Quita.

"So," I said to the guys. "I hear they're keeping you both close to home still. The police. I'm sorry it's been so harsh."

"I am over that, Madeline," Buster said. His grin reminded me of the Buddha statue in his front hall. "You know how it goes in this devilish world. You cannot escape your karma."

Trey snorted. "Right, man."

Buster ignored Trey and continued, "I figure that it is not my karma to be directing that *Warp* music video in Copenhagen. I'm cool with that. I figure there must be a higher plan. You dig?"

Actually, I did.

Buster said, "But my man Trey here is freaking."

I looked at Trey. He certainly looked bad.

"I need to get to China, brother," Trey said. "I got business, you understand? These Chinese partners don't get why I'm not over there right now. It's so stupid."

"You know what would make you feel better?" Buster asked his friend.

I quickly thought of several good answers: sleep, a change of clothes, something to consume that didn't include alcohol as its main ingredient . . .

"You should jump in the pool," Buster said. "It will cool you off, bro."

Trey drained the ice-cube melt from the bottom of his glass and stood up. "I think I will. You coming?"

"In a minute," Buster said. "Go ahead. You gotta chill."

Trey left us and walked down to the large swimming pool way down at the end of the property. I watched him in the distance as he pulled off his shirt and stripped down to his boxers. Athletic and slim, Trey Forsythe dived off the side into the pool, sending perfect aqua ripples up onto the glassy surface.

"He's been so out of it," Buster said. And then he leaned over and opened a cooler, bringing out two bottles of Arrowhead water. He set one frosty bottle before me and then unscrewed the cap of the other one for himself.

"Thanks," I said. "What's wrong with Trey? Is he staying here?"

"Yeah. Just for a few nights. I hate to be alone, know what I mean?"

"Sure."

"Anyway, he's leaving today. I've got a friend who's moving in for a while."

"Someone I know?" I asked, turning to look at Buster.

"Do you know Doris Ann? She and I have started seeing each other."

Since when? I sighed. I suppose it was inevitable. Buster had been trying to dump Quita. This Doris Ann must have already been lined up. I felt uneasy thinking about Quita's replacement.

"I don't think I've met her," I said.

"She's great," Buster said, happy. "She's not like the other babes I bring around here. She's smart. Kinda like you."

I smiled, and said, "Awwww."

"Remember Lee Chen and our mah-jongg fortunes, Mad? Mine is coming true. I'm the East Wind, don't forget. I'm one very lucky guy. Doris Ann will make a difference in me."

"What is she?" I asked. "A model? An actress?"

"A librarian."

I almost spit out my bottled water. Imagine that.

"What's wrong with Trey?" I asked.

"He and Quita used to be very tight."

"Oh. I didn't know that."

"They dated or something. Long time ago."

"Really?" I didn't know that.

"But you know, Trey doesn't fall apart," Buster said. "I just can't see him falling apart because of some woman he used to be tight with."

"He looks pretty bad," I said, sipping water.

"Tell me. He's not sleeping. He just sits around and drinks my booze. He's no fun at all. And he's been after me to borrow money. Maybe that's it. He's broke again."

"Money is tough," I said, hoping to draw out a few more answers. This is what I had come to talk about, after all. Why had Quita McBride been so desperate to get her hands on money the night she died?

"No lie. But that's why we have to make a lot. Right?"

"Quita was very upset about money, too, wasn't she? But didn't she inherit a bundle when Dickey McBride died last year?"

"Well, you would have thought so, wouldn't you? But there are still some legal things that were up in the air. These lawyers are bloodthirsty mothers. You know. And they thought Quita was dim. They were dragging her over coals. Red-hot coals."

"About what?" I asked.

"There are always technicalities. Paperwork, whatever. Quita was always tense about it."

"Buster, did Quita ask you for any money lately?"

He nodded, matter-of-fact. "Everyone is always asking Buster for money."

"That's what has been puzzling me. I barely knew Quita, and she asked me for money, too. Why? Did Quita tell you what she needed the cash for?"

"Maybe lawyers? I don't know. Verushka came up to me at the Sweet and Sour Club and asked for twenty grand, too."

"Really?"

"Yeah, she told me it was to pay off a loan or something."

"And Trey?"

"He said he was in trouble with some guys."

"So will you lend it to him?" I asked.

"He's a big boy. He'll go to work and sell another hundred containers of bicycle parts or whatever shit he sells," he said, referring to Trey's commissions from his import sales gig.

"You think?"

"It's a tough world out there, Mad. It'll all be okay. Don't you worry. Somehow, people cope."

Do they? I wondered. Did Quita "cope"?

"Say," I said, changing the subject. "Do you know if Verushka's working today?"

"She works every day. You want her address?" He pulled a pen from his pocket, and I gave him a notepad from my purse.

"You seem calmer than the last time I saw you, Buster."

"It's my new Zen thing. It works for me, don't you think?" He grinned.

"I'm glad."

He looked up at me and let the hip mahjongg master mask slip off. "It's been a rough couple of days. Really, really rough. Quita was a real pain that last week, blowing up all the time, demanding all the time. I know I shouldn't say that because she's gone now, but Quita could be self-absorbed to the point of . . . Well. And then the accident. I was pretty freaked myself, there. And then, you know, those idiot cops coming around and making like it was my fault. It hasn't been easy here. But, you know, I get the feeling everything is getting better."

"Good for you," I said, getting to my feet.

I looked over at Trey. He was still doing laps, the lonely long-distance swimmer. I said good-bye to Buster. He made a big deal about standing and giving me a hug.

"It's Doris Ann," he said. "She's amazing. Wait until you meet her. She's teaching me to meditate, and I just started teaching her to play MJ. And she beats my ass already."

"Ah, just what the world needs," I teased him gently, "another hot mah-jongg player."

I turned to leave, folding the note with Verushka's address. I had to follow up on the money angle. Verushka was desperate to get together a lot of cash. Maybe she'd tell me the reason why. Especially since I just that moment realized I had a sudden suicidal impulse to make Verushka a very sizable loan.

Chapter 23

In September of 1917, Harry Culver incorporated his own city, just east of the beach resort known as Venice, California. He was quite a promoter. He bussed people into his new burg and gave them a "free lunch." He offered free land to the winner of the prettiest baby contest. He started a marathon car race. But his biggest marketing brainstorm was so effective it forever altered the history of Culver City. He enticed early movie man Thomas Ince to relocate his Sunset Boulevard studio facilities to 10202 Washington Boulevard. In 1924, a roaring lion moved in. Metro-Goldwyn-Mayer took over the forty-acre Goldwyn Studios. And Culver City became one of the major centers of this new screenland industry.

Even now, bought out with Japanese money and bearing a Japanese name, the same venerable old studio still stands. It was to this older Culver City neighborhood that I was headed. In the shadow of what is now called Sony Pictures Entertainment, on a side street off of Washington, was an old warehouse that housed the miniature-model shop of Mars/Kirschner Industries. I pulled up and easily found a spot to park on the street, a sure sign it was Saturday if there ever was one.

The plain-front gray building gave no indication of the work done inside. You couldn't tell from the exterior of the three-story-high structure what went on inside, and that's the way these businesses liked it. The warehouse fit into its nondescript block, appearing generically industrial. I pushed the intercom button next to the front door and hoped someone working on a Saturday would hear my ring.

A few moments later, a security release buzzer sounded, and I quickly pulled open the large metal-framed door. The reception area was deserted, but soon a young African-American woman with fabulous braids came out front. She wore extralarge overalls over a skinny little tee.

"Hi," I said. "My name is Madeline Bean. Is Verushka available? We're friends."

"Oh, sure," she said. "Follow me."

I walked with her though the doorway and turned down a typical office hallway. But unlike any other light industrial office corridor, were the Day-Glo colors used to paint each office door and, on the walls between the doors, the cool eight-foot-high photo blowups depicting Paris and Dodger Stadium and the surface of the moon.

"She's in the shop," my guide told me, as we walked all the way down the hall. At the end, she opened a lime green door, and we entered a large open warehouse space three stories high.

The woman stopped in the open doorway and pointed off a ways. "She's over there. See her?"

She left me alone at the entrance to the miniature-model shop. The place was simply amazing. If you ever played with a dollhouse when you were a kid, or built a model railroad set, you'd be in heaven.

All around were incredible tabletop environments, miniaturized and perfect down to each hair-thin detail. Stretched out on two dozen worktables, I saw everything from English villages to skyscrapers and from airplanes to spaceships. In one corner, I could see some sort of alien vessel, its exterior blasted with phaser fire. On a farther table, I saw an exact replica of the football stadium at Notre Dame. These, I knew, would appear life-size on the screen.

And the skylighted work space was filled with people. About forty artists were moving about the airy workshop room tinkering on different projects. On the table closest to me, four men were rigging miniature cables. They worked on a three-foot-high, twenty-five-foot-long replica of the Golden Gate Bridge, perfect down to the minute signs of oxidation on its rust-colored paint.

"We're going to blow that one up," Verushka said, walking up beside me. "Kaboom. I'm really excited about that."

I turned and said hello.

"These days," Verushka explained, "most movie effects are CG — you know, computer-generated. It's much cheaper, but we say, you get what you pay for. We're winning them back. Sometimes the effect is worth the time and money. You know they used miniature pistons in the engine-room scenes in *Titanic*."

"This is fantastic," I said.

"Thanks." Verushka turned to me. "What brought you down here? I was shocked to see you standing by the door."

"Hope I didn't scare you," I said.

"No, but technically, as far as our top-secret clients know, we are a secure site."

"Sorry, I forced my way in with gunfire and then tied up your receptionist."

Verushka laughed. "We have Dreamworks

coming in today. If anyone asks, you're consulting on a kitchen environment for one of our space modules."

"Perfect," I said, smiling. "You know, Wesley would actually be great at that."

"Really? I should call him. So what's up?"

"Buster gave me your address. Can you spare a minute for a couple of questions?"

"Party questions? Come on out to my office," she said, giving me a big smile.

Verushka led me out of the workshop and back down the corridor. We soon stopped and she used a key-card to open a chartreuse green door. Her office was large and spotlessly white. There was a nice white-leather sofa in one corner, and she flopped down. She was dressed in casual clothes, a denim work shirt that she wore as a jacket over a T-shirt and pair of baggy shorts. It revealed a bit more of Verushka's thighs than I'd seen at the Sweet and Sour Club parties, and there was a bit more of Verushka to see in the daylight. Her makeup was neat and her pretty bow mouth sported a fresh application of burgundy lipstick.

I took a seat on the sofa next to her. "I haven't come about any parties. I've been worried about what happened to Quita."

"Oh, yeah. Quita. That was pretty horrible, wasn't it?"

"Yes," I agreed, watching how she reacted. "I just stopped by the house. I saw Buster and Trey. Buster looks like he's getting over the shock, I'd say."

"How's Trey?"

"Not great. He's been staying with Buster, did you know?"

She looked worried.

"How are you holding up?"

"Me? I'm doing okay. Thanks. I've been stressed, but that has been going on for a while . . . nothing new."

"What's the matter?" I asked.

"Money." She looked to see how I might respond. I gave her a reassuring look and she went on. "It's always money, isn't it? I love this company, Madeline, but it is a long road until we make profits. Right now, all our income goes to paying our staff and running the place."

"You looking for investors?" I asked casually.

She looked over at me, and her expression changed. "You?"

"Possibly."

"Oh, Madeline. This is wonderful! I mean, you'd really be getting in on the ground floor. We're turning the effects business around. We do pyro. We build 'em and we blow 'em up. My partners aren't here right now. They worked all last night, actually. But you'd like them. They are both master model-makers."

"What kind of capital are you looking for?" I asked her.

"Twenty thousand," she said quickly.

Here it was again. That same desperation.

"Verushka, what the hell is going on?"

"What do you mean? I thought you wanted to —"

"Look, I'm not the investor type. But tell me honestly what you need that money for. Maybe I can help you."

"What do you want me to say?" Verushka asked, her voice going up, her eyes opening wide. "I'm mortgaged up to my eyeballs here. My credit cards are maxxed. I just need a little cash flow."

I heard the same pitch of panic in Verushka's voice that I'd heard in Quita McBride's.

"Is it for someone else? Maybe for someone close to you?"

Her deep brown eyes didn't blink. Slowly she nodded.

"Who?"

"My boyfriend. You don't know him," she added. "He needs my help."

"I had no idea." This was an understatement. Verushka had always seemed like the lone strong woman type. And the guys with whom she played mah-jongg never talked about her boyfriend that I could remember. It just went to show that one really never knows. We don't always have time to pay attention. People are a mystery. "I didn't realize . . ." I said.

"I know," she said, sighing. "I've been pretty low profile about our engagement. That's the way he wants it. There are reasons." Verushka folded her plump hands in her lap.

Oh, man. What kind of guy encourages his "fiancée" to keep their relationship a big secret? Easy odds answer: a married one. Poor Verushka. I never understood women like Verushka, who allowed themselves to get involved with unavailable men. Or did I? I thought about Arlo for the first time that day.

But I felt sorry for her instantly. And on top of all that, he had money troubles.

I looked at Verushka and reassessed. In the time I'd known her, she'd impressed me as funny and outspoken and large and endearing. She reminded me of Velma on *Scooby-Doo* — quick and sincere, everyone's best friend. Only now I was beginning to worry that Velma had fallen for a bad dog.

"Why does your boyfriend need the money?"

"He's got debts. He's gotten behind in paying them off. I have to help him, Maddie."

"I see."

"I really shouldn't talk about it. He's very private."

"Oh, sure. I understand."

This always works. The trick is to stay quiet.

"It's not really so unusual," Verushka continued, after a few seconds of the patented M. Bean silent treatment. "Everyone owes money, don't they? My fiancé is in trouble. What do you think? Could you give us a loan?"

"Twenty thousand is a lot of money," I said. "Who does he owe?"

Verushka looked up. "Everyone. He's borrowed money from everyone we know. Most people look at him and think he's successful. They can't see his pain."

"I'm surprised I don't know your boyfriend from the Sweet and Sour. Does he play mah-jongg?"

She hesitated again. "Really, Maddie, I wish I could tell you his name. I just can't."

"Okay."

But of course, she wanted to tell me. "The

Sweet and Sour is not a good place for my boyfriend."

"Is that it, then? The gambling?"

At the weekly parties, I made a special point of not noticing these things, as gambling for money is illegal, but I'd suspected hundreds and even thousands changed hands at the end of the night.

She looked up at me, hesitating. But Verushka was a talker. I was counting on that. I sat there looking interested.

"Your boyfriend has a problem?" I asked gently.

After a few seconds she let out her breath slowly. "Huge."

"Oh, Verushka. You must be worried."

"You can't tell anyone this, okay? I tried to get him to go to Gamblers Anonymous. I wanted him to go to a therapist or something, but he won't. And it seems to be getting worse."

"You must be stressed," I said.

"Now he's in debt to some Chinese guys, and he's going crazy trying to pay them back. They gave him a deadline of Wednesday night, and we couldn't get the cash in time. I'm frantic worrying about what they may do. Do you think you could lend me the money, Madeline? Just until I can pay you back? I'll put up my stock in this company as collateral. Please."

"Verushka." I looked at her. I knew she didn't want to hear what I had to say. That didn't stop me. "This guy sounds like big trouble. Do you really need this?"

"Do you believe in fate, Maddie? I do. Some things are beyond our power. And even though we might be in pain, we can't always control our own destinies. Some people have money problems. Perhaps that is my fiancé's fate. And it's my fate to love him."

Throw fate in my face? This is exactly why I have hated the concept all these years, hated the excuse it provides to people who don't want to take responsibility for solving their own problems, fixing their lives, growing up and healing themselves.

"Won't you help us, Maddie? Can't you find a way in your heart to give us a loan?"

Another woman in need, begging for my help. I felt the weight of it. Just the other night, I had turned Quita down, and now I was paying that price.

"You believe in fate, don't you?" Verushka asked.

"Well," I said, "right now, I don't believe I'm fated to lose twenty grand."

"Oh." Her dark brown eyes widened,

clearly showing her pain. "I had such hope."

I had hopes, too. I hoped to find out what had happened that night to Quita McBride. We don't always get exactly what we hope for.

And then it all sort of just clicked together. Verushka was in love with a man who needed twenty thousand dollars to pay off gambling debts. Verushka had to keep her lover's name a secret. Quita McBride was also desperate to get her hands on a lot of money. Now what was the possibility that they were both trying to save the same man? And I thought, could it be Buster who is the man in need? Was Buster broke and stringing Verushka along? Is that why Buster couldn't lend money to his friends?

"Verushka, it's very important for me to know your boyfriend's name."

"Madeline," she said with finality, back to being the businesswoman. "It's very important for me to get back to work."

"Is it Buster?"

She laughed, startled at the suggestion.

I sat there, hoping she'd break down. Hoping to find out the connection. I tried one more time, speaking softly. "Please tell me," I said.

She stopped at the door and turned back to me, a smile on her sad face. "Is it worth twenty grand to you to find out?"

But just then, of course, it all clicked into place. No money would be changing hands. I figured it out myself for free.

Chapter 24

"Hey, Madeline?" Buster opened the front door. "You forget something?"

"Yeah, I guess you could say that. I forgot to talk to Trey. Is he still here?"

"Trey? I think he's sleeping. He was on the patio a while ago."

"Would you mind if I checked?"

"Oh, sure. Come in. Yeah." Buster opened the door wider.

"Trey and you go back pretty far, right?" I walked in and stood in the entry, back once again in the presence of the golden Buddha.

"Since fifth grade. Long time." Buster walked me through the big house. He was now wearing his lucky red-silk jacket with the embroidered slogan *The Hand from Hell*. I figured he was playing mah-jongg on the computer before I interrupted. "It always amazes me," he said. "He doesn't go after chicks, they come after him." Buster turned and gave me a very deliberate look.

"Well, don't worry about me," I said, startled to the point of laughter. "I'm not interested in Trey."

"Good thing," Buster said. "I love the guy, Maddie. But he is not the easiest guy to love."

Buster opened the French door out to the patio for me. "Looks like he's still sleeping. But go on over. Maybe for you he'll wake up."

I crossed the flagstone patio. The teak table and chairs were positioned just the way they had been when I had stopped by earlier. I found the path that led down onto the lawn and followed it to the pool farther off. Trey Forsythe was reclining on one of the padded teak lounge chairs at the edge of the pool. He lay motionless, eyes closed, with one knee up.

I studied him: his dark blond hair, his thin and poetic face, and the little patch of light blond beard that covered his chin. I tried to see him the way Verushka did. He was lying there with his shirt off in the late-afternoon sun. His tan was an even mocha. My eyes swept over his smooth, well-defined chest, his hard stomach. Below, a fine line of hair traveled south of his navel, disappearing beneath the open drawstring of his low-slung pants. My eyes traveled lower.

"Find something you were looking for?"

I brought my eyes back up to meet Trey's pale blues.

"I always do," I said.

"So you're back. Not enough party business to keep you busy?"

"My business is doing just great, Trey, thanks for asking. You know, catering in L.A. is a big money deal. Wes and I can't complain." I stood next to his chaise lounge, looking down.

"That's great. But I bet you could be doing better."

"Really?"

"It's all about marketing." Trey lightly slapped his flat stomach. "That's what I do, and I'm the best."

"So, you want to give me some advice?"

He took his time looking me over. "You are obviously a very beautiful woman. You work that. I've seen you."

"Ah," I said, "so maybe I should have skipped cooking school altogether?"

Trey smiled. "You can always do a better job with marketing . . . maybe take on a new partner. I mean Wes is a good guy . . . but he's not exactly chick bait. Your business could only do better if you had someone the girls appreciated more."

"Like you?" I stared down at him.

"You could do worse."

My back was to the setting sun, and Trey squinted up at me.

"I don't think you want to get into event-planning, Trey," I said, finding a seat on the chaise next to him. "I just think you are looking for a way to raise some cash."

"What makes you think that?"

"Quita McBride."

"Now, I'm not following you at all . . ."

"Let's say Quita wanted to help you out. What would Quita do to raise money fast? She didn't have anything worth selling. But then she was reminded that her husband had kept a journal that might prove valuable. She hadn't paid much attention to the journal when Dickey was alive, but now that she was hungry to get cash, it probably sounded like her only shot."

Trey looked bored.

"Of course, Dickey's old diary couldn't do Quita any good as long as it was missing. But that all changed when Wes called. He'd found the old mah-jongg case hidden behind a wall. Quita was sure the diary had been kept in that case, but she couldn't wait to turn it into cash. So she called Dickey's old movie-star friends and offered to sell them the diary, sight unseen."

"You making all this stuff up?"

"But poor Quita didn't figure on just how

badly those old ladies would want to protect their secrets. When they learned that Quita hadn't even seen the book yet, Catherine Hill and the others arranged to get the book back themselves. Faster and cleaner. The way they did it, Quita never got a chance to read any of their silly old secrets."

"Really?" Trey looked at me. "They sound pretty sharp."

"Sure." I took off my sunglasses, as the sun had begun to set. "So Quita was frantic, wasn't she? Wes and I saw her Wednesday evening. When she learned Dickey's mah-jongg case had been stolen and the red book was missing, she panicked. There was nothing to sell to the mah-jongg ladies. No more big payoff."

"And even if all this is true, Madeline, what is it to you? You think there was something wrong with a friend trying to help another friend?"

I looked at the young man, so cool and relaxed as we talked about his "friend." Nothing of her pain seemed to touch him. "Was Quita in love with you? Is that why she was so worried about the money?"

"We had a thing a long time ago. She was a good kid. I guess she couldn't get enough of me. Her old man was famous, you know? But he wasn't . . ."

Trey didn't finish the sentence, but he didn't have to. McBride may have fulfilled Quita's fantasies of Hollywood. He may have given her a thrilling last name. But he was in his seventies by the time Quita grew up enough to move to Hollywood and marry him. The reality was Dickey McBride wasn't a handsome young man anymore. Age is the enemy of any vain person, but it's worse for the famous. They trade on their youth and their energy and their sex appeal; they make a fortune simply because we want to look at them, and then when they age, we look away.

"So you were seeing Quita before Dickey McBride died."

He gave me a slow smile. "Are you shocked?"

This couldn't possibly pass for charm, but like a beautiful reptile, he was fascinating somehow.

"My friends say I'm unshockable," I said, seeing his bet.

"Quita wanted to help me get some cash. This was like a year ago. She told me her husband had a stash of money. I thought, Dickey McBride — he must be loaded. The trouble was, she couldn't get to it. Then, after he died, she couldn't find any great stash. And the lawyers kept hassling Quita.

They were never going to let her get her hands on McBride's dough."

"Why not?" I asked.

"Something about paperwork."

"That must have been disappointing."

"No shit," he said, still smiling his most charming smile. The setting sun lit the ends of Trey's short blond hair, creating a halo.

"So what did she do?" I asked.

"Come on, sit closer and I'll tell you," he said. "Quita sold that old house as fast as she could. But after paying off the mortgage and taxes and a whole load of other stuff, she didn't end up with much."

"And you grabbed whatever money she had, I'll bet. To pay off your debts."

"Don't look at me like I took it from her. She wanted to give it to me. It was her choice."

But what Trey was telling me didn't entirely scan with the fear I had seen in Quita McBride's eyes.

"Why don't you tell me the rest of it, Trey? Why she was frantic to raise money for you on Wednesday? It wasn't your fantastic body alone, was it? That's been over for months, right? Why don't you tell me what had Quita so motivated to help you out?"

"Why should I?"

I got up on one knee and moved to lean down over him as he reclined in the chaise. He looked up at me, surprised.

"Because," I said, my anger hard to contain, "I want to know." Then, to make him jump, I slammed my hand down on the side of the chaise lounge just a few inches from his ear.

But he didn't flinch at all. His face was now close to mine. I could feel his breath on my cheek. He reached up and took my other hand and placed it on the warm skin on the flat of his stomach.

"How badly?" he whispered. "How badly do you want to know?"

I left my hand where he'd placed it, not flinching myself. "What did you have on Quita? Something scared her. Was it your old affair? How could that . . . ?" I was lost. How could that be a threat? McBride was already dead.

But then, maybe we had all heard the story backward. My expression must have changed.

"Did you figure it out?" Trey reached up and slowly pulled on the clip that held my long hair back off of my face. A tumble of heavy hair fell forward.

The rumor had been slightly off.

I said, "The night McBride had that

fatal heart attack in his bedroom, he wasn't making love to Quita, was he? He died because he walked in on the two of you."

I saw it clearly. The rumors were right as far as they went. Quita was naked and Dickey's old heart couldn't take it. Only she wasn't having sex with Dickey that night. Quita was in bed with Trey when her old husband found them.

"I don't know a lot of girls who could have figured that out, Madeline. In fact, I don't know any. And I find girls with brains very sexy."

"So what did you do? Did you blackmail her? If she didn't keep coming up with money to pay off your gambling debts, you would let people know about the way Dickey really died, is that it? What could that matter, really?"

"She was fighting for a piece of a very big pie, Madeline. She was hyped to keep the movie star name and all of Dickey's money. She wanted to be interviewed on *Entertainment Tonight* when the limos pulled up for the Dickey McBride memorial auction. And Quita didn't want any investigation into how Dickey had died."

"And all you wanted in return for your silence was money she couldn't get her hands on." I moved back and took my hand off of Trey's lean body.

"You can put it any way you want to. She was just helping me out."

"What I still don't get is how Quita ended up with your best friend, Buster. That must have been awkward for you. Your old girlfriend and your best friend."

He just stared at me, waiting. Waiting for me to . . . what?

And then I got it. Quita ran out of money and Trey set her up with his oldest and dearest friend, the one who still had money but refused to pay any more of Trey's gambling debts.

I shook my head. "She never really liked Buster at all, did she?" I asked.

"Now, now. Hey. She liked him okay," Trey said. "But it is also true she was trying to help me. Buster was being a jerk about the money. He always used to be a sport about it. He was always good for a loan, you know? But then, one day out of the blue he says, 'no more.' No more. He's got a ton of it. He makes more off of directing one of those car commercials than I make in a year busting my hump arranging manufacturing deals in China. He could have solved the whole problem if he'd just agreed to give me another loan. But he wouldn't. Don't go feeling sorry for Buster. It's his own damn fault."

To support his gambling habit, good-looking Trey had used them all. First Buster, who had paid his friend's debts for years, then Verushka, who picked the wrong guy to love, and then there was Quita, whose fears about Dickey's death made her open to blackmail.

Trey watched me stand up. "You sure you want to leave?"

"I've heard enough. Unless you'd like to tell me about the night Quita died."

"What? What are you talking about?" For the first time, Trey sounded annoyed.

"Quita told me she was supposed to meet you after the party." She hadn't said anything at all about Trey, actually.

"Okay, sure. But I never came back to the house. What was the point? She hadn't gotten the money."

So, Quita had been expecting him that night. And how was I to know he really stood her up?

"Look." He sat up and made eye contact. "Lend me some money, Madeline. I know Buster. He'll get all concerned about you. He'll be raging at me. Then Buster will pay you back. You lose nothing."

"And why, Trey, would I ever do that?"

"You were looking at it when you first came outside. You know you want it."

"Oh," I said. Oh, *really*. "You're scaring me, Trey. You know me so well."

He smiled.

On some, sarcasm is entirely wasted.

"Madeline, you are really funny. Don't you remember that fortune cookie you e-mailed me the other night? It said, 'Taste everything at least once.' Follow your own damn advice, sugar. Come on down here. Take a taste."

I kept a tight rein on my rising disgust. Years of working in Hollywood had trained me well for this particular form of self-control.

"Out of respect to Verushka," I said, "who believes the two of you are engaged, I will have to fight my natural urge."

"What? You think I love Verushka? Come on."

Some slight movement, out of the corner of my eye, caught my attention. I looked aside and saw a woman standing in the shadows not far away. Verushka. She stood there, silently listening, tears streaming.

"Verushka has been a pal," Trey said. "But that's it. Jesus, where'd you ever get an idea like putting me next to her? I mean, God." He couldn't hold back a low throaty chuckle. "That's kind of gross. Have you looked at her, Maddie? She's fat. She's never gonna be a beauty. You worried about Verushka? Hell, she's a dog. She's got nothing that you've got."

I didn't dare look up again. I knew Verushka was standing there, humiliated, hating me, as Trey rambled on, reassuring me that Verushka meant absolutely nothing to him. He hadn't yet realized that another source of financing had just dried up for good.

"Come on, Maddie. I know you feel something for me."

Did he seriously imagine he was going to seduce me into giving him money?

"Come on," he said. "I'll show you love the raw way. You'll like it. You just gotta loosen up and show me what you feel."

"What I . . . *feel?*" I asked, looking down at his lank, sinewy body, almost tempted.

"Don't fight it, Madeline," he said, closing his heavy-lidded eyes.

Okay. He was begging for it.

I'd show him what I felt, all right. I hauled off and slugged him.

Chapter 25

Bellagio Road was quiet and dark as I pulled up in front of Catherine Hill's Bel Air estate. The gate was open this time, permitting access to the long driveway that was lined with old-fashioned lampposts. I followed the evenly spaced puddles of soft white light on the cobblestones all the way up to the house. Lit up at night, the home's formal pillars and classical façade gave it the look of a mausoleum. The entire scene seemed more imposing than I remembered it from yesterday's bright afternoon visit.

I noticed a couple of cars were already parked near the entrance. A Lincoln Town Car and an older Jaguar. I left my own Grand Wagoneer among them and took the steps up to the front door.

Before I could ring, the door was opened. Standing there was Catherine Hill.

"You are on time," she said, her voice pleasant, her light English accent charming as always. "Please come in."

Catherine was dressed in a long silver

lounging robe, with a zipper up the front. And if silver lamé was not enough to make her fashion statement, there were white marabou feathers at the neckline and at the borders of each flowing sleeve. Tonight she had abandoned her turban and instead sported a highly piled platinum blond hairdo complete with perky bangs. It was a wig.

"Don't you look adorable," she said, ushering me inside, showing her famous dimple.

For tonight's meeting I had abandoned the good-little-girl suit and instead wore my usual kind of thing, a long black dress with ankle-high, thick-soled boots and socks.

"I like the way you are wearing your hair down tonight," Catherine said. "It's so becoming on you. Don't you think so, Helen?"

She turned and I saw Helen Howerton standing there, wearing purple slacks with a large silk overblouse. Tonight's print featured zebras standing on red circus balls, all on a purple background. Her hair was still the shiny black football-helmet-with-a-flip 'do of the day before.

"So much hair," Helen Howerton said, looking at me. "And it's such a lovely color. My hairstylist could do something marvelous for you," she offered. What a thought.

You might have noticed that on this second visit, it was not I who was offering up the insincere praise. It is in just such minute social adjustments as these that you can most quickly detect the changing winds and the power shifts in Hollywood.

The two women showed me to the living room, which was off to the right. The walls of the room were painted the same deep persimmon red-orange as the entry, and the room was decorated in English mahogany antiques and big, down-cushioned pieces upholstered in olive damask, scattered with dozens of assorted throw pillows. The lavish living room had all the touches of a professional decorator, like the hundred silver-framed photos of Catherine Hill and her famous friends arranged artfully on the table behind the sofa. The enormous square coffee table and every other side table held bowls overflowing with fresh flowers and museum-quality displays of Catherine Hill's collection of rare antique Victorian dolls.

Rosalie Apple stood next to the large grand piano by the front windows and turned as we came in.

"Hello, Beall," she said, saluting with two

fingers touching her gray hair.

She looked much as I remembered, short-cropped hair, little makeup, and no obvious signs of plastic surgery. Rosalie was dressed in a white oxford shirt with navy slacks and Gucci loafers, conservative as before.

Eva James looked up at me from the spot where she was seated, next to the fireplace. The fire's glow softened her tight jawline and lit up her sleek blond bob. In this light, she looked almost exactly as I remembered her in her glory days as queen of the MGM musicals. I suspected she always devised a way to sit near the edge of a lighted fire.

Helen Howerton and her zebras settled down on one of the three massive sofas that formed a U around the fireplace. Catherine and Rosalie took seats on the opposite sofa, and I decided to face the fire, on a sofa of my own.

I set the red-leather book down on my lap.

"Shall we chitchat, dear?" Catherine asked. "Or would you prefer to get down to business?"

She seemed calm and friendly. I suspected my recent theft of the red book had not pleased her one bit, but her talent to hide her true feelings was a gift, one I had witnessed before, in fact, the previous afternoon. We seemed to understand each other.

355

We had both been deceptive. We had both discovered the other's deception. We were, therefore, very much alike. No need to make a scene. And besides, I had the red book and was about to return it. They dared not upset me now. Power, while fleeting, feels supremely cool.

"Could you please tell me what went on between you and Quita McBride?" I asked.

"All right," Catherine said, sounding perfectly agreeable. "She called me on Wednesday morning and told me she wanted to trade something valuable. She claimed that an old mah-jongg set had just been found. She reminded me that Dickey kept a diary and that there were many secrets in it that we girls wouldn't care to have come to the press. She said when the mah-jongg set was returned to her, she'd have the diary as well."

"She was attempting to blackmail you," I said.

"Filthy girl," Eva James said.

"She's gone now, dear," Catherine Hill said sweetly to Eva, then resumed her story. "Quita asked me to pay her twenty thousand dollars in cash and also agree to be uncooperative in a lawsuit that was pending. You see, I was going to give an affidavit that Quita did not want me to give. I agreed, of course. We all of us had reasons we wanted to see that diary. Dickey had teased us for years that he had been keeping a journal. Everyone had heard him say he kept it safely hidden in his mah-jongg case."

"I see," I said. "But instead, you sent your gardener to steal it before Quita ever got possession of it. How did he know where to find us so he could steal it?"

Catherine Hill settled her hands in the folds of silver lamé that covered her lap and continued. "Quita said there was a man who was fixing up Dickey's old house. This man found Dickey's old mah-jongg set hidden in the wall. Imagine that. She said this young man had just called her from the house but that he couldn't meet Quita and give her Dickey's old case until six that evening. Of course, we had no real interest in the mah-jongg tiles. It was the diary we all wanted. Quita suggested we meet after midnight to exchange the money for the diary."

"You agreed?"

"I said yes. But, of course, I had no intention of waiting until after midnight to get that diary."

Eva spoke up. "We couldn't allow someone else to read Dickey's diary, you see."

"And," said Rosalie Apple, adjusting her

navy slacks as she crossed her legs, "what if this Quita thought it over and decided she could get more money from us? We couldn't have that."

Catherine shook her platinum wig and continued. "I sent my man, Flax, to go fetch it for us. He drove to Dickey's old house on Wetherbee as quickly as he could — it's not far — but the man there was just leaving. Flax noticed the man wore a bulky backpack and the house itself was under construction, so Flax followed the man."

"That was my partner, Wesley," I said.

"Ah," Helen spoke up.

I tried to keep my eyes focused on Helen's wrinkled face, but they kept wandering off to check on all those zebras balancing on her big shirt.

Helen took up the story. "Flax said your partner, Wesley, was a very nice safe driver and so it was incredibly easy to follow him into Santa Monica. Flax had hoped the young man would leave the mah-jongg set in his parked car. That would have been easy. A quick little bash and bingo, another car theft in Santa Monica, and we'd have our diary. But no. Your partner took his bulky backpack along, so Flax simply had to follow."

"Your friend is very tall, Beall," Rosalie

said. "Insanely easy to follow a tall man. Flax had no problem keeping him in sight, even walking around in that crowded outdoor market."

So, it was as simple as that. It was almost just after Wes arrived at the Market that we met up and he showed me the mah-jongg set. And soon after, this man Flax ran off with it.

"But this guy, Flax, he threw the mah-jongg set away," I said. "Why?"

"We didn't care anything about that old set of tiles," Helen Howerton said. "It was the diary we needed to get hold of. Hell, if Flax had been stopped and he was still holding on to that old wooden case, he'd be arrested. And then where would we be? His family has worked for Catherine forever. They'd track it back to us."

Catherine said, "I told Flax, go get the diary and whatever you do, ditch the old case. And he did what I instructed. He always does. Good man."

It wasn't that complicated, I realized. Wes and I had just stumbled into an old storyline that had been set in motion for decades. It seemed straightforward enough. And why, really, shouldn't these old ladies have their secrets back?

"You never gave Quita the money?" I asked.

"Of course not," Catherine Hill said, her voice for once sounding heated. "We got the diary, hadn't we? Why should we pay the silly thing a cent? But that wasn't as important to the girl as my testimony. She had really been quite desperate for me to stay mum."

"Yes," I said, remembering her earlier comment. "What sort of lawsuit was this?"

"She wanted all of Dickey's money," Rosalie said.

"Of course she did," Eva James said, giving the fire another poke.

"But she didn't deserve it, did she," Helen added. "The little bitch."

I put my hand on the red-leather diary and rested it there. "Tell me about the lawsuit."

"Dickey had never really married Quita. Not legally. They had a phony little wedding ceremony on a vacation he took her on a few years back. A friend of hers got her a counterfeit marriage license from the Grand Caymans or some such place, but it was not legit."

"Wow," I said. Not married.

"I knew he never married Quita," Catherine said. "Hell, I think Dickey was still legally married to another woman from way back. Quita was fighting the estate, o course, and naturally, she didn't want me to testify. But then, of course, the attorneys for Dickey's estate did."

"Did you read it, Beall?" asked Rosalie, still giving me a steady look. "The diary?"

"Did you read what Dickey wrote?" Helen echoed, her voice almost trembling.

"They were mostly a pack of lies," Eva added, her voice oozing charm. "I'm sure he made up the most ridiculous nonsense."

I thought of the secrets these ladies were living with all these years. The money trouble Rosalie had gotten herself into. Dickey's accusations of embezzlement might or might not have been true. Many celebrities had little knowledge of their own finances. Who could say what was fact at this late date?

And with Dickey McBride's reputation as a lady-killer, it was no wonder so many famous names appeared in the little red book with stars of conquest next to their names. I could imagine Eva James, the dancer, worrying about the affair she had had with Dickey. He had noted it in his diary along with four out of five stars. I hadn't taken the time to figure out all the dates, but Dickey implied in his diary that Eva was married at the time to one of McBride's movie-star friends. Since Eva's last husband, an old

Hollywood hoofer, was now dead twenty years, I wondered why she would care so much about the diary. But shame never died.

Helen Howerton, who played the teen-aged sidekick to Catherine Hill in all those schoolgirl pictures, was another of Dickey's dates — five stars. I wondered if Dickey had to peel Helen out of her trademark loud prints when they tumbled into bed.

His book betrayed even Catherine Hill, the woman who claimed to be the one person in Hollywood with whom Dickey had never slept. McBride wrote that he'd been Catherine's very first lover, back in a dressing room when they were both in their teens, in the days when they played brother and sister in the movie *Summer Storms.*

"None of us has read the diary, you see," Rosalie said. "We couldn't."

"Then we'd see what he wrote about each other. That wouldn't do at all," Eva James said, looking eternally young next to the fireplace.

"Mama took care of it for us," Catherine Hill explained. "We gave it to Mama to keep nice and safe."

"We were going to burn it," Helen said.

"Yes, but we planned to do it all to-gether," Catherine said. "Mama hid it for us, using the same trick that Helen and I used to hide a diary in our old *Heavenly Girls* movie." She eyed me. "But yesterday, when we realized you'd actually found our book —"

"We were shocked, you know," Helen said, interrupting.

"And amazed," added Eva James. "We thought we had been so clever. We were certain we had fooled you."

"Yesterday," Catherine repeated in a louder tone, taking back the stage, "when we realized that you found the book — why I swore up and down —"

"She did, too," Helen said.

"— and for the first time in my life," Catherine Hill continued, "well, I never thought I'd say this, Madeline, but I wished the Lord had made just one less Catherine Hill fan."

I laughed out loud, and so did the others. Their secrets were so harmless, I thought. Most of them. But there was one old secret that might still hold some venom. The world at large might not care, but among this close circle of friends, one item from Dickey's journal could still do damage.

Dickey confronted Rosalie Apple about her irregular bookkeeping and his missing royalty payments. She denied any wrongdoing, he wrote. In his anger, he fired Rosalie as his personal manager.

But then McBride accused Rosalie of something that in those old days was considered even more unspeakable. The rejected playboy figured out why he could never get this one woman into his bed. Rosalie Apple was in love with her favorite client, Catherine Hill. When McBride confronted her, Rosalie never denied it. In Dickey's diary, next to the name "Rosalie Apple" there were no stars. Instead were the words, "old maid."

Rosalie was still looking at me intently. "Did you read Dickey's journal, Beall?"

"Or did you stop yourself, perhaps?" Helen Howerton asked. "Maybe you had second thoughts?"

"Well?" asked Catherine Hill.

"No, ladies. I did not read Dickey's diary," I said.

Would they believe me? I looked at each old face. There were smiles and sighs, and even a tear. It's what each of them desperately wanted to believe, so indeed, they would. How powerful it must be to want to believe a thing so badly that no matter how farfetched, you do.

"I am more concerned, really, about finding out why Quita McBride died. Quita had wanted the red book, so I tracked it down. But as soon as I realized its sensitive nature, I thought I had better return it to you."

"Bless you," Catherine Hill said.

"And you," I asked, "still have the old mah-jongg set?"

"Yes, of course. Here it is." Catherine picked it up from a spot next to the sofa where I hadn't seen it. "Is there some particular reason you want it back, dear?"

"Let's say I've gotten attached to it," I said.

"Cath?" a small, reedy voice called out. Catherine Hill's little mama came teetering into the room. She was dressed, as I had now come to expect, head to toe in a duplicate copy of her daughter's silver lamé housecoat outfit. The marabou feathers came up so high on her neckline that they reached her small chin. There are no words to describe the wig.

"We're right in here, minimom!" Catherine called to her.

By the smile on the lips of the ninety-year-old Hill matriarch, I suspected she had once again forgotten her teeth in a glass.

"Are we having a party?" Mama Hill asked.

"Yes, Mama," Catherine Hill said, her

voice sounding positively festive.

And then she took the red-leather book out of my hand and flung it directly into the center of the fireplace.

Chapter 26

I only have one television set in my house. It sits atop a pine dresser in the tiny third upstairs bedroom. My bedroom.

"How old is your VCR?" Holly asked, scooching over to make more room for Wesley and me. The three of us were crowded on top of my quilted bed, the only comfortable spot in the small room from which to view the set.

I passed the bowl of freshly popped popcorn. "Hush."

On the screen, a young and dashing Dickey McBride was singing about his affection for a beautiful maiden named Lotus Flower. The setting was a Technicolor-bright view of old-fashioned Hong Kong harbor. I had rented *Flower of Love* on my way home. Something about those days in Hong Kong still worried me. Too many coincidences pointed to *Flower of Love*.

"Didn't anyone mind that Catherine Hill played a Chinese girl?" Holly asked. With one swipe of the bowl, she grabbed a large handful of popcorn.

"That was the forties for you," Wes said. "A little slanted eyeliner, a black wig, dark makeup — that's all it took to turn Catherine Hill into Tip Tang." He pointed to the screen.

"Is that even a Chinese name?" Holly wondered.

"Well . . ." Wes began, holding up one hand.

Wes had studied Mandarin. Naturally. I felt a minilecture coming on.

Holly was currently in control of the remote, so she muted the soundtrack on the movie. On screen, Dickey McBride, in the midst of warbling, ". . . my Lost Lotus Flow . . ." went suddenly silent.

"First off," Wesley said, "Chinese is not one language, it's more like a language family. Think of Mandarin, Wu, Min, Kejia, Yue, Huizhou, Xiang and Gan, to give them their Mandarin names. Kejia is also known as Hakka, Min is also called Hokkien, and Yue is commonly known as Cantonese."

"Whoa," she said.

I peeked around and made eye contact with Holly. "You did ask."

"Well, I just thought the name of Catherine Hill's character sounded too cutesy. Tip Tang, whazzat?"

Wesley, on a roll, took on that question. "Transcription of Chinese into Latin letters has been a very tricky issue. Chinese languages have sounds that don't have easy equivalents in European languages. Also, Chinese languages are all tone-based, and how do you write that? Over the years, we've written their words using different phonetic spellings, but none of them sound exactly right."

"It confuses me," Holly said. "It seems like all the words have changed, too. Like do we still call it Peking Duck if the city is called Beijing now?"

Wes grabbed the popcorn bowl and helped himself. "We probably should. Most of the world has adopted a system of transliteration called Hanyu Pinyin, which is the official system of the People's Republic of China. That's why we now see words like Beijing, and Daoism and Mao Zedong."

"Hey, I want to watch the movie." I grabbed the remote from Holly when she wasn't paying strict attention and unmuted *Flower of Love*.

"I don't think I ever saw this one," Holly said, shifting her focus back to the screen. "It's pretty funky."

"I vaguely remember it," Wes said, "but I didn't remember how good old Dickey McBride was. He had a great voice."

The scene shifted to a palace garden, and we all made comments on the silk costume Catherine Hill wore.

"I can't believe how thin Catherine Hill was," I said. "And pretty."

"So," Holly said, "when they were making this movie, everyone on the set was learning to play mah-jongg and gambling like crazy. I love knowing all that behind-the-scenes stuff. Read another entry from the book."

I had, of course, made a photocopy of the pages from the red-leather diary. The copy was on my lap, and I picked it up again. I had been reading out some of the brief entries from the months McBride and Hill were in Hong Kong. We could not make sense out of every entry. Some were cryptic. But some were romantic. There were many notes that referred to McBride's affair with his beautiful young lover "Jade." Nothing scandalous by today's standards. Just notes like: "met Beautiful Jade for the weekend," and "Beautiful Jade makes me sing to her in bath." But many of the others referred to names we couldn't immediately recognize.

"Here's one," I said, reading from the binder. "Millie was fired for cold hands. Trina is much warmer."

"What was that about? Sounds kinky." Holly giggled. "Who was Millie? Who was Trina?"

"That note was made over fifty years ago," I said. "We'll probably never know."

Wesley was seized with an idea. He took the remote control from me and fast-forwarded to the credits.

"Hey, we're gonna miss the movie, Wes." I was the only one, apparently, who cared for an orderly narrative.

"Just wait," Wes said.

We watched the movie jerkily speed through its closing scene and then zip past the words The End. Immediately after, the credits began rolling by. The song was a warbling duet between McBride and the woman who sang for the lip-syncing Hill. It was pretty awful. Wes hit the slow-motion button. The crawl of names slowed as they floated up and off the screen. And then, yelling, "Look!" Wesley hit "pause." Frozen on the screen was the name: Trina Van Hertbruggen.

"Trina's hand *is much warmer,*" Wes quoted from the diary.

Trina Van Hertbruggen was listed as the

makeup artist, and we surmised that she probably replaced the cool-fingered Millie. Such a small item as the chill factor of hands could make or break you in Hollywood. Another mystery solved.

I gently reached over and plucked the remote out of Wesley's grip, intent on rewinding to the point earlier in the movie at which we had stopped.

"Wait," Holly commanded.

I paused the tape.

"Go in slow motion, Mad. Maybe we'll see someone listed in the credits named *Jade*."

Well. Duh.

The three of us stared at the tiny names as they crawled slowly up and off the TV screen. Many of the names of the crew and bit players were Chinese.

"No," Holly said. "No one named Jade."

"Hey, go through them again," Wes said, getting excited. "The Mandarin word for Jade is Ling. Look for Ling."

We were instantly alert. I quickly rewound the tape. Holly, on the left, sat cross-legged on the bed, rubbing her eyes. I rewound a bit too far. Wesley, in the middle, sat with a hand absently over his mouth in concentration. I hit play, and the terrible closing song began. I, sitting on the right, held my ears until we came to the names. I hit the slow-motion button and we stared again at the credit crawl.

"There." I stopped the tape. "That's not Ling, but it's close. What does that name mean, Wes?"

"Chen Liling," he read. "The name Chen is one of the most common Chinese surnames, and the two first names are Li and Ling, which mean 'beautiful jade.' "

Beautiful Jade. . . . *met Beautiful Jade for the weekend . . .*

"That's it! That's it!" Holly crowed.

"Liling was an actress," I said, reading her small screen credit, wedged between dozens of Asian named bit players. I quickly rewound the videotape back to the movie. "It said she played a handmaiden called Wing Wong."

"This is awesome," Holly said, munching popcorn again. "We rock. I want to see what Dickey McBride's Chinese girlfriend looked like."

"Yes," Wes said, equally keen. "It was this girlfriend, Beautiful Jade, who taught McBride to play mah-jongg. And McBride taught Catherine Hill and Quita and the rest."

"Right. I'll bet she's the one who gave McBride the old mah-jongg set," I said, scanning the backward-moving images as the tape rewound.

"This is ultracool, Mad." Holly's mouth was full of popcorn, so she might have actually said, "Wes's outer ghoul, Mad." Either way.

I stopped the movie at a scene we'd previously viewed. It was a large set of the palace ballroom. Catherine Hall, playing Princess Tip Tang, was singing to three hand-maidens.

Wes and Holly and I now studied all the court bit players with a scrutiny one rarely would. Each frame that held Catherine in its focus usually had one or two of the hand-maidens in the background. None of us looked at Catherine Hill. We were intent on viewing the lovely Asian faces that belonged to the background players.

On the soundtrack, the unseen woman who dubbed the singing voice of Catherine Hill hit a high note, as on-screen, Catherine's mouth opened wide to match. The courtesans and handmaidens swayed behind her.

Wait. Oh my God.

Automatically, my finger hit the pause button. Frozen on the screen was a clear close-up of one of the handmaidens. I was positive this young lady played the tiny part of Wing Wong. And I was positive, although that film was made so many years ago, that I knew the woman to whom that pretty face belonged.

Chapter 27

I sat in the little side garden of the small house in Westwood that belonged to my old cooking teacher, Lee Chen. Liling Chen, I should say. Or should I say Chen Liling, handmaiden to movie queen Catherine Hill in Chen's one and only American film.

I sipped a cup of tea as we sat together on white-iron chairs. Lee Chen had professed herself happy to receive a late-night visitor. She had not been sleeping well, she told me.

The evening was cool, and we sat under a little electric patio heater. As we talked, Lee Chen offered to read mah-jongg tiles and tell me my fortune. They lay out on the patio table before us, with the twelve tiles divided between East, West, North, and South, and the one tile in the center. She had been turning them over one by one and telling me stories about their meanings.

"You see here," she said, turning over Two Circles. "This is the Chinese character: *Sung*. It is the pine tree and symbolizes the qualities of the tree, that is, firmness and strength . . ."

As Lee talked I wondered what I was going to do. It would be kinder to leave everything as it was. It would be kinder to walk away, leave questions unasked, let things lie. Lee Chen was not a young woman. What right did I have to poke around in her past, dredging up long-buried memories? Was it honorable to disturb a woman I had been so fond of only to pay back my debt of guilt to a woman I never liked? I would think about it before I went too far.

Lee had more to say about Two Circles. ". . . and therefore is often linked to a young man. Perhaps a lover —"

"No," I interrupted with firmness, "not true. No young man lover."

"Okay, Madeline." Lee smiled. "Then, perhaps a younger brother or son."

"My brother Reggie," I said, picking the only possibility mentioned I could handle at the moment.

Lee said, "Two Circles is also linked with writing and drawing, but not painting. This is because the wood of the pine makes the finest charcoal and its soot the finest ink. It can therefore indicate a resolute person who chooses diplomacy rather than violence."

Lee sat very quietly as I pondered how

diplomatic my inquiry could be.

"When did you come to America, Lee?" I asked. "I don't remember hearing that story."

"A long time ago, Madeline. It was in 1948, just one year before the Communists took over the government on the mainland."

Lee wore a blue jacket over her simple dress. She cocked her head, her straight hair brushing against her cheek. This mannerism I knew well from long ago when I was her student.

"You were born in Canton?" I asked.

She held her hands still in her lap. "No, Madeline, I was born in Hong Kong. Before the Communists, I had been able to visit my family who lived on the mainland, in what used to be called Canton Province. But the world was changing very quickly. I could see that the time would come when my freedom to travel might no longer be tolerated. I decided to move West."

Lee turned over another mah-jongg tile. "Ah," she said, "Two Wan. You see? This is the Chinese character called *Chien*. It is symbolized by the sword."

"Oh dear," I said.

"No, no," Lee said. "It is not necessarily a bad sign. *Chien* is a double-edged sword that denotes a balance or a decision . . ."

I knew I had to make a decision. How long could I allow this woman to sit here in friendship, with all the questions I was dreading to ask? I waited for some sign of what I should do with my terrible doubts.

Lee seemed oblivious to my turmoil and continued telling my fortune. "The sword can therefore represent the joining together or the severance of something. For example, in relation to people. Either way it indicates that something is held in balance and that no progress can be made until a decision is made."

"Did you move to America because of a man?" I asked, flat and direct.

Lee Chen looked up. "What do you mean?"

"I find it remarkable that you never mentioned you had been an actress once, long ago."

I watched Lee's eyes and saw in them the look of sudden sadness. "Oh, Madeline. Is this what brings you here to talk this evening? Please, my dear, do not dig and dig at what is better left buried."

"Should we bury the past?"

"Yes," Lee said forcefully. "What is to be served by bringing up such pain? What?"

I looked at Lee, so small, so worried. I hated myself for continuing to hurt her, but would hate myself, too, if I let it all go now.

"You remember the woman named Quita McBride? You met her at Buster Dubin's house."

Lee Chen looked at me and didn't answer.

"She was married to Dickey McBride, the big movie star from long ago. You met her the other night at the Sweet and Sour Club party. And then, later that night, I think you went back to see her. You had something in common with Quita, didn't you? You had both been in love with the same man."

"I do not wish to talk of these things. I know you might mean well, because you are one of the sweetest souls I know. But you must let all this be. It is private business, which has nothing to do with you."

I stood up, worried that I shouldn't have said a word, worried that I couldn't stop myself from saying more.

"Lee, please. That night at Buster's house, you learned then about Quita and Dickey McBride. And we talked about an antique mah-jongg set, do you remember that? And you learned that night that Dickey's set had been found. And that it would belong to Quita."

She looked at me. I felt her eyes beg me to stop.

"Here," I said softly. "Here's the old set. I recovered it, and now it is yours." I pulled it out of a canvas bag that I'd left near my chair.

"Ahh," Lee Chen said, dropping to the wood of her deck, opening the lid and the small drawers, removing first this one, then another tile. "You brought it home to me," she said in a dazed voice.

"This set was yours, of course," I said, wanting to know for sure. I always wanted that. Like I had this right to find out. I felt slightly sick, but still pressed on. "Did it belong to your family?"

"You have found out many things, my dear," she said, more sadly than with anger. "Many things perhaps you would like still to learn." The old woman stood up slowly and settled down on the iron chair, holding her old game set in her lap like a toddler. "If you wish, we will talk."

I sat down, too, and picked up my teacup, waiting as she gathered her thoughts.

"I was a foolish young woman." Lee said. "I wanted to see the American movie people who had come to Hong Kong to film. My cousin took me to the set. He was working on construction and had ways to get me a pass. In those days, the men would play mah-jongg on their break times, during their lunchtime, and after work ended, often past midnight.

"I remember one day, Richard McBride, the big American film star, came to watch the workmen play. He stood by the side of the mah-jongg table, very respectful, and watched. He was a big man, Richard, and a beautiful man. I was just a girl. When he asked me if I knew how to play the game, I was too shy to speak. But when he asked me if I would teach him, I found in myself a sudden boldness. I nodded at him yes, I would.

"That's how we began, my Richard and I. The film company had leased for Richard a beautiful house in Hong Kong, and there I cooked for him and I taught him to play mah-jongg. And soon, I was asked to be in the movie. It was just a very small part. Richard wanted me to be near him, and this was a good way. My parents were very unhappy. But I was eighteen. At that time, the politics in China were very dangerous. My father was busy on the mainland. My cousin was supposed to be watching me closely, but he was too busy gambling."

"And you and Dickey McBride fell in love."

Chen smiled a very sad smile. "I fell in love with him. He told me he, too, was in love. He was an American movie star. He had already been married two times. But he told me I must trust him." Lee's smile vanished. "And I did."

"Did you want to marry him?" I asked.

"With Chinese women, marriage is a very serious thing. In the old traditional values, a wife had four responsibilities. The first is faithfulness: A wife should never consider another marriage even after her husband has died. The second is beauty: A wife should always try to make herself beautiful to attract her husband and make him happy. The third is submissiveness: A wife should understand how to talk with her husband and how to act accordingly and to make him always feel comfortable and never challenged. And last, a wife must be hardworking: She should enjoy cooking, sewing, child rearing and keeping a good, clean and orderly household."

"How terrifying," I said in a small voice, thinking of the millions of women to whom this set of values represented a life of virtual slavery.

"You can see, Madeline, why we traditional Chinese girls were taught to choose a husband with the greatest care. There was no divorce for us. We were bound by honor to only one man, even if he turned out to be a villain. That is different from the modern notions of the West, and even today in China there are many modern girls. But for a girl like me, in those days, I knew no other way."

"Yes. I see."

"When Richard left Hong Kong, he promised to send for me in one month. But two months went by, and then three months, and I never got a letter. By then, I knew I would have to leave Hong Kong. I was afraid if I stayed any longer, I would bring shame to my family. My cousin gave me money."

"Were you going to have a baby?" I asked.

"How do you know all this, Madeline?"

"I read Dickey's diary. Not all of it. But he wrote of you, Lee. He wrote that in you he found his soul mate. He called you Beautiful Jade."

Lee's eyes turned glassy. Tears. "But he did not want to be with me when I came to America. The war was over, but all women with Asian features were treated like we were the enemy, it seemed to me. Richard was afraid of what people would say in the newspapers. He was afraid of his movie-studio boss. He was afraid of his fans, you see? I understood. He tried to give me money, but I did not want it. Instead, I found a job in the kitchen of a restaurant. I scrubbed the pots and I survived. And then, I showed them I could cook. Soon enough, I opened my own restaurant. In time, I became a teacher as well. And it has been a decent life, Madeline. I cannot regret a lifetime that brought me such a daughter and such beautiful granddaughters.

"This is why I do not want to dig in the past, you see? I had some pain in those days, yes. And I did not know what the future would bring me. That was a terrible time, but it is past."

"Yes," I said slowly, setting down my empty teacup, "but I'm sure you weren't expecting to hear the name Dickey McBride the other night. You weren't prepared to hear us talking about your own mah-jongg set, which meant so much to you. You went to see Quita later that night. You wanted to ask her for the mah-jongg set. Isn't that so?"

"It belonged to my grandmother, you see," Lee Chen said softly, tears again making her eyes shine. "I never should have given away my family's old set. I was a foolish child so many years ago, and I was in love. Richard wanted the tiles, and I had been taught all my life to be submissive, so of course I gave them to him. But what do we know of the passing of time when we are children? I had never imagined that Richard would someday give away my family's heirloom. When I heard that this treasure had been passed to a silly young American girl, I knew I was getting another chance to make amends to my ancestors. That is fate, Madeline. That is why I was meant to be at that party and meet that girl. I went to her right after the party. Just after you drove away to your meeting with your young man, I turned my car around and drove back up to the house. I walked up the steps and heard fighting inside the house. Buster Dubin was fighting with his girlfriend. I kept quiet because I did not want to disturb them. But later, she came outside. I knew it was my chance. I told the girl I wanted to buy the mah-jongg set."

This was my worst fear. Lee Chen had just admitted to being on the stairs with Quita on the night Quita fell to her death. I could imagine a hatred growing in Lee Chen's heart. She had been poorly treated by Dickey McBride, years ago, used and abandoned. She had borne him a child that he ignored. In her pride, she had chosen to take no money from McBride, but how well did that proud decision sit all those long years? As a single mother in a foreign country, how had she managed when her child needed medicine and schoolbooks and clothes? How had Chen felt as years went by and she read about McBride, who continued taking lovers and wives, living a rich man's life?

Is that how her years went? If so, what a bitter time that must have been. And if Chen Liling had kept all this secret pain hidden away for decades, what action would she take when fate brought her to the Sweet and Sour Club party on Chinese New Year? How dizzying was the blow of meeting up with her past ghosts so unexpectedly? The brutal coincidence of running into Dickey's pretty young wife. His blond wife. That certainly might have unhinged quiet Lee Chen.

These thoughts made my stomach twist as I looked at her. Lee sat with her back rod-straight on her garden chair. I couldn't believe she could kill. She couldn't. And that night after the Sweet and Sour party, Lee hadn't been raging. I had detected no seething hatred.

"Tell me, Lee, please tell me . . ." I heard myself whispering. "Tell me you did not go back to hurt Quita."

I felt sick to my stomach. What had I started? Why had I come?

"Hurt her? I could not hurt anyone, Madeline. What do you think of me? I was only interested in recovering an object that was precious to my family. I wanted to give this mah-jongg set to my granddaughters. That is all. And now you have brought it here, and what was wrong has been set right."

"It has," I said.

"Why do you look so unhappy? Do you imagine I could kill someone, Madeline?" She stared at me, hurt and angry. "I think you must have more faith in yourself. You have considered me your friend and teacher for many years, have you not?"

I nodded, thoughts and memories blurring.

"Don't you trust your own judgement in people, my dear girl?" Lee Chen asked.

I felt the fever of fear drain away. I had to be certain. I couldn't let this thing go.

"Tell me the rest, Lee. What did you do?"

"I met with the girl. She told me she would sell my precious family treasure to me for a price."

"Twenty thousand dollars," I said.

Lee Chen looked shocked. "How could you possibly know that?" she asked. Her voice held a note of panic.

"She was desperate for that money," I explained, watching her. "Did you agree to pay her price?"

"Yes. She said she must have the money right away for her boyfriend. He was in some trouble, she said. Immediately. I told her I had the cash and would bring it to her."

Lee Chen looked so small. Oh, God, could she have pushed Quita? Did she have such anger in her?

"But when I returned," Lee said, "she did not have my family's mah-jongg set as she had promised. She said I must give her the money first. I told her no and left."

"When you returned," I said quietly, "it was three o'clock, wasn't it? You argued."

"No, no," Lee said. "We said unpleasant words because she did not have my property, that is all."

"Do you have your purse here, Lee?" I asked. I had gone too far not to be absolutely sure I was right. But if I was right, what had I chosen to do?

"What? My purse?" Lee was startled at the turn in the conversation.

"Yes. Could you lend me twenty dollars?"

"Twenty dollars? Of course I will. But what is this about?"

I sat there, waiting for her to fumble with the clasp on her small black-leather bag. She pulled out a wallet and unrolled a tidy stack of bills, all twenties. All, I noticed, with little frowny cartoon faces written in blue pen on the corner.

Ray had drawn that graffiti on those twenties. I had bugged him about it and made a big deal out of defacing the money he'd picked up for the party payroll. But those twenties didn't pay for party supplies. Eight of those twenties I had lent to Quita McBride as she watched her world come crumbling down. Quita's lover was deserting her, her boyfriend was kicking her out of his home, her husband had never really been her husband at all, and his estate was as good as gone.

I looked at the twenty-dollar bill Lee laid neatly down on the table on top of my mahjongg fortune hand. The stupid face glared from the corner of the bill.

In my life, I have always tried to avoid causing anyone any pain. In fact, I am moved always to protect those for whom I care from any and every pain, if I can. I am actually overwhelmed at times by my fear that some sly pain might seep through my hypervigilant protection and cause damage before I can stop it or soothe it away. I feel panicked at the responsibility of it.

I realized, here, sitting in Lee Chen's rose garden at night, that I probably would never choose to have children of my own because of this fear. How do you raise a child and protect them against every pain? The world is filled with hurts. I would go mad to prevent every single slight and insult and injury and illness and heartbreak. Soon, I suspect, I would simply be driven crazy by all the sharp things out there in the world. That is how fearsome I find the thought of someone I care for suffering.

I looked again at Lee and the marked twenty-dollar bill. When Quita's purse was found empty, I knew the twenties I'd lent her must have gone somewhere that last evening of her life. I thought she might have given the money to Trey. But Trey wasn't interested in such small change. Those missing twenties had bothered me all along. And now, at last, I had tracked down those bills. Lee Chen had to have taken this particular bill from Quita after the party. But why?

I continued looking at Lee, sitting across from me, so silent. She hadn't told me everything at all. And despite her pain, which I was clearly making worse, I found I had to push harder now. I needed something above and beyond just masking Lee Chen's pain, and even my own. I needed the truth to come out.

"You told me when McBride asked you

for the mah-jongg case back in Hong Kong long ago," I said slowly, "you were submissive."

"Yes."

"Like a good wife, Lee."

There was silence.

"You were married to Dickey McBride in China." Catherine Hill hinted that Dickey was still married to someone from long ago. "And you are married to him still, isn't that true?"

Lee did not answer.

"I know that Quita was upset about many things on Wednesday night, but one of those things was particularly distressing. The lawyers were going to prove that Quita had never been legally married to Dickey. And why didn't he marry her, I wonder. Could it be because his marriage to you had never officially ended?"

"And? If that is true — what then?" she asked, her eyes openly hostile. Her voice a harsh challenge.

"Then, I think Quita must have been very angry with you, Lee. When you came back to see her, it was three o'clock. Quita did not have the mah-jongg case. She had used it as bait to trick you to bring her the money she demanded."

"She was a lying whore," Lee said. "I spit

at her. I told her who I was, that I was Richard's wife. She called me all kinds of horrible things, hurtful things. She threw money at me and said, 'go away, old woman, and let me be.' She promised if I withdrew my claim, she would be generous with me. She would send me more twenties."

"And you pushed her. You wanted her to die," I said.

"She was a very bad lady," Lee said, as if she was tired of explaining to a child why she had been forced to step on a beetle. "She made her own terrible life."

"And you ended it," I said aghast, finally believing it to be true. "Why?" I shouted.

"I have been ill, Madeline. I don't talk about it to my daughter."

"You're sick?"

"And who will fight the whore to get Richard's money for his daughter, my Yang, and her daughters, too? Who will make the lawyers give the money? No one. I have never told a soul about Richard. Not even his daughter knows who her real father was. And there was that whore, standing on the stairway, telling me she would never stop fighting to get Richard's money, even if it meant keeping the case open in the courts for years and years and all the money in Richard's accounts were drained dry with the cost of lawyers and fees." Lee was breathing hard. "And that whore said she would tell my daughter that Richard had been her father. I yelled at her to stop, but she wouldn't. She kept telling me the most vile rubbish, and I could not let her do those terrible things she said."

"So you pushed her?" I demanded.

"Yes," Lee yelled.

"You wanted Quita to die?"

"I wanted her gone forever. I was in that place for a reason. I was in that place to end her miserable existence. I was in that place to push her hard, so her head would hit the corner of the step. I am not a strong woman, but it was the will of God that she must die that night, and that is why I was there. Do you see now? I do not care what happens to me. I am dying. It does not matter if death comes a little sooner for me. But my poor child must be spared every pain, Madeline. Can you see how important that is?"

It was perverted, twisted, inside-out logic. In a dark flash I felt the center of my soul shift. I saw it clearly — how sick and monomaniacal the whole idea of sparing others pain could be when pushed to this level. And if that was the lesson to take from my own dismal part in this drama, maybe that's why I was destined to live it out. It made me weak to see it from this view. I swallowed hard.

"Someday," Lee said, wheedling and insane, "you will have a child of your own. Two children, did the tiles tell us? And you will understand well what I had to do. You and I are so much alike, Madeline."

"No."

"You will understand someday. My daughter had to be protected. She had to be spared the shame of knowing she had such a dishonorable father and such a dishonored mother."

"No, Lee," I said again.

"Yes, Madeline, yes," she said, her voice pleading. "This is not about me and my pain. I care nothing about that. This is for my daughter Yang and her beautiful children. I had to see to it that they would never have one second of pain caused by that miserable whore."

Chapter 28

Sunday morning in Los Angeles. One of the places I like to start Sundays is the ABC Seafood Restaurant on the corner of Ord and New Hope in Chinatown. The noise and bustle of its Dim Sum rooms, the lively flavors of a dozen varieties of steamed dumplings, the sounds of Chinese languages, the faces of the hundreds of Chinese-born customers, transport me to a land where life is much different from the one I'm sentenced to live out here in L.A. It's Hong Kong, freeway close.

I needed a cheap, quick escape from a night that brought no comfort or rest. I couldn't stay home with my thoughts. Dull from exhaustion, I sought the comfort of routine. Sunday mornings at ABC.

This Sunday morning was more dramatic than most in Chinatown. In order to welcome the Year of the Snake, many of the large Dim Sum palaces, like ABC, had made contributions to neighborhood organizations. These groups brought their musicians and their lion dancers. I stood out on the sidewalk, waiting for Honnett to show up, watching the New Year celebration swirl around me.

Half an hour ago, the lady inside the large restaurant had taken my name and handed me a paper number. Meanwhile, the waiting crowds were gathering outside the front door of ABC Seafood. Not far away, the gunshot ricochet of firecrackers snapped. Firecrackers, I knew, chased away the mythical monster, Nian, which once terrorized the people.

These traditional rituals had always fascinated me in the past, and I prodded myself to focus, pay attention to the dancers on the sidewalk. One man was holding up the large stylized lion head, while his costumed legs were covered in ruffled golden pants to resemble the lion's front legs. The second man, in matching gold ruffled pants represents the animal's hind legs. Together they performed in front of the street crowd, dipping low and leaping high. The lion dance is a remarkable combination of performance art and sport. It takes years of training and practice before one can be good enough to give a public performance. I had heard that many lion dancers are also practitioners of Kung Fu.

"GONG XI FA CAI!" a voice yelled to me over the popping of firecrackers and Chinese drum music.

Even with the sound and the fury of the outdoor celebration, I recognized Arlo's voice.

"Hello," I said, looking over at him, my heart crunching only a little. All the way on the other side of the earth, my troubles knew how to track me down.

It had been four days since I'd last seen Arlo, sitting at La Scala Presto, waiting for his burger. I had been both disturbed and relieved he had never called to hash it all out. After our recent history, breaking up and getting back again, it had felt less shocking, somehow, this last parting. Like earthquakes whose aftershocks diminish until we hardly feel them.

"How did you know I'd be here?" I asked.

"Holly," Arlo said. "I threatened to blow up the ladies' room at the Hard Rock Café if she didn't tell. She knew I was just crazy enough to do it."

"You always manage, somehow," I said. "Well. What's up?"

I could only imagine. He wanted to give it another try. He'd discovered God, a new therapist, hypnosis, the healing properties of tofu. Something had changed him and now we should try again.

"I quit my show," Arlo said, his tousled brown hair played up his boyish look.

That got my attention. In all the ins and outs of our relationship over the years, he'd never blown a job. No one quits a pilot in mid-production. People get fired, but no one walks away. "What happened?"

"I figured you are always right, so I must be wrong." He smiled. "I was too obsessed with the sitcom, with the whole business. So I walked off."

The end of his speech was slightly obscured by a particularly loud drumbeat as the Chinese drummers moved closer to where we stood.

"So what do you want, Arlo?"

"I don't know," he said, looking at his boots, smiling a little. "Maybe I want a hug good-bye."

I leaned forward, wondering if I'd heard correctly. He held me for a moment and let go.

"Yep. Simple as that. I want to be your friend."

"Are you asking for another chance? Because —"

"No, no, no. I get it. We're not going to do that again. I just always thought you'd be in my life, somehow." His eyes crinkled in the corners as he stood there on the street curb in Chinatown, smiling at me, as the lion dancers swooped in the background.

"We can try it," I said, not knowing what else to say. "If you'd like. What are you going to do without your pilot?"

"That's another thing I wanted to talk to you about, actually," he said.

The outside loudspeaker emitted a blare: "Ninety-three."

I looked at the scrap of paper in my hand. Ninety-three.

"That's my number," I said.

Arlo put his hand on the back of my leather jacket and guided me through the crowd watching the dancers. He opened the door of the restaurant and walked me in.

It was noisy and crowded inside the door. The hostess was talking into a microphone mounted on a podium. "Ninety-three?" she said. "Ninety-four?"

"Ninety-three," I said loudly, catching her eye.

She gave us a small, professional smile, and beckoned Arlo and me to follow.

Inside the entry, dozens of customers waited for tables. Almost every face looked to be Chinese. They squeezed in near the large aquarium tanks in front that were filled with live shrimp and abalone and lobsters. Two little boys, their black hair in identical bowl-style cuts, stood fascinated to see one lone shrimp at the bottom of a lobster tank.

Arlo and I followed the hostess into the main dining hall, a bright room of red and gold, lined with mirrors and crowded with diners. The roar of two hundred people, talking and clicking chopsticks against plates was loud and animated. Many of the tables were large rounds, covered in spotless white cloths, holding families of twelve, from ancient grannies to tiny infants. The hostess led us in a serpentine pattern through the room. We ess-curved our way around steamy Dim Sum trolleys pushed by petite Asian women in uniforms and were soon left at a table in the corner.

"I'm actually expecting someone, Arlo," I said, looking across the square table at him. He seemed to be making himself at home, pouring hot tea from a pot into two small cups.

"Remember how you broke up with me?" he asked, finishing his chore.

I stared at him.

"Well, you probably do," he continued in a conversational tone. "I was telling the story — hey, I hope you don't mind that I was talking about it. Anyway, it turns out

Katzenberg cracked up. They have offered me high six figures to write the screenplay."

"What? You're going to write a movie?" I was stunned. Arlo had been stuck in the mines of series television as long as I'd known him. He'd always talked about moving to features. He'd never had the guts to leave his huge paychecks behind. He'd never had the creative energy to write a spec screenplay while doing all his series work.

"They loved the part where you broke up with me over the sesame seeds on the bun. What can I tell you?" Arlo gave a wry smile.

"You want me to say it's okay for you to write a comedy script about the way our relationship ended?" I asked.

Honnett walked up to the table and, without interrupting, pulled out the chair next to me. Arlo looked at him, and at once Arlo's chipper little "let's be friends" smile faded.

Arlo turned to me. "A guy? You're already seeing someone else? I thought you were meeting Sophie for lunch."

I shook my head, wondering what fresh hell was this.

The thing is, the men knew each other. Arlo had met Honnett on a few occasions. Work occasions. But by Arlo's startled sick new expression, anyone could see that everything had changed. The idea hit him hard. Honnett and me. This was clearly a whole new world of pain into which Arlo had unerringly plopped himself.

Ignoring Honnett, Arlo turned at me, his eyes reproachful. "You left me for a policeman? How does this possibly figure, Mad? I thought it was the *hamburger bun* — the food thing. I can be picky. I know this. It's like a religious difference between us."

I gave Honnett a quick look, to see how he was doing with this scene. He was clearly not having a picnic, but he wasn't bolting either. I admired his ability to take the stress.

Arlo took my glancing at Honnett as evidence of the deepest sort of betrayal. I was sharing a look with another man. He had more to say. "Madeline . . . a *cop?* A lousy cop?" His voice was getting louder, but he did turn to Honnett, and say, "No offense." Then back to me. "So how long have you been dating this guy? Must be months. How long have you been playing around?"

"Wait." I looked at him, hoping to get through before I was truly never able to come to any restaurant I liked again, having had these bad scenes with Arlo haunting me in each and every one. "We're not going to do this. I just can't. I'm a wreck. Nothing was going on behind your back, whether you want to believe me or not. Please. You know we weren't working. And it wasn't about the bun."

Arlo looked crestfallen. "What then?" He thought it over. "*The Empty Pot*? Was that it?"

I felt uncomfortable. But I suppose everyone needs to hear it one more time, spelled out. "Yes, Arlo. It was. Kind of. That little story symbolized what we were up against, you and I. The big gulf between how you think and how I think."

"*The Empty Pot*," Arlo explained to Honnett, including him suddenly in our conversation. Arlo thought he was being amusing to turn chatty to the man he had just been insulting. But I could hear the anger under his light words. "*The Empty Pot* is a charming little Chinese fable," Arlo said darkly.

"I know it," Honnett said. His first words.

Arlo looked startled, but quickly recovered his joking, angry delivery. "Maddie and I broke up over the moral of that story. It was purely a literary breakup. We're still crazy about each other, except of course when it comes to food and literature."

Who couldn't help but laugh at Arlo? It's what he lived for.

He went on. "Okay, Chuck. So you know

the story. The emperor gave all the kids bad seeds so nothing grew in their pots. The question is, what would you do? I told Maddie I would cheat and go to an expensive florist to fill the emperor's empty pot, which she took to mean I wasn't honest or something," he said, grinning at his own wickedness.

I sighed. How could I make Arlo go away? I knew of no way that wouldn't be loud and messy. So I waited him out.

"Now Madeline had a different view," Arlo continued. "She thought that little Ping had great strength of character to admit he had not grown any flowers. Honesty was moral, she said."

I smiled weakly at Honnett, wondering if he might actually be steaming under his cool exterior. By his impassive expression, I couldn't tell a thing.

"So," Arlo said, turning to Honnett. "You know the story. What do you think it's about? And if you say 'honesty,' I'll know you are a bullshitter and just trying to impress Maddie."

"Well, Arlo," Honnett said, "it does take courage to admit the hard things, don't you think? Things that you know are true, but you don't want to accept? For instance — the fact that you and Madeline are completely over now. Finished. It's painful to admit the truth to ourselves, isn't it? It takes courage to do that," he said.

Arlo shut up, finally.

Honnett continued, "But since you asked me, I do think the story says something else. I think it talks about the nature of emptiness, don't you?"

"Emptiness?" Arlo repeated.

"Right," Honnett said. "It's pretty hard to look inward and acknowledge how empty we are at times, isn't it? Without kids to love. Without a wife to love. Without a job to love. You know what I'm talking about, Arlo? Without God to love. That kind of emptiness is profound. And people tend to hide from it, rather than facing it and fixing their lives if they can."

Arlo was silent. A first. And then he asked, "Are we talking about the same kids' book, because . . ."

"Sure," Honnett interrupted in a calm voice. "Ping's power was not just in admitting he had failed the emperor's test. He had the strength to own his emptiness. He accepted himself, even in failure."

"Oh," I said, and Honnett looked at me. It might have been the most romantic moment of my life, considering the circumstances.

"Well, I gotta be going," Arlo said,

scraping his chair back and standing. "This has been great. We ought to do this every Sunday."

"Arlo . . ." I said, wondering what would come of us all, and not up to any more deep thoughts.

"Just kidding," Arlo said. "But we're going to stay friends, right? You promised me that."

I looked at him.

"Okay, I'll just wrap it up quickly," Arlo said. "One. We're going to be friends. Two. You think my new movie deal is fine."

Arlo Zar would never change. Or maybe he would. I only knew I wouldn't be there to see it.

Arlo stood by the table for a moment, staring at me. "Well. Bye, Maddie," he said, then he turned and left in a hurry.

"That seemed civilized," Honnett said, smiling at me after Arlo cleared out.

I laughed. I always appreciate sarcasm.

"Sorry for all that," I said, waving a hand weakly. "God. You okay?" I asked.

"Me? Sure. That was nothing," he said. "Besides, I'm the one who gets to stay here with you."

Honnett checked out the bustling dining room. "This is great," he said, watching the nearest Dim Sum server approach with her steam trolley carrying dozens of little metal bowls of fresh Chinese delights. "Why don't you just order one of everything so I can try it all."

Ah.

I reached out my hand and took his, holding it on the table.

"You ready for some pretty lousy news?" he asked, holding onto my hand, not letting me pull it back.

"Okay."

I had called Honnett. Eventually. What else could I have done?

I sat up all night. Long after I left Lee Chen's house, I sat at my kitchen table staring at a candle, thinking terrible things about the terrible truth. Now that I finally clasped it, ugly and brutal, what was I to do with it? Was acknowledging the truth enough? Is "knowing" the end of it? Did I have to take any action at all? I made myself think it all through, consider every aspect.

Lee Chen, my old teacher. The woman whom I had long admired. So much like me, I'd imagined — a chef, a businesswoman, a kind soul. What to do with the knowledge that she had let her past mistakes well up and drown her reason.

What to do about her admission of

murder? The woman was now so old and ill. Likely, her illness would take her swiftly. Should justice be left to God? I thought about the lack of real proof, when it came down to it. Lee had purposely pushed Quita McBride to her death, but it could never be proved unless she confessed. Would she ever admit to another soul what she had admitted to me? It seemed to me — running over and over the possible outcomes in the middle of the night — that I might merely choose to do nothing. Unlike the police, I had that option.

I spent the hours before morning turning it over in my mind. Who else had to know what had really happened on that quiet night in Whitley Heights? I tried to convince myself no one would be hurt, but the truth, painful as a toothache, would not allow such an easy resolution. There were two women to whom I was obligated in this matter. One I had cared for, one I had not, but was either of their lives more or less important? If I chose to protect Lee Chen's secret, how would I live with myself as I betrayed Quita McBride once again?

In the end, the hours spent weighing and judging and agonizing were all a waste. As dawn came and my bedroom window began to brighten, I had come up with no plan that would make everything all right. I drifted off to sleep.

When I awoke an hour later, I recognized my own truth. I was powerless to right a situation that was so wrong. Lee Chen had admitted to pushing a woman to her death. Fated or not to the lives we live in this world, I still believe we must make our own choices. It was as simple as that. This was true for Lee Chen, and also for me.

Calling Honnett was like calling the doctor when you have spent the night denying you felt a lump — that kind of anguish. There was little relief in coming forward with such devastating news.

During that phone call, Honnett remained quiet as I told him everything that I had learned, everything that Lee Chen had revealed to me the night before. We agreed to meet at eleven. I selected the location.

A succession of servers pushing steaming carts stopped at our table and left off a selection of treats. And now the table before us was covered in little metal bowls filled with four tiny Dim Sum treats each, from spicy pork Shu Mei to succulent pink shrimp Har Gow to Ho Yip Fan, fried rice wrapped in lotus leaves. There were also soup dumplings, a marvel of culinary engineering in which a portion of soup is magically sealed inside a gossamer rice-flour skin and steamed without a drop of leakage, and Chien Chang Go, "thousand-layer cake with egg topping," each small pastry tart a piece of flaky sweetness.

"You ready to hear this, or should we wait until after lunch?" Honnett asked, his big callused hand holding mine tight.

"Okay. Tell me." I sat there, feeling myself shrink.

"I called Mrs. Chen right after I talked to you. She didn't answer her phone."

I knew Honnett had planned to talk to Lee. He told me he was going to interview her. He felt she might want to make a statement, get it all off her chest. And he was pretty confident he could break her down. I wasn't so sure, but what do I know about the psychology of police interrogation? All morning, I couldn't get that picture out of my head. The humiliation of Lee Chen.

My stomach began to turn. "You know what? Can I change my mind?" I looked at Chuck Honnett, his face strong, his eyes kinder than I remembered them. "Can we discuss this at the end of the meal?"

"Sure we can," Honnett said. "Tell me about all this stuff I'm eating."

And so I did.

We also discussed a few other matters. Some police business.

"Say, you know that guy Trey Forsythe? He's one of your buddies, isn't he?" Honnett asked, oblivious to my visit with Trey.

"Not quite," I said. "What about him?"

"He was beat up pretty bad last night. I saw the report he filed."

"He's okay?" I asked, startled. Those Chinese gamblers had come to collect, and Trey must have told them he didn't have their twenty grand. "Was it the tongs?"

"Nope," Honnett said. "He claims it was a former girlfriend that beat him up. You know Verushka Mars? That's the one. She attacked him with a stick or something."

Oh, man.

"All you hear about all day is about everybody's worst moments in hell. You have such a lousy job," I said, but this time, more in commiseration than in criticism, the way I have said it in the past. "Say," I said, "I got a call from Catherine Hill. How about that?"

"Movie stars are calling you. That's perfect," Honnett said, grinning.

"The maj 'girls' wanted to invite me to their next mah-jongg party. Next Friday."

"Really?" Honnett looked up, a dumpling

poised between chopsticks, and asked, innocently, "To play or to cook?"

I had to smile at that. "To play. They want to teach me. I think I remind them of themselves as young women. Which is pretty scary, Honnett."

"You can teach them a thing or two," he said.

"Oh, and Wesley has a weird thing," I said. "You know that house he's been fixing up. He's already replaced the roof, floors, plaster, almost everything. And then guess what? He got a call from a broker who has a buyer with cash. They are making an offer."

"I thought you told me the house isn't finished," Honnett said.

"Right. But most of the major work is done. Wesley has poured a ton of money into it already. But here's the catch. The new buyer wants to tear the entire house down and start over. They're going to put up a new one from scratch."

"Ouch," Honnett said, getting the irony. "Are they offering a lot?"

"Oh, yeah," I said. "Wes will make a fortune. But he'll lose the Wetherbee house."

"Tough call," Honnett said. "Someone wants to destroy all his work."

I smiled at Honnett, feeling better than I

had in days. This felt like a relationship. This felt good.

"Will he sell it?" Honnett asked, sampling the pork Shu Mei.

"Oh, yeah," I said, smiling. "It's a lot of money. He is really aggravated and worried about it, but he can't stop the world from changing."

"I had no idea Wes had such a tough business head," Honnett said. "Guess he's not the emotional jerk I would be in that case. I'd never sell."

"You wouldn't?" What a delightful thought. Was Honnett admitting to an emotional side I had never suspected? "You're an emotional jerk? Tell me about this."

"I mean about stuff I fix up," Honnett said, coloring. "My cars. Did you know I fix up old Mustangs? I'd never sell one of those babies to a chop shop, Maddie. I can feel Wesley's pain."

Throughout our meal, I got a charge out of watching Honnett try each new Dim Sum dish. He was wildly open and adventurous in his eating. I loved that.

We carefully avoided bringing up the subject of Lee Chen, and as the meal wound down we had both relaxed. Perhaps this strange occasion had given birth to one of our first real conversations. I was telling him

414

about some of my friends, people he had yet to meet.

"I got a message from my friend Sophie," I said. "She is leaving tonight. Her adoption paperwork has finally been completed. She's going to China to get her new baby girl."

"Wow."

"Do you think there's something wrong," I asked, "for a single woman of forty-two to decide to adopt?"

"These Chinese babies are abandoned, aren't they?" he asked. "My sister adopted a little girl from China."

"I didn't know that." I didn't know much about Honnett.

"It's tragic, these Chinese orphans," Honnett said. "These baby girls, they're born in unbelievable poverty in a culture where girls are not of value. They are the least wanted human souls on the planet one minute. And the next minute, whoosh! They are sent home with these nice, loving families who are damn thrilled to have the privilege of raising these babies and making a home for them here. Why shouldn't we think that is a heroic thing to do? Whether your friend is married or not, she can learn to be a good mother. That's what's important."

"I know. I agree." I sipped my cup of tea. Well, well.

Our waiter, Sung, came over. He quickly added up our total, counting the ink marks left by each Dim Sum waitress throughout the meal as she served the little metal trays we selected from her cart. There were a dozen or more marks representing Honnett's healthy appetite for a cuisine that was new to him. The bill came to a little over twenty dollars. Honnett paid, and we walked out the door.

Another group had gathered on the sidewalk. A new set of lion dancers was performing their traditional swooping acrobatics to the sound of Chinese drums. We walked through the crowd, moving away from the entertainment.

Neither of us brought up the subject of Lee Chen. Honnett was waiting for me to tell him it was time, but I still craved our brief vacation from the real world. In a small crowded shop on a side street, we looked at many imported items, incense holders, cheap dishes, and lacquer bowls in red and black. When Honnett wasn't paying attention, I bought him a Chinese New Year gift. I tucked some cash into the little red *Hongbao* envelope, paying attention to keep it an even denomination like $8 or $12 for luck.

When we were back out on the street, I presented him with the traditional gift.

"What's this?" he asked, sounding delighted, pulling out the ten singles. "I thought these money envelopes were gifts for kids."

"All unmarried children are eligible to receive *Hongbao*," I informed him. "It's for the child inside. Find him and pay him."

"And this is for you." Honnett handed me a bag. He had also found something in the little shop.

It was a large ceramic pot.

"The guy told me red is the right color for Chinese New Year. He said red means good luck."

I couldn't believe that Honnett had selected for me an Empty Pot. Life could be weird. Truly, indisputably weird.

We walked to the corner and then I knew it was time. How long could I prolong hearing about my old teacher and her interrogation?

"Tell me."

"Okay," Honnett said. "It's pretty bad."

"You said she didn't answer the phone, so what happened? Did you go out to her house?"

Honnett nodded. "She didn't come to the door. I went out there with another officer. He went around back, looking into the windows. That's typical when a suspect is not cooperating."

Suspect.

"He called me to the side yard. There was a small frosted window. It was open to a downstairs bathroom."

"Had she escaped?" I was shocked. Why would Lee Chen climb out of a small window?

"No, Maddie. She was dead."

"What?"

"In her bathtub. We saw her from the open window."

"In her bathtub?" What?

"She cut her wrists. I'm sorry. I wish I didn't have to tell you about it. She killed herself."

I pulled away from him. I heard a loud crash. At my feet, shards of red glazed pottery.

"No."

"Hey, hey, hey," he said, soothing me, pulling me back, holding onto me. "What could you hope for, Maddie? I know this is tough. I know." He held on to me, and I didn't fight it.

How had it all come to this? A mysterious

418

red book. A theft. Old secrets. Deception. A sad love affair. Betrayals. And four days later, two women who had both loved an actor named McBride were dead. It would take more time, I knew, to sort it all out.

But for me, it had all started with an old mah-jongg set.

I hate surprises.

The employees of Thorndike Press hope you have enjoyed this Large Print book. All our Thorndike and Wheeler Large Print titles are designed for easy reading, and all our books are made to last. Other Thorndike Press Large Print books are available at your library, through selected bookstores, or directly from us.

For information about titles, please call:

(800) 223-1244

or visit our Web site at:

www.gale.com/thorndike
www.gale.com/wheeler

To share your comments, please write:

Publisher
Thorndike Press
295 Kennedy Memorial Drive
Waterville, ME 04901